BLACK BOX

BLACK BOX

a novel

Gary D. Cole

BLACK BOX

Published by
Trenchant Press LLC
Raleigh, North Carolina

This book is a work of fiction. Names, characters, businesses, organizations, places, events, and incidents are either the product of the author's imagination or are used fictitiously. Any resemblance to actual persons, living or dead, is entirely coincidental.

Book design by Susan Fecho.

Library of Congress Control Number: 2012930065

ISBN: 978-0-9850105-0-8

CHAPTER ONE

Ned held his breath as the sedan skimmed past the Christ Church cemetery. As children he and his sister Margo, the oldest, had puffed out their cheeks and banged their palms on the liner of their car as they were driven past the graveyard, where Ned's great-grandparents, grandparents, and mother were buried. Celia, the middle child, had refused to join in. On a whim Ned had started the superstition up again the summer he'd moved in with his father and now did it each time he drove that stretch of Sheridan Road, though he always kept one hand on the wheel.

He could have pounded both palms now, as he wasn't driving, but he kept his hands clasped in his lap. This was no time for child's play.

The Lexus slowed as it entered the Ravines, the winding gully that was home to some of the premier real estate on the North Shore. Ned had always felt a slight chill as he passed into the shadows of the Ravines, where the plunging terrain and dense trees left Sheridan in darkness whatever the time of day. Even at that hour, approaching midnight, he was conscious of an eerie blackness swallowing the car as it slipped from the amber haze of the streetlights by the public beach at Tower Road.

The house was less than a quarter mile into the Ravines. The entrance was marked by two massive stone monuments, thick with moss and ringed with ivy, that Ned had likened to giant rooks when his grandfather had taught him chess in elementary school. Between these sentinels stood a hulking wrought iron gate that had to be unlatched by the family chauffeur when Ned first came to visit as a child but was now controlled by an automatic security system. For the first time that he could remember, the gate stood open.

The gravel crunched softly beneath the wheels of the Lexus as it swung past the entry. Ned usually found the symmetry of the elms lining either side of the driveway comforting. Tonight, however, the trees seemed sinister in the somber light of the low torch-style lamps that stood at even intervals between them.

There was usually no illumination other than these lamps until the glittering lights of the courtyard that opened majestically before the house, a quarter mile down. But tonight Ned could see through the windshield the rhythmic flashing of a police car's lights at the end of the driveway. Arcs of light, red and blue, glanced off the passing elms and a row of shrubbery bordering the drive as it widened into a semi-circle just before the courtyard.

As the sedan approached, a uniformed policeman stepped from behind the patrol car and motioned for them to stop. Beyond the officer's outstretched hand Ned spotted two other police cars flanking the rococo fountain in the center of the courtyard. The front doors of one of the cruisers were open and a man in a suit leaned against the car, speaking into a radio.

The driver lowered his window as the policeman approached the car from his side.

"Are you Ned Prince?" asked the officer.

The driver shook his head. Ned spoke up from the back seat.

"I'm Ned."

Ned heard the gravel pressed beneath the heavy tread of the policeman's feet passing behind the car. The officer's impassive face tilted toward him as Ned pressed his window button.

"Could I see some identification please?"

Ned fumbled for his driver's license. The policeman gave it a cursory glance and returned it through the open window.

"Lieutenant Nielsen is expecting you." The officer pointed to the man in the suit.

The driver spoke to Ned.

"Do you want us to stay?"

"That's OK. You guys have been great. As always."

He reached over the seat with both hands to press the shoulders of the driver, a sturdy blonde man in a starched Oxford shirt, and his even blonder passenger, a slender woman in a white cotton blouse.

"Call us if you need anything, Neddy." The woman's hair bounced on her collar as she turned toward the back seat.

"I will. I'm sorry about the show."

The call from Celia's husband Art had come at the intermission of a performance of *Hamlet* Ned was reviewing at a North Side theater. Scott and Linda had been with him at the show. He had no car, so they had offered to drive him up to his father's house. The urgency in Art's voice, so different from his usual jollity, had made it clear there was no time to take the train.

Ned unfolded his long, limber frame from the car. The September night air held the faint warmth of a summer not quite passed. He ran both hands through his dark, flowing hair, which swept over the collar of his shirt.

The man in the suit met Ned at the mouth of the courtyard.

"I'm Lieutenant Nielsen, Winnetka Police. Your brother-in-law mentioned you'd be coming."

Nielsen was of middle height and compact. He had the sloping shoulders and barrel chest of a former wrestler.

"I'm afraid there's been an incident inside the house. Could you come with me please?"

Nielsen's tone was quiet and respectful, almost gentle. He had the deferential manner of one accustomed to dealing with those accustomed to getting their way.

Nielsen led Ned through the courtyard, also lined with gravel. The gravel seemed more dingy than Ned had remembered it as a child. Ned's great-grandfather and grandfather had insisted on replacing the gravel at the end of each summer so that it always shone gleaming white before any awed traveler who came through the gate. Ned's father had discontinued the tradition last summer.

Lamps of beveled amber glass fixed on ornate wrought iron stands hung on all three sides of the courtyard, casting a torchlight glow. Lights in the same style as those along the driveway encircled the stone fountain, into which Ned and his sisters had tossed pennies and made silent wishes. His father had cut the water supply to the fountain over a year ago.

The courtyard was framed along the back by the brick, beam, and stucco of the mansion's Tudor façade, rising three stories over an imposing entry portico. To the sides stood a four-car garage on the visitor's left and a glass-encased wing to the right, each of two stories. The servants' quarters ran over the top of the garage. Ned's favorite among the servants had been an ancient Scotswoman. She had served as his mother's nanny and had remained with the family as an honored retainer even after Elizabeth Ingram had come of age. Ned remembered many Saturday afternoons spent in Nanny's quarters sucking on the hard candy that she kept for him by the bushel and looking at old photographs of his mother.

The glass wing had originally been an enclosed porch that was remodeled by Ned's grandmother for year-round use. His mother had renovated several of the cramped storage rooms on the second floor of the wing as a suite for Ned, who had been the only child still at home when his parents took possession of the house following his grandmother's death. The airy expanse of the suite hadn't eased the stifling Ned felt on moving back in with his father after college.

Nielsen led Ned between the columns of the portico and through the massive front door, which stood open. Another uniformed officer was posted at the base of the sweeping staircase that dominated the front hall. The policeman blocked Ned's view of a Monet that hung at the foot of the stairs and was the first sight that greeted visitors as they entered the house. Ned's great-grandfather, C.W. Ingram, had acquired the Monet and a score of other Impressionist paintings in the wake of the First World War, when European aristocracy needed the cash that the Ingram family was busy minting. Ned's grandparents had donated a number of the paintings to the Art Institute, but the house still boasted one of the finer private collections in the Midwest.

Ned followed Nielsen down the hall, passing the grand sunken living room that opened to the left and the dining room, hung with tapestries, to the right. The door to the study, to the left beyond the living room, was ajar. This had been his grandfather's den, a richly paneled, map-lined man's refuge that still smelled faintly of cigar smoke. Ned's father had never used the study.

At the end of the hall, where a stately pair of French doors led on to a stone terrace overlooking Lake Michigan, they turned left into the billiard room. An imposing billiard table still stood atop an Oriental rug in the center of the room, but it was draped in a purple velour cover and had not been played on in years. Ned had challenged his father to a series of games when he had moved back home, but those had soon gone the way of the weekly family brunches Celia had proposed after Ned's return.

In the far left corner of the billiard room was a long mahogany bar, behind which stood mirrored shelves lined with spirit bottles of every description. Opposite the bar, in front of one of the room's several floor to ceiling windows that offered magnificent views of the lake, sat Ned's sister Celia, sobbing silently. As a rule she was impeccably coiffed and dressed, but now her hair lay in unkempt strands on the bunched shoulders of an old coat as she sat, huddled, with her head in her hands. Ned's brother-in-law Art stood by her side, one hand perched on her shoulder in a vain attempt at comfort. Art's doughy face, usually creased in laughter, was grim.

Nielsen left Ned and approached a doorway at the far end of the billiard room. This was the house library. As a boy Ned had been enthralled by the leather binding and ornate gold lettering of the volumes that lined the shelves. As he became more literary he grew contemptuous of the collection, which he considered lightweight and based more on the appearance of the book than its content. He thought it no coincidence that the library was tucked in a corner of the house and rarely entered.

After his mother's death his father had taken possession of the library and had moved a plain desk and chair there to serve as his office. He also brought an old upright piano out of storage and installed it beneath the one window in the room that overlooked the lake. There was a priceless Steinway grand in the music room that opened off the living room. In the evenings when Ned was still in high school his father would often spend an hour at the piano after dinner, playing old show tunes and some jazz standards. He was a gifted pianist who was always called on to play a few tunes when he and his wife entertained, which they did often. Ned had not seen his father at the grand piano in years, except at Christmas.

Art approached Ned and wordlessly put an arm around his shoulders as he led him toward the library. Nielsen called for the officer posted in the library to take a break, then stepped aside to let Ned pass into the room.

Sheet music lay scattered on the floor at the base of the piano bench. Some pages were spattered red. Ned's father lay slumped over the top of the keyboard, his blood pooled on the black and white ivory of the keys. Art remained at the door as Ned made his way haltingly toward the piano. As he drew nearer he saw that the side of his father's head was horribly wounded and that a handgun lay atop a page of music on the polished hardwood floor, beyond the reach of his father's outstretched fingers.

Nielsen noiselessly entered the room and waited for Ned to take in the scene. Ned had braced himself for something terrible, as a child tenses before some unannounced punishment, but he was not nearly ready for what he saw. He hadn't the breath to gasp. He stood rooted to the floor, his knees locked and shoulders hunched.

When Ned finally turned away, Nielsen, his hands clasped in front of him, waited a decent interval before speaking. He said, in a solicitous and practiced tone, "I'm sorry for your loss. Is there any reason why your father would want to take his own life?"

CHAPTER TWO

Ned eyed himself in the mirror. He was no judge of tuxedos, but it was clear his father's taste had been impeccable. The cut of the coat sloped elegantly from broad shoulders to slender waist. The pants tapered smartly to a narrow cuff just above shoelace level. The shirt featured fine ornamental stitching, without being frilly. The cummerbund was marbled in fantastic colors like the edges of the aged books in his grandfather's library. The cuff links and studs were nestled in a small purple velvet bag that had been tucked inside the jacket pocket. He found to his surprise that they were the faces of tragedy and comedy, one face for each cuff and two of each for the studs, presumably to be worn in alternate order. The overall fit was uncanny.

Only the shoes gave the lie to Ned as a man-about-town. They were his own; his father had not worn his size. The toes were badly scuffed, the black leather cracked around the laces, and the heels worn almost to the sole. Ned did what he could with a shoe-shine kit that had sat in the back of a closet since high school, but the polish was brittle. For a moment he flirted with the idea of chucking the dress shoes and sporting a pair of green Converse All Stars instead, but judged that his first day on the job was not the time to cut that sort of a dash. He would not have hesitated had he been in Chicago, he thought, but then he would not be attending some fancy dress affair if he were.

His daily pacing had been shot to hell. His usual routine had been to sleep until at least eleven, grab a bagel and multiple cups of the blackest coffee, then lounge around his apartment with the *Tribune* sports section. He wouldn't start work on the novel until two at the earliest, later if he had a review to dash off. Late afternoons he'd find a pick-up basketball game at the gym, and evenings he could generally scare up a high school buddy or two for burgers and beers or a ball game if the Cubs were in town. He would write a few more hours after midnight, then collapse into bed around three.

That, however, was when he had an allowance from his father. Now Brooks Prince was dead, and the monthly checks had been cut off by Tucker Farr, his father's executor. Farr had been apologetic but firm. Farr told Ned that all of his father's investment accounts had been drained and that Brooks Prince had even dipped into the trust funds set up for Ned and his sisters. Under the circumstances, said Farr, it would be imprudent to continue paying an allowance to someone capable of earning his own keep.

So Ned was now a working man. The *Weekly* in Chicago had used him as a freelancer, but they already had a full-time reviewer and no room on the staff for another. Farr had mentioned that a Yale classmate of his was the publisher of the *Columbian*, Portland's alternative weekly, whose theater critic had accepted a teaching position. Ned would have to move to Oregon, of course, but Farr had said that getting out of town for a while mightn't be a bad idea. Farr had managed to keep the cause of Brooks Prince's death out of the papers, but eventually news of the suicide was bound to leak out. Because of the place of Ned's family in Chicago society, the media glare would be intense.

Ned had been powerless to resist Farr's suggestion. He had lurched around in a daze since his father's death. It wasn't that they had been close. Other than Farr, who had known Brooks Prince since grade school, and Celia, the ever dutiful daughter, no one had seemed close to his father except the squadron of Ingram family lawyers, accountants, and investment managers who hovered over his every move.

What had stunned Ned above all else about his father's death was the boldness of the act. Brooks Prince had gone through life reading from a script written by his in-laws. Though he'd been given an impressive title and a plush office at the Ingram headquarters, he had had no real job other than to serve the family interests on a host of charity boards and escort Ned's mother through a whirl of black tie balls and do-gooder dinners. He had never made his own mark in anything, except in death.

Brooks Prince had been wrapped in a cocoon of Ingram privilege that Ned despised. Ned had escaped the mansion in the Ravines as soon as he could because to him it stank of privilege. The house had been at the core of the short story collection that had garnered Ned a winning review in the *New York Times* book section and had landed him a sizable advance for the novel. But he could not write there, not in such a monument to avarice.

Ned had bristled at Farr's implication that he was a freeloader. It was true the *Weekly* paid him a pittance and that he had long since run through the advance from the novel, which had ballooned hundreds of pages past its expected length and was more than a year overdue to his publisher. But he lived simply, flinging himself fully into the craft of writing. His apartment in Chicago was a humble one-bedroom in an up-and-coming neighborhood that had yet to up and come. He took the L all over the city and the Northwestern train on his few journeys to the North Shore. He had his vices, of course, but at least they were cheap.

But not cheap enough that he could manage without the allowance. He was dumfounded at Farr's report of Brooks Prince blowing millions of Ingram dollars on something he had managed to conceal from the phalanx of family retainers. Farr now had the usual lawyers and accountants on the case, trying to reconstruct his father's dealings, but he said the traces were few.

There were the house and the paintings and the whole lock, stock, and barrel, of course, but Farr was not about to sell these just to subsidize Ned's writing. Ned was amazed the Ingram fortune could not be tapped in some other fashion, but he acknowledged he was no man of business and in no position to dispute Farr's decision that he must make his own way. He did not want to be seen begging around Chicago for work, not in a city where he'd been his own master, so he had taken the Portland offer and left town.

His father's estate had yielded three things. The first was a late-model Lincoln Navigator that he'd sometimes borrowed when he'd needed wheels for an out-of-town expedition. The second was the tuxedo he now had on, which Celia had handed him when he was packing the SUV for the westward drive. He'd been tempted to hand it right back, as he couldn't imagine he'd ever put it to use, but she had been on-and-off hysterical for weeks and he hadn't wanted to set her off.

The third was a frayed cardboard box that his older sister, Margo, must have hidden under the rest of his stuff inside the Navigator. He'd unloaded it with the rest of his gear, but hadn't opened it until this evening when he went searching for his dress shoes. The box turned out to be crammed full of yellowing theater programs and black-and-white cast photos featuring Brooks Prince during his student days at Northwestern University, where Ned's parents had met.

Ned's grandfather had been a huge Northwestern booster - name on a library, board of trustees, fifty-yard line seats at Dyche Stadium, the whole shooting match. Gramp used to get driven in his Rolls Royce to all the home games. Gramp wouldn't have heard of his daughter going anywhere else when she got out of New Trier, although he doubted whether she'd put up much of a fight. Thankfully Gramp had been dead several years when Ned headed off to college, or there would have been hell to pay over his choice of Swarthmore. Ned had never asked his father why he'd picked Northwestern, but suspected it was the first school he'd gotten into. Dad had been a master of the path of least resistance.

Brooks Prince had evidently been a leading man. He was center stage in most of the photos, flashing a winning grin, and top billing in all but a few of the programs. He was also credited as a songwriter in some student revues.

Ned could not imagine his father in any setting so bohemian as the theater. He had always pictured his parents in their college years as partygoers at a fraternity social: his mother, in a demure pastel sweater, a little tipsy, pulling his unready father in a cardigan and penny loafers on to the dance floor. They had been at college during the Vietnam War era, but he was sure the tie-dye and bell-bottom look had passed them by.

Ned made an imperceptible adjustment to his bowtie, ran his fingers through his hair, and headed for the door of his apartment. He had rented a unit in a condo called the Brittany. Most likely, Ned thought, it was the name that had infected the developer's daughter during a decade-long, nation-wide contagion. The project was best classed as faux-loft: high ceilings, exposed beams, hardwood floors, and brick walls. The Brittany's developer, according to the broker who'd handled Ned's rental, had pioneered the conversion of industrial buildings in Portland's fashionable Pearl District. He'd apparently honed his craft to such a point that he no longer required the inconvenience of actual old buildings to achieve the desired effect. Ned found his unit antiseptic, certainly when compared with the aromatic old one-bedroom he had sublet in Chicago, but the location was ideal and the rent manageable.

He saw through the windows flanking the elevator that the skies had brightened since he'd returned from his first day at the *Columbian*. Though he knew it was just a prelude to another round of drizzle, he'd decided to walk over to the bus and take it downtown to the Hilton rather than do battle with rush hour traffic in the Navigator.

His apartment was on the fifth floor, three units down from the elevator. A middle-aged couple in matching multi-stranded rainbow-hued sweaters was already on the elevator when he entered. They were doubtless from one of the penthouses on the upper floors. He'd found the Brittany a curious mixture of empty-nesters returning to the city from suburbia and urbanistas making their first home purchase. The ex-suburbanites did not give a man in a tux a second glance.

The reaction on the No. 9 bus heading downtown was a different matter. The assortment of stolid commuters, backpack-toting students, and weary pensioners looked at him with a bafflement befitting an alien visitation. The driver gave a slight sneer when Ned announced "Fareless Square," the downtown zone where rides were free. Ned squeezed into the standing room only scrum, placing his umbrella in front of him as a shield for the cummerbund.

The bus stopped right in front of the Hilton, a skyscraper by Portland's low-slung standards that sprawled over an entire city block. The event appeared to be a youth charity benefit, as fresh-scrubbed children in white shirts brandished directional signs and cried out scripted welcomes. Ned followed their arrows to an escalator laden with dowdy matrons and well-fed burghers descending to the grand ballroom below. He shuffled along with the pack to the registration table, where a perky volunteer gushed a greeting, presented him with the evening's program, and pointed him to Table No. Thirty-Seven.

The *Columbian* was apparently not one of the event's major patrons, as No. Thirty-Seven was stuck in a dark corner of the cavernous ballroom, at the end of the very last row of tables. No one was at the table, which was festooned with bright streamers and reproductions of children's art. Ned was a little ashamed of his umbrella – Portlanders never seemed to carry one despite the constant rain – and hid it under one of the chairs before heading for the ballroom lobby in search of a drink.

The narrow lobby was packed with patrons chattering in small groups or queuing at one of several bars. When Ned finally reached the front of his line, it was clear from the modest array of spirits and the harried look of the bartendress that a Pimms, his favored drink, was not on the cards, so he settled for a local microbrew.

As he turned away from the bar and took his first pull on the beer, Ned saw amidst the bevy of buzzing three and foursomes a larger crowd hovering around a man who looked like a senator from central casting: erect carriage, unthinned thatch of silver hair, and majestic smile that at once conveyed both dignity and empathy. The well-wishers and hangers-on would approach, and the senator would clasp their right hands in both of his and utter some mot juste as his eyes locked on theirs. Ned had seen glancing through the program that the honoree of the evening was the honorable such-and-such and figured this must be the man.

On the outskirts of the senatorial throng was Roger Bolden, the publisher of the *Columbian*, in animated conversation with a woman whose strapless back faced Ned. Even from a distance it was clear that the round and balding Bolden was turning on the charm, his pink cheeks puckered in good-humored banter. Ned wound his way toward the publisher, who spotted him as he drew near the senator and motioned him over with an imperious wave.

"Welcome to the good and great of Portland, Dirk. They only come out at night, even if their bedtime is still ten thirty. Nothing like needy children to pack them in, particularly if Brutus Emeritus is willing to lend his name to the proceedings. As he has to every federal building in town."

Dirk Marlowe was Ned's pen name. He'd wanted to ensure that any success he gained as a writer was not due to family connections, so he had never written under his own name. As he had come to Portland for a writing job, he had decided to go by Marlowe.

Bolden cast an admiring eye over Ned's outfit. His first question to Ned when they'd met at the *Columbian* office earlier that day was whether he owned a tuxedo. When Ned allowed that he did, Bolden had giggled, clapped his chubby hands, and asked him to take the place of a flu-stricken editor at the evening's event.

"You do indeed have a tuxedo, don't you? You have to be careful, Dirk. The powers that be here expect the scriveners of the Fourth Estate to be meager and ragged, not clad in opulent garments that might upstage their own splendor. There is no danger, however, of your overshadowing this young woman, whose presence this evening graces the good and the great with the beautiful. Allow me to introduce Karin Bergren. Karin, this is our new theater critic Dirk Marlowe, who has descended from the Olympus of Chicago to teach us provincial mortals how to break a leg."

The woman turned to face him. Ned started at her beauty. She was perhaps an inch short of six feet, though well over in stylish black heels. Her shimmering honey-blonde hair was pulled into a simple plait that followed the graceful line of her neck on to strapless shoulders. The hue of her skin was the rich, glowing bronze that blesses amber blondes. Bolden had called her young, but she was probably close to forty. There was a ripeness to her that Ned was not accustomed to in girls his own age. A jeweled pendant hanging from a slender gold chain disappeared between full breasts that swelled above her neckline, and her black evening gown curved around sweeping hips.

She had classic Nordic features, but with hints of a sensuality that overcame the typical Scandinavian severity. The bridge of her nose was long and straight, but slightly flared and fleshy at the base. Her lips curled with a natural fullness.

"Welcome to Portland, Mr. Marlowe."

Her smile was warm and showed a set of gleaming white teeth. She took a sip of white wine.

"It's Dirk. Whenever I hear 'Mr. Marlowe,' I start looking for my father."

"You see, Karin, he already has the informality of our fair city down to a tee. We pride ourselves on not standing on ceremony out here, Dirk. The pioneers who came down the Oregon Trail checked all their stuffy Eastern conventions at the Missouri River. Not much starch in a covered wagon, you know."

"But I see you've not entirely dispensed with formalwear."

"Well, most trailblazers took at least one set of their Sunday best. We don't go to church much in these parts, so we had to put it to use in some fashion. And besides, muslin frocks – or shall we say sweaters and khakis – don't display some of our city's natural assets to their best advantage."

Bolden tipped an imaginary cap in Karin's direction, while sneaking a glance across the lobby.

"Ah, I see an account to whom some sucking up is sadly due. We live and die with our advertisers, you know, and this one has wanted to give me a preview of dying for some time. I think I can leave you two young people alone without a chaperone. But a word of warning, Dirk: Karin is on the board of Willamette Stage and will doubtless seek to ensnare you in their web."

Bolden gave a giggle and darted off.

"I don't think I've been left alone with a critic since I joined the board. Is there some sort of code of ethics I need to follow?"

"Sexual favors and bribes in excess of $1,000 are frowned upon. I believe anything else is fair game."

Her laugh was throaty and deep.

"So what do you think of Portland theater?"

"I'm afraid I'm a Portland theatrical virgin. This is my first day on the job, and I've yet to attend a single play here. At this stage, my mind is frighteningly open, though not for want of trying on my predecessor's part."

Milson, the departing theater critic, had briefed Ned on the local theater scene over lunch. He had bemoaned a prevailing mediocrity, though he'd singled out a few companies that he'd called burning coals in the overall ash heap.

"Milson? He hated everything."

"I would say that he yearned to love, but set the bar of his affections rather high."

"And I would say the man's a pompous ass. He's panned nearly every show we've done since I joined the board."

"Perhaps you should leave the board."

She grinned. "No, I understand our losing streak with him started well before me. But I may take your advice anyway. My term is up at the end of the year."

"Are you tired of theater?"

"I could never be tired of theater. But there's very little theater in board life. The actors have all the fun, and all we do is foot the bill. I do that drill with my children every week, but at least I have some say in what they do. Our artistic director will gladly take my check, but he would never take my advice."

"Have you tried?"

"I did when I first came on the board. Dylan – that's our artistic director – couldn't have been nicer, but I could tell he wasn't going to listen to anything I had to say. I soon learned that it was his job to choose the season and ours to applaud whatever he chose."

She had a way of turning out her full lower lip in a girlish pout.

"According to Milson, most people in town thought that was his job as well."

"Oh, I'm not saying he has to cheer for everything, no matter how awful. But if people pick up the theater section and see nothing but negative reviews, they'll just go to the movies, which is what most of them really want to do anyway."

"So a critic has a duty to save the theater, at the price of his integrity?"

"Now you're putting words in my mouth. But wouldn't a critic want there to be plays to review?"

"My experience has been that theater people are strangely compelled to perform their art and will continue to do so, regardless of the obstacles placed in their path by empty bank accounts, oppressive landlords, and unflattering critics."

"And so you critics should feel free to make life as miserable as possible for these poor deluded creatures."

"No, we should encourage the best among them to brave the obstacles and fight on. We should steer that dwindling but hardy brand of theatergoers to what is worthy of their support and be unsparing as to what is not."

"Is that what you did in Chicago?"

"In Chicago I did what I could. I was a freelancer, not my paper's theater critic in chief. My editor kept my pontificating to a dull roar."

"So you've come to Portland to hold court?"

"I've come to Portland for the money."

"Don't you have it backwards? I thought people left minor cities like ours to make it in major cities like yours."

"Not struggling novelists in need of a full-time job."

"So you're not just a critic?"

She drew a little closer to Ned.

"I'm afraid I am also a poor deluded creature, albeit in another line of goods. Scratch most critics and beneath that brittle exterior you'll find an artist's soft underbelly."

"Have you had anything published?"

"I had a nice run of beginner's luck. Now I'm paying for my good fortune with a wicked sophomore slump."

A roar of laughter came from the politician's entourage. The senator himself was the only one not convulsed in hysterics, a wry chuckle apparently being the closest he came to laughing at his own jokes.

"Perhaps you'll find inspiration here. You know we're quite a center for writers."

"So I understand. I've been trying to figure out whether it's the weather or the coffee."

"I'm afraid I couldn't say. I don't know any writers."

"Well, now you do."

"Yes, I suppose I do." She smiled, almost to herself. "And what inspires you?"

"If I knew that, I wouldn't be in such a slump."

The lights of the lobby flickered on and off, signaling the patrons to head to their tables.

She raised her glass. "Here's to finding inspiration in your new city. Oh, and high praise for Willamette Stage."

Ned hoisted his microbrew bottle in answer. "I knew there had to be a catch, but I'll drink to that all the same. Hopefully I'll see you at a show around town, Karin."

"I don't get out much, I'm sorry to say. And most people under thirty call me Mrs. Bergren, Mr. Marlowe."

She flashed a dazzling smile, turned on her heel, and with a wave of her wineglass over a bare shoulder disappeared into the ballroom.

CHAPTER THREE

Ned took a moment to collect himself. There was a low murmur as the crowd filed toward their seats. He got his bearings, took a slug of his beer, and made for the double doors at the far end of the lobby.

By the time he reached the *Columbian*'s table all of the seats but one were taken. The only chair remaining had its back to the dais. Ned as unobtrusively as possible collected his umbrella from under one of the occupied chairs and slunk into the empty seat, stashing the umbrella beneath his legs.

Bolden spotted him and gave a knowing wink from across the table.

"Have you pledged rave reviews for the rest of Willamette's season?"

"My criticism is not for sale."

"Neither is our newspaper, but it doesn't mean we can't be bought."

"The lady did not offer."

"She honored you with her time. I would say that consideration has passed. Watch out - she may yet try to collect on the bargain."

Bolden turned to a woman in a red dress seated to his left. A graying, curly-haired man in a black dress shirt who Ned guessed was the paper's editor in chief was deep in conversation with a woman in hexagonal eyeglasses to Ned's right. The man on Ned's other side, left out of the conversation, was chewing on a roll.

"Who's Bolden talking about?" he asked, his jaws still working on the remains of the roll as he spoke.

"A woman he just introduced me to in the lobby. Her name was Karin Bergren, I think. He's yanking my chain a little because she's on the board of a theater company and I'm the new theater critic." He extended his hand. "Dirk Marlowe."

"Sorry. Anthony Selvaggio." His handshake was a vise grip.

Selvaggio was about Ned's age. His stumpy frame was stuffed stiffly into what was obviously a rented tux. Ned spotted an undershirt that was just visible beneath the crack in his dress shirt collar. He was pale, with a thick mat of black hair that resisted brushing.

"That's Jerry Bergren's wife, right?"

"I don't know. She didn't say anything about a husband."

"I wouldn't either if I were her. Bergren's a liar and a con man."

Selvaggio almost spat the words out in a heavy New Jersey accent.

"You know the man?"

"Never met him. But we've been keeping an eye on him for a while. I work the business and financial beat, do a lot of investigative work."

Selvaggion spoke in an intense staccato.

"How long have you worked for the paper?"

"Three years in January. Moved out here from Trenton."

"Is that where you're from?"

"Nah. Got started out of Rutgers at the paper there. I'm from Asbury Park."

"You must be a Springsteen fan."

"You got that right."

The evening's master of ceremonies approached the lectern, which was decked with the same streamers and art that were featured on the tables, only larger. Ned took him to be a TV news anchorman. He made a few glib jokes at the expense of local personalities that were lost on Ned, then introduced the charity's board chairman. The chairman, a lean, bald man with a lawyerly air, earnestly thanked the assemblage, then delivered a flowery tribute to the senator. He built to an obvious ovation point, and the patrons obliged by rising to their feet in ringing applause. The senator, seated at the center table in the first row, responded with a wave that was royal in its economy. Ned, who joined in standing ovations only when moved to some exalted plane, was one of the last out of his chair.

"The cult drinks the Kool-Aid," hissed Selvaggio.

"Is it always like this?" asked Ned, as white-clad servers brought out meager salads.

"Never been to a black tie event before, so I can't say. But if you're asking if the entire city will put its nose up the ass of the senator at the drop of a hat, then yes."

Selvaggio slathered his salad in thin Italian dressing.

"The senator, you see, is the high priest of the cult of the Good Person. There's not much religion out here, at least not compared to where I come from. Fewer people go to church here than just about any place in the US. The Catholic Church is a joke. People here don't worship God; they worship at the altar of the Good Person."

"And what's a Good Person?"

"Just look around you. They're progressive. They're tolerant. They're enlightened. They give to environmental groups, even if they drive an SUV that gets twelve miles to the gallon. They swear by mass transit, even if they never ride it. They denounce racism, even though you can count the number of blacks in their kids' schools on the fingers of two hands. Some of their best friends are gay or lesbian. They think guns are for rednecks and the military is for fascists."

His salad was gone. Selvaggio grabbed the last roll in the basket, ripped it in two, and dipped both halves in the dregs of his dressing.

"They're all about grassroots and consensus. They can't stand political machines. They think smoke-filled rooms and back-room deals are for Neanderthals in Jersey or Chicago."

"That's my city," slipped in Ned.

"Cubs or White Sox?"

"Cubs – all my life."

"You'll fit right in."

"Fit in? There's no major league baseball out here."

"You call a team that hasn't won the Series in a hundred years major league?"

"Yankees fan?"

"You got that right."

Both oil-soaked halves of the roll had vanished as well. The servers, who were working the ballroom front to back, arrived with the main course.

"So what's wrong with being a Good Person? Other than a mild dose of hypocrisy, which you'll find anywhere you look."

"Wrong? I didn't say there was anything wrong. They're on the right side of just about every issue I give a damn about. They vote right. They give to the right causes. They eat right."

"Then what's this about cults and Kool-Aid?"

"Because they think they've somehow trumped human nature. They think because they wear Patagonia and saved the spotted owl, they're a different species from a guy who wears a cheap suit and plays the ponies in Hoboken. They think because there are no fat guys named Louie making payoffs in thick envelopes, there's no greed or corruption out here."

"And I gather there is?"

"It's subtle but, oh yeah, it's here. You need to know where to look, though. When I first came out I thought I'd go nuts. I got my ticket out of Trenton after we rolled up a judge and his clerk in Mercer County who were taking payoffs from lawyers for case assignments. I thought I'd get out here and rack up a few crooked pols and bureaucrats in the first year easy. No dice. There's not much in that line in Portland.

It took me a while to learn, but I started to see that if you were a certified, true blue Good Person, all sorts of nice things would fall your way. It was almost like being a made man in Jersey. It might be a sweet development deal, it might be a no-bid city contract, it might be that people looked the other way if you did something a little naughty – maybe even a lot naughty. No one would ever admit there was anything crooked going on, and some of them might not even think there was. 'Joe's a Good Person,' they'd say. 'He's one of us. He's not some bigoted, gun-toting, Bible-thumping right-winger. He'd look out for us, and we should look out for him.' And believe me, they do."

The conversation around the rest of the table had turned general. Bolden noticed Selvaggio's buttonholing of Ned.

"Is Anthony telling you about the notches on his laptop? Don't cross that man, Dirk. He's an ex-wrestler who's perfected the 'grab him by the family jewels and don't let go' hold. It doesn't work so well on women, but then all women in this town are above reproach, aren't they, Deirdre?" He turned to the woman in red on his left.

Her answer was interrupted by the breezy anchorman, who had returned to the lectern as dessert was being served to the patrons in the front row. Ned did his best to remain awake and respectful through the evening's program, which featured a breathless video; a children's chorus, whose high-pitched paeans to peace and harmony were met with resounding applause; and yet another gushing testimonial to the senator, this time by the charity's executive director. After a period of straining his neck, Ned followed the lead of several other patrons in his area and turned his chair around to face the dais. In this position he could barely make out the arch whispers of Bolden, who provided a sotto voce running commentary on the festivities to the muffled amusement of the table.

At last the anchorman delivered his parting quip and the lights of the ballroom came up. Ned noticed as he started to turn his chair around that Karin Bergren was taking her leave. Her stride was fluid, her neck held high. The heads of a number of middle-aged men turned as she passed their tables. She stopped to press a few hands, paused as she approached the double doors to reach for something in her purse, then turned along the back row and headed toward the *Columbian* table. Bolden spotted her as she approached.

"Karin, you honor us humble journalists here in the cheap seats."

"I just wanted to congratulate you on your new theater critic, Roger. I don't know how you managed to pry him away from Chicago. He's promised to keep an open mind, which we don't often find in a critic around here."

Her comment drew a few knowing chuckles around the table.

"I'll be sure to send you an invitation to Milson's retirement party, Karin. Perhaps you'd like to audit some of his courses – he's going into academia, you know."

"We've learned quite enough from him, thank you."

She circled around the table toward Ned.

"I hope you'll enjoy your new job, Mr. Marlowe. Don't let the publisher influence your artistic good sense."

"I never interfere on the editorial side, do I, Deirdre," said Bolden with a giggle. "If I did I would have to call myself a writer instead of a publisher and my self-image would suffer terribly."

"Our new show opens next month. I hope to see you at the opening, Mr. Marlowe. Good night."

She shook Ned's hand with both of hers. He felt the outline of a small slip of paper squeezed into his palm. He quickly closed his fingers on the piece of paper as she turned and left the ballroom.

CHAPTER FOUR

Ned closed the latch of the bathroom stall and leaned his back against the door. He had ducked into the men's room to escape the crush of patrons storming the escalator. He hadn't even attempted to look at the slip of paper, as no part of the lobby offered privacy.

Ned uncurled the clenched fingers of his right hand. He could tell from the texture of the paper that it had been torn from the evening's program, which had featured a collage of the ubiquitous children's art and streamers on the cover. It was folded in half.

"Meet me at the Lowbrow Lounge in the Pearl at ten tonight. Cell 971-570-3378. Karin."

Her handwriting was all sweeping strokes and flourishes. It was evident from the ragged slope of the letters that the note had been written hurriedly and in the dark.

Ned looked at his watch. It was almost nine forty. He knew about the Pearl District from the boasts of the broker who had handled his rental, but had never heard of the Lowbrow.

He was startled by a flush from an adjoining toilet. Ned heard the ringing footfall of a patron's dress shoes across the bathroom's tiled floor. As the water of the sink hissed behind him, he wondered whether this was an invitation he should accept. He took Bolden's chaff with a grain of salt, but he was a new critic in town and did not want to be seen as playing favorites. Then he remembered those strapless shoulders and swelling neckline and any scruples faded fast.

He didn't have time for mass transit. There was a cabstand just around the corner from the Hilton's main entrance. Ned noticed a long line of luxury sedans and SUVs pulling out of a parking garage across the street, but there was almost no queue for the taxis. When he asked for the Lowbrow Lounge, the cabdriver, a square-faced man with an unplaceable Eastern European accent, cast a glance at his tuxedo and gave him an odd look. As the driver pulled out of the stand and switched on the cab's wipers against the drizzle, Ned remembered that he'd left his umbrella under the ballroom chair.

They drove past sleek office towers, which soon gave way to squat low-rise buildings. Scattered second and third story lights shone a hazy yellow through the mist.

They crossed Burnside, the street that he'd learned divides north and south in the city's grid. Chicago may have named one of its chief thoroughfares after an infamous Indian killer, Ned mused, but at least Sheridan had been a competent general. Suddenly, the cab was dwarfed by sprawling facades of brick and glass. Ned asked the driver whether this was the Pearl District. He received an affirmative grunt.

They stopped at an intersection that looked like an architectural rendering for an urban theme park. The amber-lit storefront of a chic restaurant faced off across the street from an upscale chain coffeehouse. The other two corners were occupied by a lighting boutique, whose magnificent fixtures dazzled through the store windows despite the lateness of the hour, and an antique store whose name, stenciled in an elaborate script with burnished gold letters, ended in "Ltd." Glistening white sidewalks were punctuated by perfectly placed benches and street lamps. A well-dressed couple in black, positioned at the light as if to give the scale of the site, clutched the leash of a small dog.

The light changed, and the driver turned at the next block and pulled over to the curb. Ned checked his watch. It was nine fifty-eight. He paid the driver and stepped out into the soggy night.

The Lowbrow Lounge was worthy of the name. Its stature was low, a one-story structure of dubious construction towered over by the brick behemoths a block away. Its lighting was low, a dim glow that filtered through narrow storefront windows bathed in red neon. Its furnishings budget was low, as evidenced by a stack of cheap white plastic patio chairs to the right of the entry secured by a plastic-cased chain that snaked through the cracks of the seatbacks. He would not have placed a wager on the Lowbrow's provenance, but felt a converted pawnshop to be as good a bet as any.

There were two battered doors facing on to the street. Ned chose the left, as that side of the Lowbrow was less dimly lit than the other. He found himself inside a cramped vestibule that in turn offered a choice of two doors. Again he went to the left, which led him into a low-ceilinged, shag-carpeted lounge area with a mirror-backed bar set back along the near wall and rough wooden booths running along the far wall. A handful of empty tables sat just inside the door before the window. The bartender, a lean man with a shaved head hunched over the bar reading a newspaper, looked up as Ned came in and eyed him with a wry grin.

"Getting married tonight?"

Ned looked down at his tuxedo and laughed.

"Afraid not. My boss hooked me as a last-minute fill-in at some charity event."

"And he told you the gig was here? We don't do much in the charity ball line."

"No, I managed to survive the ballroom at the Hilton. Someone invited me to meet her here afterwards."

"We don't have much of a rep as a post-gala watering hole either. Is she also dressed for a wedding?"

"Only if your brides prefer black, strapless, and low-cut."

"I've been down the aisle twice and neither time with someone like that. I might still be married if I had."

Ned did a quick scan of the booths. Two pale college students dressed in standard issue grunge work shirt and jeans were in animated conversation over empty beer glasses. A lone woman with heavy mascara nursed a Mai Tai. A biker couple sat in silence, the man's black-booted feet stretched out alongside the booth as he slouched in his seat.

"What are you drinking until she shows up?"

"Can you manage a Turbo Pimms No. 1 Cup?"

"You bet. I probably get one Pimms order a month, though not usually on a Monday night from a man in a tux."

"What's your usual crowd here?"

"Not you. Unless you're a pretender too. We get a lot of slumming yuppies pretending to be blue collar, ex-hippies pretending to be counterculture, and high school punks pretending to be drinking age. And some tough old bastards who've been coming to this place for years and haven't noticed they're not part of the Pearl District marketing plan."

He cocked his thumb in the direction of the bikers.

"So you haven't been gentrified out?"

"Not hardly. The developers and the planners and the realtors have created something so totally fake down here that people have a desperate need for something real. We're authentic, almost like a museum piece except that admission is only two bucks a drink at happy hour. If I had any brains I'd get out a sledgehammer and beat the place up even more. The more we look like a dive, the better business seems to be."

"You're the owner?"

"Co-owner. My partner owns the building. One of these days a developer is going to make him an offer he can't refuse, but for now we both love the cash flow and thumbing our noses at these snotty assholes who'd love to get rid of us and put in a truffle salon."

"I'll be back. You mix a great Pimms. Most places I go think it's some sort of prescription cold medicine."

"My pleasure. Why do you drink that stuff anyway? I have to say it's not my cup of tea."

"'Cause I'm pretending to be a snob."

"You're doing a helluva job. Whoa." The bartender's head jerked in the direction of the door. "Is that your date?"

Ned swiveled in his barstool. Karin stood just inside the doorway, the red neon light in the window behind her glinting off raindrops beaded on a long black raincoat with gold piping. She was stunning. She spotted Ned and came towards the bar.

"I'm so sorry. Have you been waiting long?"

"No, no. Just long enough to get the lowdown on the Pearl District."

The bartender gave a short bow.

"It's nice to see you, Karin. Or should I say 'Mrs. Bergren?' Are you still drinking Aquavit, or is that not on Jerry's approved list?"

"It's mostly Chardonnay these days, Mick. But why don't you bring me an Aquavit for old times' sake. And 'Karin' will do just fine."

"You got it. Make yourself at home. You see I give you the run of the place on your once-every-fifteen-year visits."

"You were always too good to me, Mick."

Ned followed her to an empty booth between the college students, who stared in awed silence as she passed, and the mascara woman, who mournfully stirred her Mai Tai. The biker couple took no notice.

"I'm sorry I'm late. I meant to arrive first. The truth is, I've been circling the Pearl District for the past half hour."

"You couldn't find the place? It sounds like you were a regular."

"Oh, I knew where the Lowbrow was. I couldn't decide if I should come in."

"After you'd invited me?"

"Because I'd invited you. I'm a married woman with two teenage children and a house in the West Hills. I'm not supposed to be out in seedy bars after hours with young writers."

"So why did you invite me?"

"Because I'm a married woman with two teenage children and a house in the West Hills."

Her full mouth eased into a slow grin.

"You're not going to lobby me for four-star reviews?"

"I wouldn't even try, Mr. Marlowe. I can see that you are a writer above corruption. That's why I invited you."

"Because I cannot be bought?"

"No." She reached for her pocketbook and pulled out a $50 bill as the bartender arrived with the Aquavit. "I believe this should cover Mr. Marlowe and me, Mick, unless you've inflated your drink prices to keep up with the cost of real estate down here."

"That would cover a round for the entire house tonight, Karin. Should I make an announcement?"

Ned noticed as Karin's head was turned toward the bartender how smooth and supple her skin was. There was just the hint of a wrinkle where her chin sloped down to her neck, but it hardly marred the view.

"I think I'll keep a low profile this evening, Mick. If there's a balance after Mr. Marlowe and I have finished, I trust you can put it to good use."

The bartender reprised his earlier bow and returned to the bar.

"You asked why I invited you. It's because you're an artist."

"Thank you. I'm flattered. But you've spoken to me for what, all of ten minutes? How do you know me, to quote *It's A Wonderful Life*, from Adam's off ox?"

"I know an artist. It's been a very long time, but I used to be one myself – well, sort of."

"A painter?"

"No, no. An actress."

"Where?"

"Here. In Portland. Well, not originally. I grew up in Astoria."

"Isn't that a swanky hotel in New York?"

Her smile dimpled only one cheek, Ned noticed.

"It is if you're eating Waldorf salad. No, Astoria is a wet, gray, miserable little fishing town on the Oregon coast. It has more overcast days than just about any place in America."

"You're a hometown booster."

"I hated it. I couldn't wait to get out of there. I kept hoping my father would take a job in California or Hawaii or Florida where it was warm and the sun shone all the time and all the colors were bright. But he never did. He just retired after forty years as an engineer for the county.

There was a children's theater though, thank God. I got started when I was eleven. I tried to get my mother to take me sooner, but she thought theater was frivolous. She wanted me to be a singer, which she considered a serious art."

Ned pulled on his Pimms. "She's right there. Singers practice scales. Actors practice drinking."

"You're going to be worse than Milson."

"You mistake my meaning. Drinking exposes you to the seamy side of life" – Ned made a gesture that embraced the whole of the Lowbrow – "which is invaluable training for theater. Scales expose you to the inside of voice studios, which is invaluable training for a serious art."

She reached up and undid the plait of her hair, which fell in a honeyed swirl around her suntanned shoulders.

"I'll drink to that." They clinked glasses.

"So you conquered the stages of Astoria?"

"I had the lead in all of our high school plays. I was ready to go off to UCLA or Florida State and be a theater major. But my parents are both strict Lutherans – my whole family is Norwegian – and they wouldn't pay for college unless I went to a Lutheran school no more than three hours from home. That didn't leave much of a choice. I ended up at Concordia here in Portland, which didn't even have a theater major."

"And you got married, had two children, and lived happily ever after."

"No, no, I dreamed my theater dreams and read the audition notices in the *Oregonian* religiously. It was about the only thing I did do religiously the whole time I was there. My junior year, I saw a notice from a new company that was holding auditions for *Hedda Gabler*. The only playwright my parents would even mention without frowning was Ibsen – because he was a son of Norway, of course. I didn't think I had a prayer of being cast, and even if I did I had no intention of telling my parents. If they ever did find out, though, I didn't think I'd get in much trouble for doing Ibsen. So I studied the play and put everything I had into Thea, as I was sure they had pre-cast Hedda and Thea, of course, is a blonde Norwegian girl in her twenties. I went to the audition, which was in some hole in the wall just a few blocks from here. Incredibly, I got cast."

"I'm not amazed, although if I were Hedda I would be afraid of being upstaged."

"You're too kind, Mr. Marlowe. I'm not sure you're really cut out to be a critic. So I was twenty, in the big city, and getting paid to be an actress. It was fantastic. I would finish my classes, speed through my homework, swallow my dinner in fifteen minutes, and then catch a ride to the theater. I call it a theater but it was really just an empty storefront that belonged to somebody's relative. It was a dump when we started in there – dusty, dirty, and damp. We had cleaning parties where the whole cast pitched in to scrub the place, then we painted it all black. The utilities had been shut off for a year. We did our first few weeks of rehearsals – in January – with space heaters because they couldn't afford the deposit to turn the gas back on.

We used to go out after rehearsal for a drink, as much just to get warm as for the alcohol. We always went to the Lowbrow. Mick was one of the bartenders here. He's the one who suggested Aquavit; he used to call me the Norwegian ice princess. I'd never had more than a glass of wine in my life.

The show was complete chaos. Hedda and Lövborg were sleeping with each other and broke up a few weeks into rehearsal. They wouldn't speak to each other offstage. The company had no money. It turns out they expected to raise the money for lights, sets, and costumes from advance ticket sales, but they had no one lined up to do promotion. The actress playing the maid quit two weeks before we opened because the dust and the cold were giving her asthma attacks. The director walked out during a tech rehearsal and didn't come back for three hours. The fire marshal came in a few days before opening and wrote us up.

The whole thing should have crashed and burned, but somehow it didn't. No one had done *Hedda Gabler* here in years, and there's a huge Norwegian population in Portland, so the *Oregonian* and the *Columbian* actually gave us a decent write-up before we opened. Opening night we had a full house. Of course that meant about forty people, mostly friends and family, sitting in folding chairs on platforms, but we could still say we were sold out. The audience gave us a standing ovation, and we went out to the Lowbrow afterward to celebrate."

"What did the critics have to say?"

"They loved it. Well, not completely, but on the whole. They had a few complaints. They didn't much care for the director, and they thought Lövborg was over his head."

"Minor quibbles. What about you?"

"The *Oregonian* said I was 'appealing.' Your paper didn't say a thing about me."

"Ah, so you don't just have it in for Milson. You want revenge on the whole institution."

"No, no. It was one of those reviews where the reviewer spends ninety percent of his time showing off his knowledge of nineteenth-century theater and about ten percent on the play he actually saw. He barely said anything about the actress playing Hedda, let alone the smaller parts."

"No offense, but I usually write that sort of review when the history of nineteenth-century theater is more interesting than the play I actually saw."

The two college students let out a whoop and exchanged high-fives. The bartender looked up briefly, then returned to his newspaper.

"I didn't really care about the reviews. I was an actress a long way from Astoria getting paid to be in a play that people were paying money to see. That's all that counted to me. I didn't get paid what I was supposed to, though. At the end of the run the producers came to the cast and said they were way over budget and could only pay us half of what we had been promised. I just took what they gave me. I wasn't doing it for the money."

"Outside of a few sharks in New York, nobody in theater <u>is</u> doing it for the money. That's why nobody makes any."

"Is that wrong?"

"No, it couldn't be more right. It means that artists are in charge, and you know how we artists love our poverty. It's the surest validation of our integrity. If theater were a moneymaker, we'd have to cut businessmen in on the deal, and then they would force us to produce crap that the common man might actually want to see. Poverty enables us to keep our standards up and the great unwashed out of our theaters."

"So cynical so young. So what would you do?"

"Not a thing. Most days I love theater just as it is. But let's be honest and admit that contemporary theater is for the elite and that we put up barriers to entry just like any other industry. Except our barrier to entry is poverty. Fortunately, we have a steady stream of stage-struck youth who keep us afloat because, just like you, they're not in it for the money."

Ned stretched his legs outside the booth, loosened his tie, and ran his fingers through his hair.

"So what was your next show after *Hedda*? Did you corner the market on Ibsen blondes?"

Karin paused, looking down at the scarred table top.

"A man who was at the opening came and sat at my table at the Lowbrow after the show. He knew all about theater in Portland and said he went to New York every year for a week to see the hot shows. He bought me a few rounds of Aquavit and offered on the spot to take me on a New York theater tour. I told him I was still in college. He said we could go over spring break. I put him off, but he came to every performance and went out with us to the Lowbrow after every show. I'd never been east of the Mississippi, let alone New York, so I finally gave in."

"Now can I say it?" asked Ned. "And then you got married, had two children, and lived happily ever after."

She pouted. "Are you always in such a hurry to jump to the end?"

"No, I'm a writer, which usually means I'm stuck in the middle. But when the road to the ending is well marked and well paved, I'm all for taking it."

"Is it really that obvious?"

"It's obvious from your impressive level of personal grooming that you did not take the path of the starving artist. I surmised from your auspicious introduction of a leading man with sufficient wealth for New York theater junkets, buckets of charm, dogged persistence, and, in the bargain, a passion for theater, that he was likely to remain on stage for the duration. You already confessed that you were a married woman with two teenage children. As to the living happily ever after part, that always has a nice ring to it, particularly when the leading lady is a ravishing Norwegian ice princess."

She gave him a searching look. "Are you always this full of yourself?"

"Hey, you invited an artist for a drink. If you wanted a passive audience, you should have gone to the movies."

"The week after the show closed I went to New York with Jerry. We stayed at the Plaza, went to the best restaurants, saw a Sondheim show, an Arthur Miller, a David Mamet. We had champagne after every show, then slept 'til noon. It was fabulous – about as far away from Astoria as I could possibly imagine."

"He swept you off your feet."

"He did. We came back to Portland, and he sent me flowers every day. We went to every play in town. My friends at college were so jealous. He proposed that summer. My parents were thrilled. He's Norwegian on his mother's side, Swedish on his father's – they made allowances for that.

We were married that fall. I didn't much care for Concordia and didn't see any reason to go back to school. I was an actress now, and I wanted to act. But then I got pregnant right after our honeymoon. Jerry said he didn't want me going through the strain of rehearsals with a baby on the way. I thought he was being over-protective, but I really couldn't argue."

The bartender sauntered over.

"Can you manage another, Karin? If it won't breach your marital vows, of course."

"I'm about eighteen years out of practice, Mick, but I'm good for one more and I don't need a note from home, thank you very much. I'm sure Mr. Marlowe will join me for another round."

Ned silently inclined his head.

"Your wish is my command, milady," said the bartender.

"He didn't approve of your husband, did he?" asked Ned after the bartender retreated.

"No. When he heard about our engagement, he sent me a single black orchid with a card that said, 'Break a leg closing night.'"

"Ouch."

"I suppose he thought I'd sold out."

"Had you?"

"I didn't think so. I'd fallen in love with the man of my dreams – handsome, successful, and a huge theater fan. And I wasn't planning to stop acting."

"But circumstances got in the way."

"Which I think Mick knew would happen. He could be scary that way."

"So you took a rain check on the Lowbrow for fifteen years."

"It didn't fit with being a wife and a mother. I suppose Mick would have said it didn't fit with being the wife of Jerry Bergren and a mother to his children."

"But now it does?"

"I'm not sure why, but a few years ago I began to get cravings for the theater. I'd missed it terribly at first, of course, but being a mother filled that hole. I rarely went to a play, almost never picked up a review. Jerry still went all the time, but somehow I either wanted to be on stage or out of the theater. I was never much good being in the audience.

I guess it's a cliché, but when my youngest became a teenager the theater started to pull me back. Even my husband picked up on it. His answer was to get me on the Willamette Stage board."

"Now there's an artistic outlet."

"Don't be mean. He meant well."

"So do all the doctors and lawyers and tinkers and tailors on those boards. I know – my father must have been on a dozen. But it's no place for an artist."

She gave a rueful smile. Ned noticed that single dimple again.

"I know that now, which is why I'm getting out. Why was your father on all those boards?"

"It was sort of his job. Family interests and all that."

"He wasn't a doctor or a lawyer, or a tinker or a tailor?"

"He was a pillar of the community."

"You said 'he was' – is he still living?"

"No. He died recently."

"I'm sorry."

"Thank you. I've been thinking about him today, actually. This was his tuxedo."

"Roger was right about the cut. Your father had great taste."

"If it weren't for his dying, I wouldn't have been at the event tonight. Bolden is one cheap bastard. He wanted somebody with a tux to fill a seat at the table so the paper wouldn't have to pay to rent one."

"That's Roger. I hear he pays his writers next to nothing."

"You heard right. But at least he offered me a full-time job. I was only a part-timer in Chicago."

"What did you do with the rest of your day?"

"Experienced life, of course. I'm a writer, for Christ's sake. I collected the stuff of living for future use. Cubs' games and drinks with beautiful married women in seedy bars were my chief pastimes."

"So you do this often?"

"As often as I'm asked. Which reminds me: why was I asked?"

"I already told you: because I'm a married woman with two teenage children and a house in the West Hills. And because I wanted to drink with an artist. And because it was time to come back to the Lowbrow."

"Damn straight." The bartender sidled up to the booth brandishing a drink in either hand. "It's never too late."

"It's past my usual bedtime, Mick. This was about the time we used to show up, right after a screaming match at the end of rehearsal. Cold, starving, and beside ourselves at the producers. And I wouldn't have had it any other way."

"But you do now."

"You really know how to hurt a girl, don't you?"

"That's what they said in both divorce pleadings. But I've been true to you, Karin. Stayed at the same barstool for fifteen years, waiting for you to come through that door. Kept saying to myself, 'We'll always have *Hedda*.'"

"And now I've come back."

"With a guy in a tux."

"Mr. Marlowe is actually the theater critic for the *Columbian* and an accomplished writer," said Karin.

"Is he now? Well, all critics claim to be writers, don't they. That's why they're so nasty – they can't bear to see someone else's work get an audience."

"Mr. Marlowe has actually been published."

"Then what's he doing in a town like this reviewing plays?"

"He says he came here for the money."

"Then he's deluded as well as resentful."

"So he's the perfect Lowbrow customer."

The bartender roared. "No, Karin, you're our perfect customer. That's why we've been pining away all these years."

"An old school barman," said Ned as the bartender withdrew. "Wicked libations with a twist of lip."

The Mai Tai and mascara woman was preparing to leave. She rose, unsteady, from the booth behind them and reached for a cheap plastic raincoat that hung forlornly on a tarnished brass hook on the side of the booth. As she passed them, she stumbled slightly, then righted herself with a certain dignity and, turning a raddled cheek in their direction, nodded an approving smile as if to bless their presence together.

"So where are you with your novel?"

"I don't remember the first word. The last word seems an infinite distance away. The words in the middle are breeding at a fearsome rate."

"What's it about?"

"I have a strict policy of not spilling the beans until they're fully cooked. Unless you're an esteemed publishing house offering a hefty advance. And these beans are a salmonella and E. coli cocktail at the present moment."

"What about your first book?"

"I'll let it speak for itself. Last I looked, which was two days ago, there were precisely three copies on the shelf at Powell's. I'll write down the name for you."

He took the scrap of paper from the breast pocket of his tux. He wrote the title in one corner, then tore it off, taking care not to rip the part that showed her cell phone number.

"Do you think a place by the ocean might help you sort out the novel?"

"It helped Scott Fitzgerald with *Tender is The Night*. That's a good enough precedent for me. Unfortunately, Portland is not an easy commute from the Riviera."

"There is an ocean about two hours from here, last I looked. We have a place there. I almost never use it."

"Why not?"

"Remember that I was born and raised on the coast. It was almost always damp and gray. It still is. I don't need to go back there to be reminded."

"So why buy a house there?"

"My husband always wanted one. He's from Portland, you see. Somehow you're not a success here unless you can get rained on in your own beach house. We used to go down there a lot when the kids were younger. Now it just sits empty most of the time. There's a big desk right in front of a picture window overlooking the water. It would be a great retreat for a writer."

"Is that a proposition?"

"It's an offer to help a struggling artist."

"That's very gracious of you. And I don't have to promise to submit my reviews for your approval?"

"No strings attached. Just don't invite a bunch of theater people over and trash the place. Or if you do, make sure you invite me."

"And don't forget the Aquavit."

"It wouldn't be a theater party without it."

They eyed each other playfully.

"You're serious?" asked Ned.

"It's the least I can do for dragging a prominent critic out on the town at all hours of the night. Why don't you try it out some weekend? If it suits you, we can see about making it a regular thing."

"I'm not sure about my schedule, but I'd imagine I'll be reviewing most Thursdays, Fridays, and Saturdays. I could go down on Sunday, or maybe even after a show Saturday night. I could pump out the reviews on my laptop and take a few days to work on the book. I should probably wait a bit and make sure the paper isn't too fascist when it comes to showing up at the office. If it's anything like the Chicago paper, they don't really care if you disappear for a day or two as long as the work gets done."

"Good. I'll check our calendar over the next month or so and make sure my husband has nothing scheduled. I doubt he will."

Ned raised his glass. "To a true patroness of literature. Thank you."

Karin raised hers in return. "To a cure for the sophomore slump. And you're welcome."

She looked at her watch.

"I'd better be getting home. I called my daughter from the Hilton and told her I'd be having a drink with a theater friend. That's almost the truth, anyway. She laughed – she said she couldn't remember the last time I'd gone out for a drink without Jerry. He's out of town."

She rose and reached for her raincoat. Ned noticed the sinews of her upper arm gently flex just beneath the smooth, bronzed skin as she pulled the coat up to her shoulders. He stepped out of the booth to help her with the coat.

"How did you get over here?" she asked.

"I took a cab from the Hilton."

"I would offer you a ride, but married women with two teenage children and a house in the West Hills are definitely not supposed to be seen together with young writers after dark."

"Outside of the Lowbrow, you mean?"

"Anything goes inside the Lowbrow, Mr. Marlowe."

She turned towards the door.

"Thank you for not forgetting me, Mick. Would you please call a cab for Mr. Marlowe? He's had a big night."

CHAPTER FIVE

Ned backed the Navigator into a parking space on a darkened side street lined with scrawny trees. To his surprise, he'd been unable to find a space on the street where the theater was and had been forced to go around the block. This was the fourth show he'd been slated to review since arriving in Portland, and the turnout in the first three had ranged from modest to pathetic.

As had the productions themselves. So far he'd had no quarrel with Milson's assessment of the local theater scene. There had been displays of undeniable talent, but it seemed to gush forth, unchanneled.

His greatest frustration had been the under-powering of the plays, a failure to crank the work to a dramatic voltage that would buzz the audience to life. The venues had all been black boxes, confining cubes of darkened space where actors offered up their lines on a flat floor before a cramped audience crammed into platform seating. But a black box, Ned knew, could literally captivate an audience. Caged in a colorless cocoon, robbed of the ability to distance themselves from the spectacle unfolding before them, they were at the mercy of the theater master who could assault them into sensory submission. Sound could carom off walls or gurgle through the seats, light could blaze the players to a terrifying clarity or fade them to a murky obscurity. Most of all, actors at such close quarters could, without hamming or bellowing, graft themselves on to the skin of the audience, then push through their pores to tap the veins beneath.

These productions had failed to use the theatrical means at their disposal. It was not a matter of budget. Ned had seen plays mounted on the most threadbare of shoestrings in Chicago that had boxed the audience into a claustrophobic delirium of wonder the roomy palaces of the big time companies could not hope to match. The plays he had seen here had instead called attention to the companies' empty pockets. The mind wandered and in wandering remarked upon the peeling paint, the unraveling insulation, and the fraying curtains. In the hands of these struggling troupes, the black box had become not a chamber of intimate intensity but a seedy testament to a poverty both economic and artistic.

Ned had thus far spared the rod in his reviews. He wanted to plumb the baseline of theater in Portland before denouncing new lows or, for that matter, proclaiming new highs. His measured criticism had drawn gentle jesting in the *Columbian* newsroom. Bolden had stopped by his cubicle the day after his first review had come out and asked, with a giggle, if Milson had taken his whetstone with him. Selvaggio, a white T-shirt peeking out from beneath the collar of his patterned flannel shirt, said that he thought Chicagoans were supposed to be tough, if you didn't count the three million Cub fans. He hadn't smiled when he said it.

He and Selvaggio had gone to lunch that day at a New York-style pizzeria a few blocks from the office. They had jousted good-naturedly over the merits of thick and thin crusts. After they had returned to the office, the reporter had probed Ned about Karin. They were on to something about her husband, he'd said, and wondered if Ned had picked up anything useful at the gala. They'd talked mostly about theater and writing, Ned had said, and Jerry Bergren's name had barely come up. Out of a certain chivalry, he hadn't told Selvaggio about the Lowbrow. His job was reviewing theater, he'd said to himself. Let the hard news guys lay their own traps.

The next day, Karin had called Ned at the office. In a matter of fact voice she had not used at the Lowbrow, she'd said how much she had enjoyed meeting him at the gala and wished him well in his new duties. She also asked if there were another number that Willamette Stage could reach him on in case they needed to make contact when he was out of the office. At first baffled by her tone, Ned had finally caught on and had given her his cell phone number. He'd thanked her for her good wishes and offered his in return for a successful season.

She had called him on his cell phone that evening. With a laugh, she had apologized for the precaution, but said she never trusted office phone systems, particularly not when Roger Bolden was nearby. She had checked the family calendar and found that the following weekend looked good for Ned to use the beach house. Her husband was playing golf in Astoria, and the kids were going skiing with friends and spending the night in a cabin on Mt. Hood. There was a new Willamette Stage play opening, and she was staying in town for opening night.

Ned had given a wry chuckle. He was scheduled to review the Willamette Stage play the Saturday night of that opening weekend. It was to be his first major Portland review. There was no point in keeping the assignment from her, as she would be reading about it soon enough. He'd made a clean breast of it.

"I knew they'd give you the review. They don't send the freelancers to our shows."

"And am I to gather it is pure coincidence you're offering me the beach house that weekend?"

"The thought of a conflict never entered my mind."

"I'm sure it didn't."

"You accept then?"

"Well, I can't very well ask Bolden what the paper's theater board member beach house policy is. It might be something of a giveaway."

"Is that a 'yes'?"

"I suppose it is. Thank you."

"You're welcome. I'll leave the keys and directions at the front desk of the MAC Club. For obvious reasons I don't want to come by your office."

"The MAC Club?"

"The Multnomah Athletic Club.The center of the West Hills universe. You've not been?"

"I've not been asked. I guess they don't roll out the red carpet for the new theater critic of the local alternative weekly."

"We'll see about that. After you write the Great American Novel, of course. Enjoy the show, Mr. Marlowe."

"Thank you, Mrs. Lincoln. I'm sure I will."

The Willamette Stage performance was tomorrow night. In the meantime, he had this evening's opening of *A Doll's House* to review. He did not have high hopes. In Nora, Ibsen had written a female lead with unlimited potential for scenery-chewing. And in the press packet that had been sent to him by Vox Unum, the theater company producing the play, he'd seen that the company's artistic director was not only playing Nora, she was directing as well. He recalled the old adage about a lawyer who defends himself having a fool for a client. It seemed the worst sort of vanity project.

Still, Milson had said that Vox Unum was among the companies that bore watching. And judging from the mass of patrons streaming toward the theater as he turned the corner, they had a following. The performance was in the SoHo Theater, which Vox Unum shared with the venue's namesake company.

Ned found little that was Soho-like in the theater's surroundings. The overall sensibility was of a light industrial district turning its back on its past but not prepared for a clean break. Windowless tilt-up concrete buildings predominated on the theater side of the street, while across the way a glossy shower and bath fixtures showroom and a stylish clothing boutique signaled a surge in redevelopment. Still, there was an authenticity to the area that was a far cry from the faux urbanism of the Pearl District.

The streetlights were spaced far apart and left dark pools between dirty washes of light along the street below, making the bright glass storefront of the theater all the more inviting. Despite the damp edge of the early November evening, a clutch of hardy smokers huddled on the walkway that sloped gently down to the right of way in front of the theater.

Ned glanced at his watch as he pulled open one of the double doors that led into the lobby. It was seven forty-five, fifteen minutes before curtain. He was making a point in his first circuit through the local theaters of arriving early, at least by his standards in Chicago. He knew how it threw the box office into a tizzy when the reviewer didn't arrive until the last minute. He'd decided to make this modest gesture during his honeymoon period. He was curious in any case to get a sense of the venues and the make-up of their audience. In Chicago, he knew each theater's crowd and made sure to minimize the moments he stood idle in the lobby or sat bored in his seat waiting for the play to begin.

Like the neighborhood outside, the SoHo was on the verge of shedding its industrial skin. The high ceilings, whitewashed walls, and storefront glass of the long, narrow lobby formed an airy contrast to the gritty unfinished cement floor. Jagged expressionist paintings hung on pockmarked concrete.

Ned took his place in the queue in front of a red marbled box office counter manned by a harried ticket manager. On the walls surrounding the counter was an array of framed posters, presumably of prior productions, that were cocked at odd angles. When Ned identified himself as Dirk Marlowe, the box office manager reached for an envelope marked with his name and handed it to him with a smile that was obliging but not servile.

"Welcome to Portland, Mr. Marlowe."

"Thank you. And it's Dirk. Whenever I hear 'Mr. Marlowe,' I start looking around for my father."

"Dirk it is. We've reserved a seat for you. The usher will show you where it is. Enjoy the show."

The box office manager stepped around the end of the counter and gestured toward a slight older woman taking tickets at the double doors into the theater, as if to say "This is the guy." It took several waves to get her attention. She nodded nervously in response.

Arcs of pre-show conversation collided with the lobby walls. The concrete construction made for live sound. He took in the several clusters of patrons chatting in front of the menacing canvases. He found it difficult to typecast the audience by age, attitude, or wardrobe, other than to observe a prevailing informality. There was no sign of either a tie or a dress.

Ned wound his way past a chic young couple in black earnestly engaged with a donnish-looking man in comfortable middle age and a companion Ned guessed was his graduate student lover. Ranged behind them against the wall were two older husband and wife pairs, each tall, erect, and clad in well-knitted sweaters. Ned judged them to be emissaries from the local Scandinavian heritage society, come to pay homage to the great Norwegian playwright.

The usher blinked anxiously as Ned approached the doors to the theater. She pointed to a seat in the center of the middle row on which an orange laminated "Reserved" tent sign was perched and in a creaky voice identified that as his place. She, too, encouraged him to enjoy the show.

Ned passed into a dim vestibule. He felt the hard surface of the concrete lobby beneath his feet give way to more forgiving plywood. Before him, a single black curtain draped on a length of metal pipe set over the passageway into the theater had been pulled aside and lashed to the wall to allow the audience to pass freely.

Ned entered the theater and was struck by its intimacy. Three ascending rows of blue cloth seats were configured in a gentle horseshoe around the floor-level performance space. The patron seated farthest away could not have been more than fifteen feet from the stage. Each turn of the horseshoe was bisected by aisle stairs leading up to a curtained doorway. Ned wondered whether each gave on to passages running behind the audience flanks. He took the near aisle and, with murmured apologies to those already seated in his row, negotiated the narrow channel to his seat.

The towering ceilings of the lobby carried over into the theater. A tightly spaced lighting grid caged nearly the full expanse of the ceiling, interrupted only by two massive support beams that, to Ned's surprise, had been left in their natural wood tone rather than painted black. The lighting booth was embedded in the wall above the curtained doorway to his right. Behind its dark glass windows Ned saw the board operator, hunched in a headset over his cue sheet below a hooded amber light.

The looming back wall behind Ned was painted a flat black, as were the low walls over each side of the audience. Above these side walls, fenced in by black railings, were catwalks leading to the lighting booth on Ned's right and to nothing he could discern on his left. He saw that the ceiling height and the catwalks offered a resourceful director a number of staging options.

The stage wall was covered from floor to almost ceiling in an elaborately patterned wallpaper. The style of the paper recalled William Morris. In the center of the stage wall were French doors done in a light Scandinavian-style aspen or birch. The performance space was set as a Victorian-era drawing room, with heavy furnishings in mahogany and walnut, voluminous upholstery, and densely woven Oriental rugs. Christmas holiday decorations adorned the room.

Music wafted softly over the audience. Classical was not Ned's musical forte, but he thought the theme echoed one of Grieg's *Peer Gynt* suites. The houselights bathed the set in a dusky glow.

The front cover of the program given to him by the jittery usher featured a glossy color background in the same ornamental pattern as the stage wallpaper. Ned placed the program inside his reviewer's packet. He did not read programs prior to writing his reviews, if at all.

The chic couple in black and the well set up don and his graduate consort filed in, still in conversation, and took seats in the front row that they had saved with long coats. The usher drew the curtain behind them. The music stirred briefly, then faded out.

Ned had seen *A Doll's House* once before. The actress playing Nora – the sheltered banker's wife harboring a dark secret from her bourgeois husband that could provoke a scandal and shatter their marriage – had resorted to melodrama, careening around the stage, convulsed in spasms of angst. This emotive excess diluted one of the most wrenching final scenes in the canon of Western theater: Nora's decision to leave her husband in spite of a concession from the play's villain that will leave their reputations intact. When the husband in the previous production heard the door slam behind Nora, Ned had silently congratulated him on being rid of an incurable over-actress.

But Vox Unum's actress distilled with a breathtaking purity the child-like essence of the part. In her hands, Nora was a spoiled little girl, alternately naughty and nice, playing dress-up to bewitch the grown-ups around her. She displayed the literal thoughtlessness of children at play with impulsive abandon.

Most crucially, she grasped that Nora's fear of discovery is the terror of a child left alone in the dark, not the bodice-heaving agony of a damsel in distress. The actress was possessed of a mortal dread befitting a child beset by bogeymen. As the forces of darkness bore down upon her, ghostly fingers constricting her windpipe were almost palpable.

The lights of the theater transformed the black box into a true dollhouse, initially spacious and festive, then remorselessly drawing inward to become a chamber of confinement for Nora. The bright beams of the first several scenes slowly lost their luster, shrouded in malignant shadow.

The gloom abated for a while when the husband, unaware of the peril facing them, assured his wife he would take on his shoulders the weight that was crushing her. Nora's frame stretched and lightened, just like a child's on hearing an adult say that everything was going to be all right.

But the great marvel of the performance was Nora's transfiguration in the play's final act. She became a woman. It was as if the spirit of the child had been expelled from her body when she learned that her husband would not make good on his promise. He would not take on their burden, but would instead consign her to a stifling servitude. Her figure grew fuller, her face heavier, as the child-like adoration she had for him was shattered by the recognition of his weakness.

The actress playing Nora was a doll personified. Pale, with flaxen hair gathered elaborately and huge, luminous blue eyes, she was an exquisite plaything. Her fragility cried out for protection from the cruel world outside the cloister of her home. As she took her accustomed positions in the family drawing room during the early scenes of the play, it was if she had been placed in each spot by her husband, who liked to pose her just so. When she practiced the tarantella, a Spanish peasant dance that enraptured the guests at a fancy dress ball the couple attends offstage, it was if someone had pulled a string, triggering one of a doll's handful of pre-programmed tricks.

At intermission, Ned did not wander about the lobby, as was his usual practice. He had to admit that he generally enjoyed sipping his coffee and taking in the furtive glances from the theater's house staff as they tried to gauge his reaction. But this evening he stayed in his seat and pulled the program from his press packet, on a quest for information about this mesmerizing actress.

There was little to be had. She was not given to the numbing recitation of previous credits or breathless acknowledgment of fellow cast members and family that marred so many program bios.

Her name was Robin Story. She had co-founded Vox Unum several years before and served as its Artistic Director. This was the first production where she had both directed and performed. This was her first encounter with the work of Henrik Ibsen. She had graduated with a degree in theater from Portland State University. That was it.

As the slam of the door reverberated across the theater and the house went dark, Ned shot up from his seat, his hands pounding together in driving rhythm. The audience rose with him as one. Light flooded the stage as the cast members strode in from the wings, arraying themselves across the set. There was no hierarchy to the curtain call. The actors came in not according to some size-of-part-based sequence, but all together. Nora and her husband were not even positioned in the center of the stage. The cast took three bows in unison, one to the audience in the center section and one to each wing. They then departed as an ensemble and did not return, despite the cascades of applause that swept across the theater, unleashing a roar pierced by several shrill whistles.

The ovation died away to a preternatural silence as the stunned audience remained standing. Then a furious buzzing erupted as the house lights came on. Each audience member seemed locked in disbelieving dialogue with his neighbor. Other than a few stray patrons, no one made for the theater exit, where the meager usher had drawn the curtain.

Ned stood alone in the middle of his row, patrons engaged at full tilt on either side of him. He looked out over the set, now once again an unremarkable bourgeois drawing room. His face felt flushed. He stooped to collect the press packet from beneath his seat.

His mind was racing and yet strangely blank. Ordinarily his review would have started to compose itself as the curtain call came to a close. But not tonight. Instead he shuttered rapid-fire through images of Nora at each stage of her performance. He was transfixed, to a degree that he found almost embarrassing.

He was tempted to join, at random, in one of the conversations seething around him. But he decided he did not want to temper his exaltation by sharing it with strangers. Clutching his packet, he excused his way through to the aisle, then wove around several other audience clusters to the vestibule. A tasteful basket, vaguely Scandinavian in design, had been placed atop a side table covered with a black cloth. A card showing in simple calligraphy the symbol for recycling was fixed to the basket handle.

Blinking as he entered the whitewashed lobby, he made a beeline for a drinking fountain he spotted below the most jarring of the expressionist paintings. His thirst was great. He never loitered in a lobby after a performance he was reviewing, but this evening he could not bring himself to leave. He saw the door to the men's bathroom in a small alcove off the lobby and went in to splash come cold water on his face. The bathroom's harsh fluorescent light gave him an unsettling pallor as he stared at himself in the mirror against the dingy backdrop of the concrete wall behind him. He had not really looked at himself in a mirror since his gala evening in a tux. He felt somehow smaller now.

He went back into the lobby and pretended to inspect the paintings. He knew what he really wanted was to see Nora again. Audience members were gradually relocating to the lobby, still joined in earnest conversation. Then he saw one of the actors, the would-be villain, stroll triumphantly through the double doors, to be greeted by admiring friends. After several minutes of congratulations, he heard the actor tell his entourage that the cast would be gathering for drinks at McMenamins Tavern.

Ned made a point of not patronizing bars where casts were known to socialize after a performance he was reviewing. Even if the review were likely to be positive, his presence there could make for awkward encounters that were best avoided. It was not an especial concern of his, but he knew that the actors would spend the rest of the evening gazing anxiously in the direction of his table, wondering what might be running through his mind instead of enjoying the party.

Ned recalled seeing an ad for McMenamins in the *Doll's House* program. He pulled the program from his packet and thumbed to the page with the ad. The tavern was only one street over from the one where he had parked.

Ned headed toward the doors of the glass storefront. Opposite the box office counter he noticed a half moon-shaped table, also draped in black, on which racks holding season brochures for Vox Unum and SoHo Productions were neatly perched. He reached to grab both brochures. As he did, he heard a voice behind him.

"Please take as many as you like, Dirk."

It was the box office manager, beaming at him from behind the counter.

Ned turned around as he placed the brochures inside his packet.

"Thank you."

"Thanks for coming. I hope you enjoyed the show."

Ned paused. He never tipped his hand before a review was published.

"I did. Very much. Good night."

The box office manager gave a slight shudder. A rejoicing smile creased his face.

"It's been a great night."

Ned nodded, then pushed his way through the double doors into a chill drizzle outside. He'd left his umbrella in the car. He thought of going back to the Navigator and heading home. He went down the short walkway to the sidewalk, then pulled up the collar of his coat and turned in the direction of McMenamins.

CHAPTER SIX

Ned cast furtive glances toward the tavern door as the Vox Unum party streamed in. He cursed silently as he saw that Nora was not among them.

McMenamins was dark and dense. Black upholstered booths lined the windows overlooking the street on either side of the entry door. An imposing bar stretched along one wall of the tavern, then jogged toward the center of the room. Opposite the curve of the bar was a pool table, its rich green felt lit by a colored glass fixture overhead. Flanking the pool table was an array of broad tables and long benches in matching battered oak. Beyond these against the far wall were a few cramped wooden booths, less inviting than those by the entry.

Ned had guessed that the Vox Unum cast would claim one of the free-standing tables. He had snagged a booth in the far corner that would give him a discreet view of the theater party. The walls around his booth were hung with Summer of Love-era concert posters from the '60s, baroque psychedelic memorials to unfamiliar bands: Moby Grape, Captain Beefheart and His Magic Band, Quicksilver Messenger Service. The collection was incongruous in what otherwise seemed a standard issue neighborhood tavern.

He had correctly anticipated where the cast would gather. The party pulled together two of the wooden tables. This seemed a familiar ritual, carried out with much good-natured banter.

Ned took several slugs from a weak Gibson, his standby when a bar offered no Pimms, and opened his press packet. While he had no burning desire to revisit the program, he was not accustomed to drinking alone in bars and needed something to occupy his eyes while he waited for Nora to arrive.

He re-read Robin Story's bio. There was as little subtext as there was text. Its understatement only whetted his appetite to engage her, somehow.

He scanned the bios of the other cast members, who had all been solid though clearly playing in Nora's shadow. He was struck by the near exclusive listing of Vox Unum acting credits. He was accustomed to actors showing how in demand they were around town.

Ned found himself suddenly hungry. He'd grabbed a quick pasta dinner with Selvaggio after work, but that might have been yesterday. He looked over the menu, which offered unexceptional fare leavened by traces of clever naming. He decided to bypass the Communication Breakdown Burger and the Stormin' Norman in favor a hummus plate. He tried to signal the attention of his harried waitress.

Instead his gesture caught the eye of a woman who was approaching the Vox Unum gathering. At first Ned did not recognize her. She was certainly not part of the *Doll's House* cast. He assumed she was just one of the many hangers on who take part in an opening night post-show celebration, but as he looked closer he saw that she had played a lead in the show he'd reviewed last week.

Her production had suffered from serious depth problems. This actress had surpassed the rest of the cast, and his review of her had been quite favorable – in contrast to his damning-with-faint-praise treatment of the others in the company. What stood out from her performance was a certain fearlessness.

She had noticed him. Although she circled around the theater crowd, dispensing the ritual hugs and kisses, he saw over the top of the *Doll's House* program that she stole several glances in his direction. After a few minutes among the celebrants, she broke away and came toward his booth.

"Aren't you Dirk Marlowe?"

"I confess it. And you're Elena Devlin?"

"You remembered."

"I'd be lying if I said I never forget an actress's face, but having seen yours just last week it still sticks in my mind. Particularly as the drinks here are not strong enough to make me forget much."

She laughed a deep smoker's laugh.

"Thanks for the review. It was very nice."

"No thanks required. I called it as I saw it."

"I thought you were fair, much fairer than that prick Milson would have been. It's a good show, but it should have been a lot better. We lost some actors just before rehearsals started. They got offered bigger parts in other shows and split."

"An old story."

"I know, but it hadn't happened to me for a few years."

"If I may ask, how did you know who I was? I've only been doing reviews here for a few weeks now."

She gave a throaty chuckle.

"I keep a sharp look-out. The house manager pointed you out to the stage manager, who came backstage and told me who you were."

"I thought you actors didn't want to know if a critic was in the house."

Her face flashed contempt.

"There's a lot of superstition in this business, but not with me. I'm the only one the stage manager told, because she knew I wanted to know. I always want to know. I'm not into acting with my head in the sand. I want to know who's doing my review, and where they're sitting. And what they fucking had for dinner – pardon my French."

"It was pasta, in my case. You make it sound like opposition research."

"If you'd been acting in front of that asshole Milson all these years, that's how you'd see it too." Her tone softened. "Is it OK if I join you? Or are you expecting someone?"

Ned hesitated slightly.

"No. I'd be delighted."

She was dark and heavily made up, with a bold red lipstick that broadcast the sensuousness of her lips. Her face had a squarish shape that Ned associated with Eastern Europeans. Her eyes, set wide apart, were a speckled gray that gave her a feline quality at odds with her thick neck and jaw. Her hair was black and coarse.

"Can I get you a drink? Or are you the only teetotalling actress ever to take the stage?"

Another hearty laugh.

"Not hardly. The party's just beginning. I'll take a vodka gimlet. If you can find someone to serve you."

Ned renewed his efforts to attract the waitress's attention. She finally acknowledged him with a weary look.

"They seem to be stretched a little thin."

"They always are. It's part of the charm of the place."

"It sounds like you're a regular."

"I was. Not any more, though."

"What brought you back?"

"I wanted to be here for Robin. This is a big night for her. I knew our show would get out before hers, so I decided to come on over. Show the flag, you know."

"That's a rare gesture of solidarity in the theater community."

"She's an old friend. We worked together in a bunch of shows, then I joined Vox Unum right after she started it."

"But you're not with them any longer?"

"Nope. I'm a free agent. Open to the highest bidder. Not that that's anything much around here," she sneered.

Ned noticed a stirring among the theater party. His pulse quickened as he saw Nora approaching the tables, alone. Conversation in the group stopped among those who had spotted her, and they began to clap. Within seconds the whole of the rear section of the tavern exploded in applause as the gathering rose to its feet. Ned and Elena Devlin joined them.

Nora smiled. It was a smile more of quiet satisfaction than of triumph. She took a seat on the far end of one of the benches, well away from the center of the party where the two tables had been joined. As she sat she brushed her fine blonde hair away from her face. It lay simple and straight atop her shoulders, a far cry from her character's elaborate hairdo on stage.

The applause continued for half a minute, then the group took their seats again. The buzz of celebration quickly resumed around the tables.

"That's quite a tribute," said Ned as he sat down.

"She's amazing. You saw the show. How was she?"

"I don't like to give my reviews away."

"Then don't go drinking in bars with the cast."

"Touché," said Ned. "She was magnificent. One of the finest performances I've ever seen. On any stage, anywhere."

The actress bowed her head for a moment, then looked up at Ned.

"I should be jealous, but I'm not. Well, not most of the time, anyway. She works so damned hard, and she gives up so much."

"Gives up what?"

"Her life, basically. Vox Unum is everything to her. It's all she really cares about. As long as I've known her she dreamed of having a company totally dedicated to ensemble. Actors who know each other so well that, as she says, their hearts beat together, they breathe together, they blink together. All for one, and one for all. You know how hard that is to pull off in this business?"

"Almost impossible."

"Something always gets in the way. It's like a rock band when the lead singer or the guy who writes all the songs ditches the group and goes solo. Too much ego. But not with Robin. She has more talent than anyone else in that company by far, but she never puts herself above the group. Ever. To her it's all about the craft."

"She must have had other offers."

"Christ yes. Just after she started the company they were shooting a Hollywood movie up here. The director came to one of her shows and flipped out. Came backstage after the show and offered to pull every string he had to get her into the movies. She listened to him and then very politely told him to get lost. I was there, heard the whole thing. I would have jumped the guy and offered to fuck his brains out on the spot. But not Robin.

She gets calls all the time for commercials. The way she looks, that blonde innocence thing, they drool all over her. Her mother started her in modeling when she was like five, and she worked all the time. When her dad got laid off, that modeling money saved their bacon. But she hated it, and now she turns them all down. She says it compromises her art."

"Where's she from?"

"Some piss-ant mill town down the Valley near Salem. Her dad was a saw mechanic or something. The whole place went down the tubes with the spotted owl thing. They ended up shutting the mill down."

"How did she get into theater?"

"How do we all get into it? They had a theater in high school. She didn't want to be a cheerleader, so she went out for drama. Same with me. She loved it, and I guess she had a great teacher who told her to stick with it. He helped get her into Portland State. She worked her way through school doing modeling and commercials."

"Is that where you met?"

"Nah. I never made it to a four-year school. I did two years at community college, and that was more than enough school for me. We met on a show. They put it on in some dump over in Northeast. We both saw a notice in the paper and got cast out of a cattle call. The company folded right after we closed. Never got paid. The only good thing that came out of it was Robin. We did some more shows together, and she directed me once."

The waitress, pudgy and tongue-pierced, finally made it to the booth. She looked spent, and the bandana masking her hair was coming loose.

"Sorry. Busy night. What can I get you?"

"The lady will have a vodka gimlet. I'll have another Gibson, but easy on the ice, please. And I'll take one of your hummus plates. Do you need anything to eat?"

The actress waved him off. The waitress trundled away.

"How was she as a director?"

"Jesus was she prepared. The show was *The Monogamist* – you know it?"

"Sure. Christopher Kyle. Baby Boomer couple falls out, sleeps with Generation Xers, with unfortunate results."

"Right. The wife's a professor who's just written a book about Emily Dickinson. Robin actually read most of Dickinson's poems just to get a better feel for the part."

"Damn. How was the show?"

"Great, all things considered. The Emily Dickinson actress dropped out two weeks before rehearsals started. Surprise – more money on another show. It didn't faze Robin. She was ready to do the part herself, if she had to. We told her that was crazy."

"No crazier than what she did tonight."

"She's been working up to the acting/directing thing for a long time. It's not showing off. She wanted to see just how deep she could go into a script. Total immersion, you know."

"They do it in film. But there the director gets to see himself as an actor every day in the rushes. It's hard to get that distance when you're on stage. Particularly when you're playing Nora, who's always on. But however she managed it, it worked. Flawlessly."

They both looked in the direction of Nora. The celebration swirled around her. She was listening intently to the actor seated to her left, her eyes locked into his.

"How did the company get that space? It's one of the better black boxes I've seen."

"SoHo built the theater. They only do three shows a year, so they were looking for another company to share the space. Robin knew them from *The Monogamist*. They partner with people on shows. You put in a proposal, and if they pick you they give you the space, put up the money, and do the publicity and the box office. You basically do the rest. They chose Robin as their partner on *The Monogamist*. We did it in a storefront in the Pearl District before they built the theater. When she heard they were looking for someone to share the new space, she went for it.

We couldn't believe it. Vox Unum had only been around for six months. We'd only done one show. Signing a lease seemed crazy.

We had these endless company meetings because we wouldn't do anything unless we all agreed.

Finally Robin came back and said she'd lined up enough money to cover our rent. She said she was so sure it would work out that she would sign the lease personally, which SoHo wanted because our company had no track record. We all trusted her totally, so when she said that we decided to do it."

"That was one hell of a gamble," said Ned. "But it looks like it's paid off."

"Big time. In a few years we went from nothing to a couple hundred subscribers. The reviewers always see our shows opening weekend, not two or three weeks into the run like some of the smaller companies. Even Milson came to our openings, that sonofabitch. So did you."

"Milson told me the company was capable of great intensity and bore watching. That was enough for me to make the opening."

"That's what he said, uh? He wasn't always so nice."

"I don't mean to pry, but I notice that when you talk about Vox Unum you still use 'we' and 'us.' What made you leave?"

The actress cast another look toward Nora. The square lines of her jaw hardened, but her eyes seemed mournful.

"I'm getting out of Portland. As soon as I can raise the money I'm going to LA. By next summer, I hope.

I'm so sick of the scene here. You can't make a living as an actress, not even if you're lucky and get some commercials. I wait tables up at Kornblatt's. They're great and a lot of actors work there, but it just wears you down. I'm always tired when I show up for rehearsal at night. My feet hurt, and I just want to go home and take a bath.

I know that's what a struggling actress is supposed to do. I know you have to pay your dues. But it's never going to get better. You're never going to get your big break. The most you can hope for is that some of those stuck-up pricks over at the big companies finally pay attention to you and cast you enough times so that you can get your union card. But once you get that, you've pretty much priced yourself out of the market, so you can't work unless you've fucked somebody up in Seattle and can get in some shows up there.

So you probably give up your union card, but then you're back to working with the smaller companies. Sometimes the rest of the cast is OK, but a lot of the time there's people who make you cringe when they open their mouth. Nobody knows how to run the company, so there are always fights and people leaving. Everyone wants to act and direct. Nobody wants to do PR, so you're lucky if you draw fifty people, even on a Saturday night. And the theater's usually a mess, and you freeze your ass off in the winter and sweat like a pig in the summer.

You barely have enough money to pay your rent, and you're tired all the time. So you keep going until you can't take it any more and you give up and get married and have kids and forget about theater, or you end up some sad old actress with no life and nothing in the bank and no insurance if you get sick. And a scrapbook full of reviews from assholes like Milson telling you what a miserable piece of acting shit you really were.

So I'm going to LA. I'm going to some place where there's a pot of fucking gold at the end of the rainbow. I don't care if my odds of making it are a hundred-to-one or a thousand-to-one or ten million-to-one, I'm going where at least I've got a shot of leaving this all behind. I don't care if the town if full of backstabbers and phonies and perverts. We get all that here, without the money."

She spoke furiously but in a near whisper so as not to be overheard. Her hands, which had been gesturing wildly, dropped to the table.

"I'm sorry. You asked why I left the company. I left because I needed to act for me. I wanted to get noticed for me, because that's the only way I was going to get out of here. There are agents and casting directors and even some actors from LA who live up here and have connections. They come to the theater sometimes and you hear stories about people getting noticed.

Vox Unum was all about ensemble. It was great – amazing really. But it was all about the company, get rid of your ego, no stars. It was hours every week of movement exercises, breathing exercises, trusting exercises – all so we would be like one cosmic actor, so no one would stand out. God, it was intense. It was a fucking cult.

But it worked. We did great stuff. But let's face it. Vox Unum was all about Robin. She was Snow White, and we were just a bunch of fucking dwarves. Not because she put herself above us. She never did. But she's such an incredible actress. Unreal. So she could do all this ensemble stuff, but she was still going to be the star. It's like when you put a great dancer in the chorus line. She's doing the same moves as everyone else, but she doesn't really belong there, you know?

So I had to get out. It was an amazing little company, a miracle really, but it was taking me nowhere. It was incredible art, but art's not a team sport."

The disheveled waitress spun into view. She unloaded the drinks and the hummus plate, then bolted. Ned raised his Gibson.

"To your future success, in Tinseltown or wherever your rainbow may lead you. Your departure will be the Portland stage's loss."

"I'll drink to that."

She tipped back the gimlet glass and drank with gusto. Ned raised his eyebrows, pursing his lips in mock disapproval.

"Sorry about that. I'm Serbian. We don't sip our drinks."

"Serbian? Devlin?"

"Stage name. My real name is Elena Divac. I got tired of trying to spell it for everyone. And I look so much like an East European peasant anyway that I don't need my name to finish off the typecast. I've got to get to LA before my hips start to look like my mother's."

With a raspy laugh she reached for a piece of pita and dipped it in the hummus. Ned steered the conversation back to the only topic on his mind.

"So how did Robin take your leaving the company?"

"I was terrified to tell her, even though we'd been friends for so long. But really because we'd been friends for so long. I knew what the company meant to her, and I'd be telling her I didn't want to be part of her dream.

I finally worked up the nerve after we closed our last show last season. I came up to her just as we'd finished strike. Everybody in the company helps with strike. She saw the look on my face and she knew.

'You're leaving,' she said.

She'd seen right through me. She said she could tell for months that my heart wasn't in it. She could see it in my work, even though I hadn't noticed any difference. I told her that I had to get out of Portland and go to LA, that I had to go for it.

I tell you, I felt like Judas with Jesus fucking Christ. She wasn't angry at all. She told me that she understood and that I had to do what was best for me. She said she would do anything she could to help. She thanked me for everything I'd done for the company. She gave me a big hug and said we'd always be friends."

"And you still are?"

"We still are. It's not the same though. But it's not her, it's me. I don't think she's changed toward me at all. But whenever I see her now, I feel like I have something to make up to her.

I guess that's why I'm here tonight. I don't usually go to other casts' parties, especially not opening night. It's their show, not mine, and they're all psyched about something that's got nothing to do with me. But I knew how big a deal this show was to Robin, so I wanted to show her I cared. So, of course, here I am talking to a critic.

I should get over there. Hey, how was Rachel Talbert, you know, the one who played Mrs. Linde? I'm pretty sure that would have been my part."

She rose from the booth, cradling her drink in her hands.

"She was fine. She didn't stand out, but I suppose that was the point."

She had already turned away from the booth toward the celebration. His response barely registered.

Ned tried to sound casual.

"Hey, ask Robin over if you'd like. I'd love to meet her."

"OK," she said over her shoulder.

Ned watched her as she circled around the joined tables and came up behind Nora, who was still deep in conversation with the actor to her left. Elena placed a hand on Nora's shoulder. She turned and with apparent delight sprang from her seat and gave Elena a big hug.

Ned took a pull on his Gibson, which was just as watery as the one before, and slathered a few pita pieces with the punchless hummus. He took up the *Doll's House* program again, but his focus was on Nora. She had engaged with Elena as she had with the actor next to her, wrapping them both in a warp of intimate conversation removed from the tumult of the party.

Elena soon gestured toward Ned. Nora looked in his direction, and he pretended to be consumed by the program. She nodded, and the two of them began a circuit around the tables. Unlike Elena, Nora carried no drink glass. Ned felt his stomach muscles tense as they approached his booth. He caught himself chewing on his lower lip.

"Robin, this is Dirk Marlowe from the *Columbian*. You probably heard he's the new Milson. Except that he actually enjoys theater. Especially tonight, he told me. I had to beat it out of him, though – he said he doesn't like to give his reviews away."

Ned stood up in his booth, though the narrow space between the table and bench made the footing awkward. Elena had stolen his thunder. He had intended to pay tribute to Nora, but at a moment and in a manner of his choosing.

Nora's eyes locked in on his. He might have been the only person in the tavern.

"Welcome to Portland, Dirk."

Her voice was warm. It was a voice he had to hear more of.

She wore no make-up, but needed none. Her skin was unlined and unblemished. She had the pallor typical of flaxen blondes. The huge, shining eyes that had given her such a doll-like appearance on stage were not the product of artful lighting or eyeliner. They were of a startling turquoise and so liquid as if to be on the verge of tears.

She was slight, even fragile. She wore a baggy, faded pullover and loose-fitting jeans that seemed to engulf her.

"Thank you," said Ned, trying to recover his composure. "I'm glad to be here."

"I heard you came from Chicago. A great theater city."

"Yes," he managed.

"A place where you can be devoted to your craft."

"I agree."

"I'm afraid I've never been there. Too busy trying to learn everything I can here."

Ned saw an opening. But as he was shaping a compliment, Elena broke in.

"And teaching all of us." She made a gesture embracing the whole of the Vox Unum party.

"I'm sure I learned more from you, Elena, than whatever you were able to pick up from me. We're an ensemble, Dirk. We both teach and learn from each other. I'm sure there must be many companies like ours in Chicago."

"Sure. It's hard though."

"It's never easy being an artist. But I would imagine keeping an ensemble together is more difficult in Chicago. More opportunities, more distractions. I'm afraid our horizons are more limited in Portland, but in some ways that's good. Not for everyone though." She gave Elena's hand a squeeze.

"Yeah, not if you're interested in minor things like making a living."

Elena's tone was biting, but she placed a hand on Nora's shoulder as she spoke.

"I'm afraid Elena's less of a fan of our city than I am, Dirk. But then she's a native. I suppose it's familiarity breeding contempt. I'm from a small town. I'm still getting used to having half a million people so near to me. I don't mind so much if only fifty of them come to our plays, as long as we're able to touch at least one."

From the mouth of someone else the lines might have seemed clichéd, the humility strained. But to Ned she was in compelling earnest.

"What brought you to Portland?"

She was taking an interest in him. Asking about Chicago, about his move here. If only he could get Elena out of the way.

He considered giving his stock "for the money" line, but ended up answering weakly, "The job. I was only reviewing part-time in Chicago."

"Milson was only reviewing part-time in Portland, even though he had a full-time job," Elena spat.

"The critic who had your job was not a favorite of Elena's, I'm afraid."

"Or anyone else in town."

"You're harsh, Elena. If he had a sin as a critic, it was that he cared too much. I think at times he cared so much that he asked for more than we could deliver. If that's a sin, it's one I can forgive. I hope you'll care as much about our community's theater as he did, Dirk."

It dawned on Ned that he had not invited Nora to sit down. She'd spent enough time with her company. He wished he could get her out of there.

"I'll certainly try. Would you care to join me?"

Elena was standing closest to the opposite bench. Without comment she began to slide into the booth. Ned silently cursed.

"You're very kind, Dirk," said Nora. "I'm afraid I was just about to head home when Elena came over. There is great energy in this play, but when it's over I'm just spent. We have another performance tomorrow, and I need my sleep. We're delighted to have you here in Portland. I hope you enjoyed the show."

He thought this might have been a signal, an invitation for him to escort her out, to continue the conversation elsewhere. He was trapped, though. Elena had already taken a seat in the booth. He tried to come up with a way out, but in that instant Nora kissed Elena on the cheek and turned away. His eyes followed her as she circled the tables, quietly pressing hands and shoulders. Then, without fanfare, she was gone.

CHAPTER SEVEN

Wind lashed the flanks of the Navigator as it emerged from the woods on to an exposed overpass. Ned had checked the forecast for the coast, which called for smallcraft warnings and heavy surf. He figured he was still twenty to thirty minutes from the ocean, but it was blowing hard already.

He was wide awake and needed to be. The narrow highway jogged and dipped, and several times trees had loomed in his windshield as he'd taken unexpectedly sharp curves. The trees seemed to claw at him in the glare of his high beams, which he'd had on almost the entire trip since leaving the main coast highway west of Portland.

The note Karin had left at the Athletic Club desk with the beach house keys urged him to stop for coffee if he decided to take off after the Willamette Stage show. He had, at a diner where he'd also ordered some apple pie. Her note had presumably been based on driving a dark and unfamiliar highway late at night and not on the sleep-inducing qualities of her company's performance.

To be fair though, his mind had not really been on the play as he sat in the middle of the fifth row in Willamette Stage's plush venue. In fact, since he'd made his way unsteadily out of McMenamins after his fourth Gibson last night, his mind had not really been on anything except Nora. He knew her real name, of course, but he had seen her first as Nora and that was the name that captured her essence shimmering in his mind.

He had never freebased cocaine, but wondered whether the purity of her performance was anything like that rush. As a critic he'd had plenty of good buzzes, performances that stayed with him, moved him, reminded him why he kept coming back to review shoestring productions seated in the threadbare seats of rundown venues when he hadn't needed the money. But the warm glow of those encounters was as a sputtering candle to the white heat that had seared him in the theater last night.

He was bewitched by her artistry and amazed by her devotion to craft. She seemed to him a vestal, the white-robed guardian of a decaying temple who stood ready to sacrifice herself on its altar. Her child-like fragility, that white-blonde hair, those luminous eyes, all suffused her with an otherworldliness befitting a votary.

He had connected with her last night. Of that he was sure. There had been no chance to take it anywhere, of course, not with her cast all around and Elena making herself at home in his booth. But something had passed between them that was more than just an actress giving a reviewer his due.

He knew how he would go after her. He'd take advantage of being new in town to ask her out for coffee. He'd say it was just so he could get to know the companies making an impact on the local scene. Get the scoop on mission, history, etc., etc. He'd wait until after the review came out, of course, but not long. He couldn't wait long.

There had been no one with her last night. She'd made no mention of a boyfriend. Surely if there had been someone in the picture he would have put in an appearance at the cast party. It looked as if the field were open.

That wasn't surprising. Elena had said all Nora cared about was Vox Unum. She was completely immersed in her work, so it only made sense her social life would suffer. He appreciated that as only a fellow artist could. He'd make sure she understood that he understood.

It would be a bit awkward as a new critic going out with the artistic director of a leading local company. He'd made a point of not dating theater people in Chicago, although that was as much because they were all head cases as it was reviewer protocol. They'd have to be discreet, at least at first, and he'd probably have to assign stringers to Vox Unum reviews. So be it.

He'd rolled out around eleven this morning. To his surprise, he had no hangover. He'd planned to complete the *Doll's House* review that afternoon so he could focus on the novel at the beach, but in two hours he'd electronically balled up and tossed a dozen or so lead sentences. None was suitable to the task.

He had decided to give it up and go for a walk when the phone rang. It was Tucker Farr. After some bantering about the foibles of Roger Bolden, Farr turned to an update on the estate. The executor's team had been all over the house and through his father's files and safe deposit box and had come up with little in the way of additional documentation. While they did not yet have a definite number, they were close to nailing down the amount his father had invested. It ran into the multiple millions of dollars.

"I'm sorry to have to tell you that your father did touch the principal of the trusts for you and your sisters. He didn't exhaust the funds, but he made a pretty sizable dent. It's clear, Ned, that he drew on just about everything he could without having to sell off any artwork or other property. I think he knew that would attract attention, and he obviously wanted to stay below the radar of the family advisors. We've interviewed them all, and none of them had any idea what was going on."

"Do you have any better sense where the money went?"

"Not really. We've picked up a few clues, but I'd like to have a complete picture before I give you and your sisters a report."

Farr had wrapped up the call by asking about Ned's love life. He and Bolden shared a sophomoric idiom for discussing women.

"I'm sure those Portland actresses must be swarming all over you, Ned. Beautiful women in their twenties, all looking for their big break, and their fate is in your hands. I don't know why I didn't become a theater critic."

Ned said nothing about Nora. That was his affair. He suggested that Farr probably preferred a well-appointed office to shabby theaters and a salary that would support a yacht instead of a rowboat. Farr rang off with a laughing "Touché."

The SUV was entering the outskirts of civilization. Ned figured this must be Tillamook, which Karin had said was the nearest town of any size. He pulled over as he came into the deserted downtown, clicked on the driver's light, and studied Karin's directions and a map he'd picked up in Portland. The beach house was in a development called Three Capes, outside of a little coastal village called Netarts. He got his bearings and set off again.

He'd almost phoned Karin earlier in the day to cancel for the weekend. He was in no state of mind to make headway on the novel. Since he'd arrived in Portland he'd been unable to generate any creative momentum. As a writer he was a creature of routine, and his routine for years had been based on the modest demands of part-time freelancing. The need to show up in an office and juggle multiple reviews in a weekend had played havoc with his writing.

That was why a retreat at the coast had seemed appealing. It was a chance to reset his course. Since last night, however, his focus was shot.

But his editor had already granted him leave to spend Monday and Tuesday out of the office and send in his reviews electronically. Bolden, who seemed to know his staff's every move, had stopped by his cubicle and joshed him about a romantic getaway with some fresh-faced ingénue. Having run that gauntlet, he thought, he might as well carry on and make the best of it.

The wind buffeted the Navigator as he crept along the Netarts Highway, his eyes peeled for the Three Capes entry monument. He spotted it as he rounded a dark curve, an understated beacon of stone and beam that hinted at wealth beyond. Three Capes was a gated community; Karin's directions had included the security code. The sentry box was unmanned at this hour. He punched in the code, saw the gate swing open, and rolled slowly in.

Ned wanted to clear his head. He did not drive much, and the coast roads after midnight had tested him. Not to mention that planning his campaign on Nora was trying, though exhilarating. A short distance into the development he saw an overlook. He pulled the Navigator over and got out.

The surf was pounding below. The moon was nearly full. Its rays speckled the foam of the waves crashing on the sand. Ned saw a set of wooden stairs descending to the water. Visibility was good. Despite the heavy surf there was a wide swath of dry beach. He zipped up his windbreaker and headed down.

From the base of the stairs he followed a sandy path through thick coastal grass. A gentle dune then took him down to the beach. Most of the development extended to his left, so he went that way.

As a boy he'd loved to run at night on the Ingram's private beach along Lake Michigan. That beach was at most several hundred yards, but beside the immense blackness of the lake it had seemed endless. He felt a sudden urge to sprint. The wind sliced his face as he ran. Images of Nora tumbled through his mind: slamming the door in her final *Doll's House* exit, basking in adulation at the cast party, then fixed on him in that way she had across the table of a Portland coffeehouse near his place. He'd already picked out where they would go next.

He was winded quickly. His only exercise routine had been basketball and he hadn't yet made the time to look for a game in Portland.

He pulled up and caught his breath. The front rank of beach houses, perched along the dunes above him to the left, sat dark, the moon glinting in their picture windows. Then Ned noticed a dim light four or five houses down the beach. He drew closer and saw that it was coming through the window of a house with a striking second-floor balcony.

Karin had said that he would always be able to tell their house from the beach by the distinctive balcony on the upper floor. She'd said it would have been perfect for the Romeo and Juliet "Wherefore art thou?" scene had the two lovers been Oregon beach bums. The design, according to her, had been Jerry's idea.

This had to be the house. Ned assumed the Bergrens left a light on for security, although Karin hadn't said anything about it. He saw a narrow path heading up the dune to the house. He felt ready to leave the beach. The wind was biting, and the run had eased the stress of the drive down. He had the beach house key with him on the SUV key chain and figured he could walk on the street back to the entry area and retrieve the Navigator after he'd had a look at the house. He veered up the dune.

The path crested next to an imposing deck. Ned turned back toward the ocean. For a few minutes he took in the magnificent moonlit view. He had to get Nora down here. Karin wouldn't have to know. He'd still get some work done on the novel, so it wouldn't be a complete lie. Theaters were always dark on Monday. They could come down on a Sunday night and come back early Tuesday. He'd feel her out on the idea at the coffeehouse.

He made for a concrete walkway running alongside the house that looked like it led to the front. Just as he gained the walkway, he caught a flicker of light dancing off the pane of the sweeping picture window that opened on to the deck. That was no security light. He had to check out its source.

Ned found a small set of steps leading on to the deck. Sand ground under his shoes as he edged toward the picture window. Wind flapped the canvas of an umbrella that was drawn shut in the center of a patio table. As he came closer he could tell that the light was from a fire inside the house. Then he caught the murmur of voices.

He scurried over to the siding that extended along the back of the house. It smelled faintly of cedar. He crept toward the picture window. He noticed the ruffled shape of curtains bunched at either end of the window inside the house. It looked like his best bet was to slip in behind the cover of the curtains, then peer around them into the room.

The surf crashed down on the beach below. Ned pulled the collar of his windbreaker up around his neck. He drew even with the bunched curtains, then craned forward, his nose just off the chilled window pane.

A fire burned low inside a towering stone fireplace that dominated the back wall of the room. The stone disappeared up into the room's cathedral ceiling. In front of the fireplace stood a low-slung wooden table; the fire glowed in the table's glossy finish. At an angle to the left of the table were matching overstuffed chairs, each draped in blankets. At the same angle on the other side of the table was a long, deep sofa. An Arts & Crafts style lamp was lit beneath amber glass atop a side table at the far end of the room.

A man and a woman were stretched out together on the sofa. The man's stocking feet were crossed on the table. His left hand held a wine glass, his right cradled the head of the woman in his lap. The limp body of the woman lay against the man, her feet just reaching the left arm of the sofa. Her eyes were closed.

It was Nora. Her flaxen hair fanned out in the man's lap. Her smooth face was reposed. Music that recalled the Grieg pre-show theme from *Doll's House* played in the background.

Ned gave a violent start. He pitched forward and as he did his chin knocked against the glass of the picture window. The man's head snapped toward the sound. Ned did not recognize him, but the face was remarkable even in the dim light for its jutting chin and piercing eyes, which bore in on Ned as he straightened up and regained his balance.

Ned backpedaled, then spun and dashed across the deck, skidding on the sand as he pulled up to take the steps. He careened down the dune, the coastal grass scraping his ankles. He looked back over his shoulder as he hit the beach and saw the man silhouetted above him on the deck. Ned took off down the sand, the wind stinging his eyes as he tried to make out the stairs up to the lookout. Twice he broke toward the dunes to his right thinking he had seen the way out, only to find it was just the steps to another beach house. Finally he found the stairway and bounded up the steps two at a time, at one point crashing into the railing as he slipped on a sandy landing.

Panting, he reached the overlook and fumbled to unzip the pocket of his windbreaker where he'd stowed his keys. He punched the unlock button as he sprinted toward the Navigator. The SUV flashed its lights in recognition. He ripped open the door, slammed the key into the ignition, wheeled around, and floored it past the abandoned sentry post and the sleek entry monument on to the highway.

CHAPTER EIGHT

Ned turned back the way he'd come, his eyes darting to the rear view mirror for signs of pursuit. There were none. His grip loosened on the steering wheel, and he tried to catch his breath. He noticed that his cell phone, which he'd left in the trough between the front seats, was beeping. He waited until he'd made what seemed a safe distance down the highway, then pulled on to the narrow shoulder and switched off his lights.

The toneless female on the voicemail announced he had one message that had arrived at 11:32 that night. It was Karin.

"Good evening, Mr. Marlowe. You probably won't get this until you reach the beach, because reception is awful on the way down. I just want to make sure you're settled in safely at the house. Call me on my cell when you get in. I'll be up. You know I won't be able to sleep until I hear something about our review. I understand you don't like to give anything away, but I hoped you might drop a few hints to an admiring reader. Roger Bolden will never know."

Her voice was warm and playful as he sat, dazed, in the darkness of the roadside. He re-played the message, grateful for its humanity.

He was stunned at Nora's betrayal. The field had been open, his for the taking. He'd had it all laid out. It would be a perfect communion of fellow artists. Nora shared his devotion to craft and his willingness to forego material comforts in the service of a higher calling.

But now she was lounging in a high-end beach house with some middle-aged asshole. It did not fit. It was the place one might expect to find a mere actress, a starlet on the make, but not her.

A car hurtled past him on the coast highway. The driver cast an uncaring glance in Ned's direction as he passed, then turned away.

He had to call Karin. It was nearing one a.m., and she'd said she would be waiting up for his call. What was he supposed to say? That her husband was shacked up with a younger blonde? He knew the man had to have been Jerry Bergren, although he had never laid eyes on the guy. The man's proprietary sense of the room had been obvious.

He saw little use in lying. He could say he had decided against going to the coast that night, but then he would have to come up with a reason to beg off for the whole weekend. He couldn't very well return to the beach house tomorrow knowing what he knew. He could say he'd been unable to find the development or the house, but then he would look like a moron and in any case she would surely insist on guiding him over the phone until he'd arrived. He could pretend he'd made it there, but then she might call him on the beach house phone tomorrow and get someone else on the line, or later ask him questions about the house that he couldn't answer.

There seemed to be little mileage in not telling what he'd seen, and why would he want to anyway? He would be lying to protect Karin from the nasty truth about her marriage, and he wasn't inclined to engage in that sort of chivalry. From everything he'd heard so far –

from Selvaggio, from the bartender at the Lowbrow – Bergren was a rogue and a hypocrite. Philanderer could now be added to the list. She was no fool, but evidently she had a blind spot when it came to her husband. It was time she saw clearly.

And he had to get Nora away from Bergren. She had no business being with a sleazeball at least twenty years older than she. She didn't need whatever Bergren had to offer. He would shine a little light on Bergren's cheating and spring her loose.

Ned hit the call back button on his cell phone. After two rings she answered. There was no weariness in her voice.

"You're late, Mr. Marlowe. Too busy singing the praises of our production to call?"

Ned was not in a bantering mood, but he decided to play along. He would not lie, but he would try to break the news gently.

"I had to keep pulling off the road to jot down more superlatives. It must have added an extra hour to the trip. The back of my program now looks like the thesaurus entry for 'fabulous.'"

"Do *Columbian* computers allow theater reviews with more than three positive adjectives?"

"I'll have to check with Bolden. It may never have happened before. Thankfully I brought my own laptop, so there's no danger of it exploding when I say something nice."

"It wasn't very good, was it?"

He paused, wondering whether to keep up the charade.

"No. No, it wasn't. It was thin soup instead of a main course."

"It sounds like your review's already been written."

"Pretty much. Though I'm always open to suggestions from admiring readers."

"I wouldn't dream of interfering."

"I'm sure you wouldn't."

"Enough of our miserable opening. Did you have any problems finding the house?"

"No, your directions were perfect. Though that highway to the coast is a bear at night. A couple of times I thought the trees were going to reach through the windshield and pull me out. You were right to get me caffeinated. I needed my pupils fully dilated."

"So do you have a fire going?"

Karin's instructions had included tips on getting a fire started.

"Yeah, there's a fire going."

"You should have plenty of wood."

"I'm sure there is."

"Have you decided where you're going to write?"

"I didn't really get a chance to look around. It's a beautiful house, though. My compliments to the designer."

"I'll pass that on to my husband. It was mostly his doing. So where are you now – curled up in front of the fireplace, plotting your next chapter?"

Ned paused. He did not relish the moment of truth.

"Karin, I'm not in the house."

"Are you out on the deck? The forecast said high winds, so I wouldn't stay out there too long."

"No, I'm not on the deck."

"What is this – twenty questions? Are you in some place bigger than a breadbasket?"

"I'm in my car."

"In your car? Are you unloading your bags?"

"No. I'm a few miles down the highway from Three Capes. I never made it into the house."

"I don't understand. I thought you said my directions were fine. Was there a problem with the key?"

"I never got to try the key. There were already people in the house."

"People in the house? Are you sure?"

"After I drove in, I decided to take a walk on the beach before I went to the house. I saw the house from below. I could tell it was yours because of the balcony. I thought I'd go up, let myself in, then head back and get the car. I went up the dune to the deck and heard voices. I looked in from the back window and saw two people. They had a fire going in the fireplace. I didn't know what to do, so I took off."

Karin seemed to suck in her breath.

"What did they look like?"

"It was a man and a woman. I didn't get a good look, but I'd say the man was in his mid-fifties. He had a full head of hair and a strong chin. The woman was younger."

The muscles of his jaw clenched as he mentioned Nora. He had no intention of giving a fuller description of her. That wasn't necessary for the business at hand.

There was a long silence at the other end of the line.

"I'm so sorry you drove all this way for nothing. We need to find you a place to stay. At this hour it's probably better for you to go back into Tillamook. You should have no problem getting a motel room there this time of year. Of course I'll reimburse you. Call me when you get settled into a room so I know you're all right."

"I could just drive back to Portland."

"No, no. It's very late, and it's a hard drive. You need sleep. You can drive back tomorrow. I don't suppose you'll want to do much writing now."

"I haven't made much progress anywhere else. Maybe a Tillamook motel is just the place."

Ned regretted the levity as soon as he spoke.

"I'll wait for your call," said Karin, in clipped tones.

Ned felt he should offer some sort of condolence.

"I'm sorry this didn't work out."

"So am I. More than you know. Drive safely."

The line clicked off.

Ned dropped the cell phone on to the passenger seat and started the Navigator. He looked into his rear view mirror before pulling back on to the road. There was no sign of anything behind him on the dark highway.

It hadn't been a pleasant task, but it needed to be done. He'd let the axe fall as lightly as he could. She had nothing to reproach him for.

Bergren had best enjoy his night of nookie at the beach house. It would likely be his last. Karin didn't strike him as the sort of woman who would just look the other way. Old Jerry would have some 'splaining to do when he got back to Portland.

He retraced his route into Tillamook. The wind had subsided, but a few gusts still caught the SUV and forced Ned to tighten his grip on the wheel. He felt a need for air and decided to crack both front windows.

His mind arced back to one of the scenes from *Doll's House*, where Nora puts all her charms on display to win her husband's favor. She minces and prances, flitters and flutters. She is a child's caricature of feminine wiles, and yet it is because she seems a child in need of protection that she wins the man over.

That was no child lying on the beach house sofa with Bergren. There was no mistaking that look on her face as she lay there, her head in his lap. That was a mature woman who was fucking a married man in his own house and seemed damned pleased with herself.

What the hell was Nora doing? He couldn't imagine she was shacked up with Bergren out of anything resembling love. The man was beneath her. Did her sacrifices for art's sake leave her that starved for companionship?

The call with Karin had stanched the seep of hurt, if only briefly. Now the bitter current quickened as he sped down the road. As it did he found the cells of a plot beginning to coalesce. Not just an explanation, a plausible string of facts, but a plot, the meshing of characters in an artful fabric.

It was Nora, of course, and he and Bergren. The two men were locked in an unwitting battle for her soul. Bergren had money, status, things. He had the purity of his vision of her and the critic's power to anoint or consume.

Ned reached the outskirts of Tillamook. His head swiveled as he surveyed each side of the empty streets in search of the neon glare of a motel sign. Finally he spied glowing red block letters announcing a vacancy. He swung into the motel's parking lot, his headlights illuminating the unlit "NO" in the lower left corner of the sign.

The motel was laid out in a two-story courtyard that framed three sides of a cracked asphalt parking lot. The office was an architectural afterthought grafted on to one end. A rickety carport offered the registering traveler scant shelter from the elements.

A hand-lettered cardboard sign urged late arrivals to ring for service after midnight. The night clerk, a thick-set man sporting an "Oregon Is For Lovers" T-shirt, emerged from a back room after Ned pressed the cheap white plastic doorbell. He checked Ned in, then from an undusted slot plucked a keychain of oblong green plastic marked "7" in red marker scrawled on masking tape.

The night wind was no longer oppressive but welcome after the fetid air of the office. There were a handful of other cars in the hotel lot. Ned parked the SUV in a faintly striped space. He pulled his laptop case and overnight bag out of the back seat.

The door to Number Seven required several pushes before yielding. He flicked the switch, which turned on both a nightstand lamp and a dim overhead light sheathed in a square fixture of frosted glass. The bed, a queen covered by a faded floral spread, drooped against the white stucco wall to his right, opposite a particleboard bureau with tarnished brass fittings. A gauzy beach scene print in a thin brown frame hung, slightly askew, over the bed. The carpet appeared cut from the same roll of rusty shag that covered the office floor.

Ned threw his overnight bag on top of the bureau and deposited his laptop on the bed. The bathroom, tucked behind a half wall a few feet beyond the bed, was tan throughout and very cramped. He splashed some water on his face leaning over a hairline-cracked sink. He kicked off his shoes, feeling the scrape of sand against his socks, and dropped on to the bed, which sagged under his weight. He drew out the cell phone that he'd placed in his jacket pocket, scrolled to Karin's number, and pressed the call button. He tossed his jacket into one of two folding, fabric-backed chairs to the right of the door that flanked a round table matching the bureau.

He was put into voicemail after the third ring. He left a message saying he'd found a hotel. He gave the name and room number and promised to call again after he got back to Portland on Sunday. He started to offer something more, but decided he was unlikely to improve on his earlier lame regrets. He signed off with just "Good night, Karin."

He rolled over toward a nightstand that completed the particleboard ensemble, unplugged the clock radio, and plugged in his laptop. He had meant to get the Willamette Stage review out of the way, but he could come back to that any time. He had caught hold of something, and he meant to ride it.

There was no headboard, so he tucked a pillow behind his back, sat up against the wall, and drew up his knees, cradling the laptop.

He clicked to open a new Word document and started flinging out notes.

"A masterful actress, at center of it all. Art conferring beauty, beauty endowing art. Slave to theater. Craved by two men. Corrupt philistine, jaded critic. Hackneyed stage door romance – flowers, wooing? Love triangle, but no love."

His riffing gathered force. His jottings, at random points within the frame of the laptop monitor, grew almost manic. There was a surge of release, then a deep weariness.

CHAPTER NINE

The sound of knocking, remote yet insistent, jarred him awake. He was sprawled on the bed. The laptop was perched at the bed's edge, still open, jags of text spilling across the white computer page. Daylight filtered through the filmy motel curtains.

He struggled to right himself in the limp droop of the motel mattress. The knocking sounded again. Now he could tell it came from his door. He called out hoarsely.

"Just a minute."

He staggered stiffly to the bathroom and threw some water on his face. He rubbed his cheeks with a coarse face towel, then finger-brushed his tousled hair. He checked his watch, which showed almost nine o'clock. He recovered his still-laced shoes and jammed his feet into them.

The motel door was equipped with a security peephole. He placed a sleep-lidded eye to the glass and peered through. Karin stood outside, her face turned away from the door, as if scanning for pursuers. He fumbled for the latch, then with a few extra tugs pulled the door open.

She wore sunglasses in the hazy morning sunshine. Her rich blonde hair was brushed but unarranged. She had on a white blouse under a pale blue cashmere sweater, oatmeal-colored corduroy slacks, and loafers. She wore no make-up.

"May I come in?"

"Of course." Ned, blinking in the daylight, stepped aside. "I'm afraid it isn't much," he said as she crossed the threshold.

"And whose fault is that?" She made a failing attempt at a smile.

Ned pulled his jacket off the near folding chair and invited her to sit down. He took the far chair.

She removed her sunglasses. He recalled how her looks had startled him when she had first turned his way at the Hilton. There was none of the gloss of that night. Her face was drawn, her skin drained of its tawny color. Her eyes were puffy and red-rimmed. There were the crow's nests of a creeping middle age not evident in evening light. But for all that her beauty was still striking and, in her present state, perhaps less formidable.

"You've been working." She had spotted the laptop, screen still glowing, on the right corner of the bed.

"I came to the coast to write. Fancy beach house, cheap motel – it doesn't matter to us serious writing types."

"It matters to me. I'm so sorry you had to stay here."

"Don't be. It's done me good to get out of town and down to the water. Remember, I'm a Lake Michigan boy, used to having big bodies of water around, not those skinny little Portland rivers. And I slept great, even though it was my own writing that put me to sleep."

He couldn't help the humor from nudging its way into their conversation, even though he wasn't sure he wanted to cheer her up.

"How much did the room cost? I brought my checkbook with me."

She was carrying a thin leather handbag which she placed on the round table next to her sunglasses.

"Please let's not worry about that now. It wasn't exactly Ritz rates. We can take care of it later."

"No, please, I insist. While it's on my mind."

Ned shrugged. He pulled his wallet from his hip pocket, extracted a crumpled credit card receipt, and wordlessly handed it to her.

She stretched it out on the table, then began writing a check. He saw that her hand shook slightly.

"It's Marlowe with an 'e,' right?"

"Right. Like Christopher. Though I understand he spelled it about a dozen different ways himself."

"Christopher Marlowe? Should I have heard of him?"

"A great playwright. Contemporary of Shakespeare's. Some still think he might have been Shakespeare – the man who wrote his plays anyway. Not Scandinavian, however, so probably not on your parents' approved list."

This coaxed a wan smile. She handed him the check.

"Thank you for driving all the way down here to deliver a check."

Ned winced as the words came out of his mouth. She sat in silence, her shoulders hunched.

"I'm sorry, Karin. I feel like I'm treading on eggshells and crunching every one in sight."

Tears welled in her eyes. A shudder passed through her. She made a visible effort to compose herself.

"I came here to confront him. And her, I suppose. I made it as far as the entry gate. But I couldn't go on with it. I knew I'd just look like a fool. The older woman always does. So I turned around and left. I didn't know where to go. So I came here."

"I'm glad you did."

She raised her head and turned toward him.

"Why? Why are you glad to see a miserable middle-aged woman like this?"

He struggled to back up the platitude.

"You've been a good friend. You cared enough about me to help me get my book going again. Maybe I can return the favor."

He found his words hollow. She stared vacantly at the pale glow of the laptop screen.

"She has to be an actress. That was his pattern, for years before he met me. He hung around theaters. He knew actresses were easy prey. We were young and broke and dying to be stars. He was all the things you never find in theater people: rich, stable, knew everyone. He was going some place, some place far away from the cheap dumps we were stuck acting in.

And he loved the theater. He knew what was playing all over town. He kept track of everybody. He knew which companies were up and which ones were falling apart. He had a good eye for talent. He'd say that they'd miscast a part in a show he's seen and that this other actor would have been perfect. From what I knew of the scene, which was less and less after the kids came along, he was usually right.

I have no idea who it might be. I don't know who's acting in the smaller theaters these days. You've only been here what, a few weeks, and you know more about what's going on than I do. You may have already reviewed this woman, for all I know. These actresses are just names on a page to me unless they've gotten a part at

Willamette Stage, and that's usually people who are already in the union and not nearly needy enough for him.

I never stopped him from going to the theater. What's the expression? 'When he stops looking, he starts dying?' I never came along to police him. I told you I don't like being in the audience. I didn't think I needed to go just to keep an eye on him. I trusted him. Why wouldn't I? He's been a good husband, a great father. I've heard some talk about his business, but I thought that was just jealousy. He did so well so young and he knew all the right people. Of course they were jealous. He had everything ..."

Her voice trailed off. She squeezed her fingers into tight fists, her knuckles protruding and white.

Ned pivoted out of his chair into a crouch on the carpet before her. He took her hands in his.

"He's a damned fool. He has a beautiful wife who loves him and is a wonderful mother to his children. Most men would kill to have what he has. Jesus, he's selfish. He married a talented actress who sacrificed her career to stay home and raise a family. After all she's done, he goes out and plays the field. Shame on him. To hell with him."

He'd started off just wanting to say something, anything. He had a part to play. But as he spoke his intended expressions of sympathy came tumbling out as real fury. He wasn't ripping Bergren for Karin's sake, but for his own.

He squeezed her hands. Slowly he felt her fingers unclasp and interlace with his. He could sense her body soften.

He'd get that bastard. Bergren might have snared Nora, but it would come at a price. Karin might have been too weak to confront the sonofabitch, but he had a chance right in front of him to make the man pay. If you go sleeping around, don't be surprised to come home and find someone else in your bed.

He rose from the floor, pulling her gently out of the chair. Without prompting, her arms circled around his shoulders. Even in loafers, she stood only a few inches shorter than he. He drew her closer. He felt spasms of silent sobbing. He let her cry, rocking against him, the honeyed swirl of her hair splayed on his shoulder. His hands slipped to the small of her back, his fingers alive to the swell of her hips.

Her breasts, full and rounded, pressed through her soft sweater against his chest. He could feel himself growing hard. Her sobs subsided. He drew one hand away from her back and placed his palm against her cheek. He tipped her tear-stained face upward. The glassy look had left her eyes. In its place he saw a longing, a deep ache certainly, but also a longing.

There was nothing to think about. He could settle a score and bed a beautiful woman in the bargain. It was as easy as that.

He brought his lips to hers. At first she did not respond, but didn't resist either. Then she shuddered, as if shaking off some unseen constraint. She kissed him, hard, and her fingers dug into his back.

He backed her up to the foot of the bed, his hands now cupped around the cheeks of her rear. They fell to the mattress. She paused for a moment, eyes locked on his in an unspoken question. Then suddenly she rocked up, knees flexed as she straddled him, and arched her back. She pulled the blue cashmere over her head and undid the buttons of the blouse, her fingers fluid but unhurried. She reached back to unhook her bra and, with a shake of her hair, let it drop on to the bed.

Her torso was long and tanned, the curve of her belly soft beneath the fullness of her breasts. Ned trembled slightly as she bent toward him and began to unbutton his shirt, her hands working in easy rhythm. She massaged his chest, then dragged her fingers over his belt to the zipper of his pants. She pulled the pants and shorts down almost languidly, then angled forward, her weight balanced on her palms on either side of his chest.

He reached both hands up to her breasts, his fingers stroking her nipples. She swayed, her eyes closed, the slight flare of her nostrils pronounced. She leaned back, pushing herself off the end of the bed into a standing position. She seemed to tower over him. She drew the slacks, then her panties, over the sweep of her hips.

She mounted him and rocked into a driving motion. Her head dropped back, her tongue pressing against her full lower lip, her breath escaping in short bursts, her breasts shaking. Ned tensed, his fingers bunching the faded flowers of the bedspread. His eyes widened. They came within seconds of each other, her climax a sharp gasp, his a low moan. She tumbled to the bed beside him.

He lay still on his back, his fingers finding hers. After a minute or two she turned away from him and curled up, her arms folding over her knees. As she did she noticed the laptop still perched on the corner of the bed. Ned sat up, folding the bedspread over to cover her. He saw that she was starting to train her eyes on the computer screen. He remembered the torrent of his notes of the night before. He reached over her and in swift succession hit File/Save/Close.

"Trade secrets," he murmured, stroking her thigh.

CHAPTER TEN

Ned headed straight for Selvaggio's cubicle. Even at this early hour on Monday morning, he knew the reporter would be there. His running joke was that Selvaggio may have left New Jersey, but he still came to work on Eastern time.

True to form, the reporter was hunched over his keyboard, the remains of a doughnut spilling over a napkin beside it. Selvaggio's cubicle was devoid of either psychedelia or irony, two features favored in *Columbian* interior decor. Laminated copies of his stories were tacked beside concert photos of Springsteen and Yankees' memorabilia. A vintage movie poster of *All the President's Men* hung over his computer. There was a framed photograph on the desk of a thick-set, black-spectacled couple in unsmiling middle age that Ned took to be his parents.

"Tell me everything you know about Jerry Bergren," Ned said.

"What the hell?"

Selvaggio spun around in his chair.

"Are you dreaming? You must be, 'cause you're never up at this hour."

"Sad to say, but I'm wide awake."

"So why do you suddenly have a hard-on about Bergren?"

"This morning I'd like to ask the questions, if you don't mind. But fair is fair. I think I may have come up with a source for you."

Selvaggio squinted at him.

“Hmm,” he snorted. “Give me ten to wrap this thing up. I’ll come see you.”

He swiveled back to his monitor.

Ned wound his way through the clutch of vacant cubicles to his desk. The stillness was vaguely oppressive.

He had decided to approach Selvaggio during yesterday’s drive back from the coast. He’d taken off around noon, just before the motel’s check-out time. Karin had left a half hour before.

They’d had sex twice more that morning, each as intense as the first. There had been little conversation. After the last, she said she was going to take a shower. He playfully followed her to the bathroom, but she gave him a solemn look and closed the door behind her. She stayed in the shower almost twenty minutes. When she finally emerged, her skin puckered from the hot water, she was subdued. She dressed quietly. He watched hungrily from the bed as she bent to put on her panties.

He came to her as she stood at the door. She took his hands and gazed at him for a minute or more. Softly she said, “Thank you,” then put on her sunglasses and left without looking back.

She was a good lay. Better than he’d had in a long while, even if it had been in a dump of a motel. But what had taken the sex over the top was his rage. There was nothing quite like getting laid and getting even. The image of Bergren and Nora cuddled on the sofa had been with him each time he’d come. Then, as he fell back on the cheap mattress, his mind would scroll back to a moment from *Doll’s*

House. He'd swirl it around, savor it, until the beach house memory overtook it and he felt himself getting hard again.

Karin would call him. He felt sure of that. She now had a gaping hole in her life, and he could fill it for her. He would wait for her to make the next move, though. That was the way to play to it.

He wasn't so certain that she would confront her husband, at least not for a while. She had a lot to process – kids, lifestyle, Portland society. At this point all she had was his word that anything was going on. It was obvious she believed him, but she would want something more solid before crossing the point of no return.

The drive back had been a whirl of plotting, both real and dramatic. He needed to take the measure of Bergren. It was a matter of honor, his and Nora's, and also now of the making of his play. For it had flashed on him as he lay on the sagging bed, the ripeness of Karin beside him, that the strands spooled out in his notes meshed in the form of a play.

He had never written one, never even had the inclination to try one. Despite, or perhaps because of, his years as a critic, he'd viewed playwriting as something less than pure. It was an applied art rather than a true one – because of the overlay of performance. Fiction was written to be read, in direct communion between writer and reader. Plays were meant to be produced, which brought an unpredictable dimension into play (so to speak) – not to mention a tangle of awkward business relationships.

But this was a play. Not because an actress was at its center, though that was of course suggestive. No, it was an ancient discipline of dramatic art that had unexpectedly imposed a structure on his disordered thoughts: the classic Greek unities of place, time, and action. He had rarely considered these since an introduction to theater course his sophomore year at Swarthmore, but yesterday they had, without warning, shaped and set his material.

The place, he'd decided as the SUV wound through the dark forests, was a theater. A black box very like the SoHo – simple, unadorned, and uncorrupted. Just the players and the audience, cheek by jowl, breath on breath.

The time would be twenty-four hours starting with the end of a performance. The Greeks preferred a single day, of course, but a few thousand years later he could take some liberties. A monologue by the actress would kick it off, a speech distilling the essence of the play and showcasing her mastery of the art. Another monologue, at the beginning of the following evening's performance, would close it out.

The action, well, that was still in the formative stages. He knew it would begin with the critic confronting the actress in the wake of the monologue and that a rendezvous between the businessman and the actress would follow. Beyond that, as of now, was only speculation.

Which was why he had to get a bead on Bergren. He knew that Selvaggio was out to nail the bastard and needed sources. Karin had been married to the man for over fifteen years. She had to have some idea of what he was up to, despite her claim to be clueless about his business. He would see what she knew and feed it to Selvaggio, in return for being cut in on the reporter's investigation. It was ungentlemanly, of course, but he didn't really give a damn.

On returning to his apartment, he'd dashed off the review of Karin's company. The Willamette Stage folks would wonder if Milson had left the *Columbian* after all. So much for the honeymoon period.

Later that night he'd finally been able to frame out the *Doll's House* review. Nora in the flesh may have eluded him, at least for now, but Nora in the theater seemed more approachable after the events of the weekend. Before he put the piece down on paper, though, he wanted Selvaggio's debriefing on Bergren. The reporter's account had nothing to do with the review, of course, and yet it was now all strung together. Ned was bumping up on his deadline, but he still had a little time left to pry.

Selvaggio steamed into his cubicle, traces of the powdered doughnut still visible on his pale cheeks. He had the rolling, hulking gait of a former wrestler. His barrel chest was encased in a flannel work shirt. A white undershirt peaked out from his collar.

"Let's take a walk," he spat. "The walls have ears in this place."

The morning was sharp and damp. The sidewalk still bore the spatters of a late night rain. Selvaggio led him in silence until they reached the leafy precincts of the Park Blocks, a stretch of statue-studded greenery flanked by many of the city's cultural landmarks.

"So you and Karin Bergren got something going on?"

Ned froze. "You really are an asshole, aren't you?" he managed, after a pause.

"Yes sir, I am. That's why they hired me to do the job I do."

"It suits you."

"Thank you. So she's your source?"

Ned ignored the question.

"What makes you think we've got something going?"

"You're theater people. You screw like rabbits. I don't know much about theater, but that much I know. And I've seen the woman. You don't have to be some theater nutball to want to screw her."

"Why do you say she's a theater person?"

"I know she was an actress when Jerry Bergren made his move on her. Bergren had had a lot of stage door romance practice before he met her. That was kind of his M.O. Looks like he's got nothing on you."

Ned raised his hands in mock surrender. "All right, all right. You got me."

Selvaggio flashed a broad grin and clapped Ned on the shoulder. "Hey congratulations, buddy. That's one helluva notch for a guy who's been in town for what, a month and a half? Just don't say anything to Bolden. He'll crap his pants. So now you want the goods on her no-good husband, uh?"

"Something like that."

Selvaggio looked over his shoulder, then narrated in a low voice as they strolled.

"Bergren's a native. Grew up on the east side with the working folk. Way on the wrong side of the river. Raised by a single mother. His father died in a factory accident when young Jerry was around three. Only child. His mother kept him pretty much on the straight and narrow: sports and church. Played baseball and basketball in high school, then on to Portland State. Paid for college by hawking encyclopedias in the sticks during the summer and pushing a broom on the late shift at the MAC Club during the school year.

Working nights at the MAC he got to know some of the lounge lizards there. One of the guys who regularly closed the bar was a piece of work named Arthur Gibson. Art Gibson was a West Hills blue blood from way back. A Gibson ancestor went out the Oregon Trail, which is like coming over on the frigging Mayflower around here. Gibson failed out of some fancy Eastern prep school, barely made it through the U of O, then was stashed in a back office at the family brokerage house.

Turned out he had a talent for sweet-talking old ladies into blowing their nest eggs on wildcat stocks. The next sure thing, right as rain, don't miss out – you know the spiel. He gets quite a bucket shop operation going and when old man Gibson kicks the bucket, Art muscles his older brother out of the way and takes over the firm.

Fast forward about twenty years. Gibson is on his third wife and God knows what bottle of Scotch. His drinking spills into business a bit, but the brokerage is still minting a nice chunk of change. He's impressed with young Bergren's gift of gab, which Jerry's perfected pitching World Book to hayseeds in Idaho. He takes the lad under his wing, buys him a few nice suits, and gives him a desk and a phone at Northwest Equities. Jerry's a natural at separating marks, I mean clients, from their money.

He also picks up Gibson's taste for the high life. Tailored suits, five-star restaurants – all the usual frills. The one unusual pastime Gibson introduces Jerry to is theater. Gibson is a genuine buff who apparently got turned on blowing off prep school to spend nights in New York. He and Jerry take in shows all over town and always spend a week a year in New York trolling up, down, and off Broadway."

Two lawyerly types in starched white collars, gray pinstripes, and black wing tips passed them from the opposite direction, clutching soft leather briefcases. Selvaggio broke off and did not pick up again until they were out of earshot.

"One ex-buddy of Bergren's told me Jerry was fascinated – being a master pitchman himself – by how actors can sell their part to an audience, even in the cheapest of dumps. The whole illusion thing, you know. I heard he's hired theater people to work the phones on his deals. I guess it beats waiting tables or phone sex as your day job.

Gibson had kind of a sideline loaning money to hard-up West Hills types. Very discreet, but nasty terms. He cuts Bergren in on some of these deals, so Jerry gets to know Portland society from its seamy underside. Then during a junket to Vegas, Jerry happens to run into some top Northwest union guys in the bar. They're bitching and moaning about the lousy returns on their pension money. Jerry buys 'em a few drinks and persuades them to send a few bucks his way to manage.

He takes that dough and puts it out at hard money rates to a timber baron in a tight spot. The loan pays off, fat fees and all, and the union boys are thrilled. Jerry wines and dines 'em at some hunting lodge and they decide to turn over a nice slice of the pension fund to Northwest Equities. This puts the firm on steroids, and Gibson makes him a full partner.

Right around this time Jerry grabs Karin out of some dive theater. She wasn't West Hills, of course, but you couldn't get much better arm candy for social climbing. Hey, no offense, buddy. So he starts to master the Good Person racket: the boards, the charity auctions, the whole nine yards. He jumps on all the right bandwagons: the Cancer Society, the Opera, the Nature Conservancy. Solid, old line, with a taste of the progressive they all love around here. Gibson was probably laughing his head off, 'cuz he was born into all that crap and couldn't give a shit.

Jerry picks up the mansion of an old Portland family when the mother kicks over and the kids get into an ugly squabble. He buys a condo at Gearhart, which is the old money capital out on the coast – definitely where you want to see and be seen in your sandals. Then he trades up to a kick-ass beach house when they develop this Three Capes project. You're a theater guy; you should check it out. They tell me it's got some Romeo and Juliet-type balcony on the second floor. You know, 'Wherefore art thou?' and all that."

Ned did not comment. By this time they'd ventured on to the concrete-laden campus of Portland State. Selvaggio didn't appear concerned by the bleary-eyed, backpack-toting students passing by. He kept talking, his New Jersey accent growing thicker as he gained momentum.

"By this time Jerry's pretty much taken over the firm. The old bucket shop part of the business is still ticking along, but it's the juice loan operation that really wears the pants by this point. Jerry's pretty damned good at sizing up a deal, and he'll take on risk that would pop a banker's green eyeshades. He knows where the bodies are buried all over the West Hills, who's been naughty and who's been nice, and he can usually tell who's going to come to him for a bail-out before they're even in the door. The union boys love him, and believe me he doesn't forget to express his gratitude in some very tangible ways, if you catch my drift."

Selvaggio didn't even glance at Ned to see if his drift had been caught. He looped around a towering tree and started them back the way they'd come.

"But even the best juice artist rings up some bad loans. Jerry's been drinking his own Kool-Aid, though, and doesn't want the union brass to think he ever gets his feet wet walking on water. Instead of writing off the bad debts, he keeps rolling them over or turning them into stock in the deadbeat's company. On the books everything looks hunky-dory, but there are some definite cracks in the foundation. The problem with taking pension fund money is that it brings the feds into play. Some regulator types start sniffing around, but Jerry's able to keep 'em at bay.

He decides he needs to make a splash. Something so grand, so perfect, that it will make him pretty much untouchable. Plus he's tired of just playing Shylock to all these clowns. He wants his own deal, his own frigging monument.

This was before your time, but you may have heard about this nutbag Indian guru who set up a commune on a ranch down the Columbia Gorge. The guy called himself Bhagwan Shree Rajneesh, and old Bhagwan was even better than Bergren at separating marks from their dough. I guess it's a better racket if you promise being at one with the universe instead of just a pile of cash. His followers bought him fifty some Rolls Royces and put all their worldly goods at his disposal.

At first the Rajneeshees seemed pretty harmless, but then they started rigging local elections. They glommed on to this little town called Antelope and changed its name to Rajneesh. When the authorities started nosing around, a few of the Bhagwan's buddies decided an investigation might be a roadblock on the road to enlightenment. So they cooked up a plot to bump off the federal prosecutor. The feds caught up with them before they could do much damage, threw the head honchos in jail, and put the Bhagwan on a plane back to India.

The ranch, all sixty-four thousand acres of it, sat empty for years. It changed hands a few times, but nobody could figure out what to do with it. Enter Jerry with a big idea. Why not turn the ranch into a theme park for peace, love, and understanding? Sort of Disneyland meets 'Can't we all just get along.' Take this sorry chapter of Oregon's history and turn it into a triumph of humanity.

I know it sounds wacko, but Central Oregon is booming. Hordes of Californians fleeing smog, traffic, and Hispanics. The place has great weather: sun and golf in the summer, snow and skiing in the winter. There's an airport north of Bend, and a bunch of Portlanders already cruise their SUVs out there on weekends to play at being rugged. Plus Oregon already thinks it's cornered the market on world peace and harmony, so what better state to host Six Flags over Nirvana?

Of course, if he really wanted to audition for sainthood, Jerry would have done this thing nonprofit. Set up a foundation, pass the hat at some black tie shindigs, nail up a wall full of plaques. But Jerry wants to have his cake and eat it. He thinks he can make a mint and come out smelling like roses at the same time.

He somehow comes up with the dough to buy the ranch. We're not sure how he did it. I'll bet he was tempted to raid the pension fund piggybank, but with the fed vultures circling he'd had to play it very safe.

Anyway, Jerry buys the place and sends out a whopping press release about how this project is going to save the planet, raise global consciousness, yadda, yadda. He's mighty vague, though, about what he's going to actually build out there. Hints at big plans on the drawing board, of course, but won't say what.

He has to tip his hand a little, however, when he goes to do up an environmental impact statement. A bear can't take a dump in the woods out here without an EIS. He puts in some pretty plans that show a Unity Pavilion here, an East-West Restaurant there, some Around the World rides for the kids. The big mystery, though, is a humongous building in the middle that's just labeled 'Museum.' The press asks Jerry what sort of museum he's putting up, but he's very coy. Just says that he and his team are 'evaluating a number of appropriate themes.'"

On this line New Jersey dropped out of Selvaggio's voice in favor stilted upper crust. They passed beneath the somber gaze of Abraham Lincoln, his bronze figure bowed atop a granite base.

"So Jerry's got a lot on his plate right now, what with fending off the feds on the pension funds and trying to get a sign-off on his EIS by the spring. The union boys are nervous. They're starting to ask questions they were too busy taking junkets to think about before.

And now some mangy theater critic's sleeping with the poor bastard's wife."

Ned, who'd been taking in this account with his eyes on the pavement as they strolled, jerked his head up.

"Asshole."

"You already called me that. Try another naughty word. Hey, I'm from Jersey – I can help you out if you're having trouble."

"Asshole."

"All right, all right. Listen, that's the least of the guy's problems right now."

"What's happening with his wife is the least of his problems?"

"With his track record, adultery is the least of his problems. Karin would have to get it on with about a dozen theater critics before she caught up to him. From what I've heard, he's sampled at least that many dishes on the Portland actress buffet."

"All actresses?"

"Just about. Hey, they're cute, young, and broke. Nice combination if you're a middle-aged guy with dough. Not to mention they're surrounded by a bunch of gay theater guys, so there's not much competition. Sorry for the stereotype."

"I'd expect nothing less from a sensitive Yankee fan investigative reporter."

"You got that right."

They had arrived back at the start of the Park Blocks. The morning bustle of Broadway, downtown's main street, was visible over Selvaggio's shoulder as he pulled up and turned to face Ned.

"So you got the picture on Bergren?"

"Pretty much. When are you going to run something?"

"Soon. We don't have a smoking gun, but we're getting there. We know the feds are close on the union stuff, but they're not there yet. We think something strange is going on with Bhagwan Land, but we're not quite sure what. We're trying to get some people close to Bergren to open up. We'll get 'em, but no loose lips yet. If you can pick up any pillow talk from Karin, that'd be great."

"I could do without the quaint expressions."

"OK, OK. Hey, you sure you really want to rat out your new girlfriend?"

"She's not my girlfriend, and I'm not ratting her out. Her husband's the rat. Getting him will only help her."

"She might not see it that way."

"I think she will. You'll keep me posted if you get anything new?"

"You got it, Mr. Undercover Man."

"Thanks. I'm going to grab some coffee. You need something?"

"Nah. I already had my fix. See ya."

Ned started for the sleek coffee chain across the street. After a few steps he heard Selvaggio's staccato voice fire off behind him.

"Hey Dirk. You know, you're a real upgrade in the theater critic department. From everything I heard, Milson only slept in his own bed."

"Asshole."

CHAPTER ELEVEN

Ned braved a long line to pick up his usual double espresso, then headed back to the *Columbian* office. He'd considered a caffeinated ramble through downtown to digest Selvaggio's briefing, but he had a review to write.

He ran into Bolden past the receptionist's desk. The publisher greeted him with a smirk of mock surprise.

"Dirk! I'd heard you were going to be cabling in your reviews from some exotic location the next few days. Was it Maui? Monte Carlo? Is the airport closed?"

"It was the Oregon Coast, actually. My plans fell through."

"Bad weather? I heard it was a bit rough down there over the weekend."

"No. Some relatives ended up using my friend's beach house, so there was no room at the inn."

"Too bad. But I'm delighted to hear you're making friends who have beach houses. No old Portlander would be caught dead without one, even if they only use it once in a blue moon. Anyone I know?"

"I'm sure you don't. An old actress."

"Ah, a bohemian at the beach. Curious. Even curiouser is your gravitating toward older actresses, Dirk. Remember that I'm counting on you for vicarious thrills romping with the young and shapely. Don't let me down."

"I'll do my level best, sir."

"Well, I mustn't get in the way of editorial progress. I never do, you know. Better luck with Monte Carlo next time!"

With a giggle he darted into his office.

Ned meandered back to his cubicle. He grabbed the Vox Unum press packet for *Doll's House* from the corner of his desk and pulled out the program. While flipping to the actor bios, he passed by the company's donor list. He paused for a moment and noticed that at the top of the list was "Anonymous." He straightened in his chair.

He dug his wallet out of his back pocket. Stuffed in a corner was the scrap of paper with Elena Devlin's phone number. He hadn't asked for it. She'd jotted it down a little tipsily at the end of that night at McMenamins and thrust it into his hand, telling him in that throaty voice to call if he wanted the ins and outs of Portland theater.

He unfolded the paper and dialed the number, guessing on the last shaky figure. From the look of the number, it was a cell phone. She answered on the third ring with a wary "Hello?" She obviously didn't recognize the incoming number.

"Elena?"

"Yeah?"

"This is Dirk Marlowe. From the *Columbian*."

Her guard came down quickly.

"Dirk!" she gushed. "Are you buying another round of vodka gimlets?"

"If I am it's not at McMenamins. That much water I can get outside in the rain around here."

"Ah, that's the charm of the place."

"So you said. I guess I have a high charm threshold."

"Some of the best actresses in town come there to drink."

"Now there's a much better reason to go back."

"So what's up, Dirk? You looking for the skinny on the Portland theater scene?"

"As a matter of fact, I sort of am."

"Good for you. Milson never got into tittle-tattle. He was too busy quoting dead white men to dish the dirt. Even though that's most of the fun in theater. Shitty pay, fabulous gossip. Whose skeleton you looking to rattle?"

"What can you tell me about Robin and Jerry Bergren?"

She was silent on the line for a good ten seconds. When she came back on, her voice was a hoarse whisper.

"How much do you know?"

"I know they're an item. I know he's bad news."

More silence.

"I can't talk about this now. I'm on the bus to work."

"Can I buy you a cup of coffee? Or a vodka gimlet?"

"I can't talk about this in public. That guy's got ears everywhere."

"You want to come to my office?"

"Oh yeah, that's much better. As if he doesn't have every paper in town wired. Why don't I come to your place?"

"OK. When could we get together?"

"Today's as good as any. I get off around three thirty, then I'm free 'til rehearsal at seven."

"I'll get us a pizza. I can run you over to rehearsal after we finish up."

A brief pause.

"We wouldn't want people to talk."

"Wouldn't we?"

He gave her his address at the Brittany. They agreed on four thirty.

Ned was finally ready to write up *Doll's House*. He had never agonized so much over a review. Part of his usual nonchalance in reviewing, he had to admit, was contempt for theater criticism. As he pegged playwriting a notch or two below writing short stories or novels, the critiquing of plays fell a few rungs further down the literary ladder.

The power he exercised over hapless theater companies also served to speed his reviews. They were so dependent on what he said that he found it precious easy to say it.

Nora had turned the tables. At first it had been awe at her performance. Then, at McMenamins, he had witnessed her indifference to critics. No, not indifference, but an artistic devotion that rendered her impervious to criticism – although, he had thought, not to him personally. Of course, his comments on the printed page might bring patrons to her theater, or make them stay away, but they could not touch her as an artist. He held no sway over her.

He resented his powerlessness, as any slave resents his master. Yet he acknowledged the mastery, even reveled in it. But he could not make this acknowledgment in writing, in his own idiom, until he had seen her on the sofa at Bergren's beach house. That sight, of her yielding to the blandishments of that bourgeois bastard, had lent her a mortality that unblocked his review.

Now that he had her measure, he was prepared to do her justice. Even more, as he grasped her frailty, he was resolved to protect her. Not just from Bergren, but from herself.

The review did not gush or embellish. It did not serve up excisable snippets of the sort Hollywood loved to fling atop banner ads with exclamation marks. It did not even make Nora the center of attention. Instead, it focused, as he thought she would have wished, on the seamlessness of the ensemble, on the fluidity of motion and the unity of voice that had given Vox Unum its name. He observed in the review that the company had achieved a degree of feminine grace striking in a production most celebrated for nascent feminism.

It was his best work as a reviewer, he thought, though a bear to finish. Around noon he rushed out for a sandwich that he wolfed down at his desk. He finally e-mailed a draft to his editor around four fifteen, barely in time to jog-trot through a misty drizzle back to meet Elena at his place.

She was waiting for him in the Brittany lobby.

"I caught an early bus," she explained.

"You always ride the bus?" Ned punched the elevator button.

"Until I move to LA and get me a Beemer." She gave a raspy laugh. "On non-union scale and a waitress's tips, it's the bus for now."

Her coarse dark hair was beaded with rain. She was made up, but not so heavily as at McMenamins. Without the slashes of color the shape of her face appeared even more square. Her wide-set gray eyes took in the tastefully appointed elevator.

"Nice place you've got here. Though a couple of West Hills types came through the lobby and looked at me strange."

"We don't get many actresses here. Maybe they wanted your autograph."

"Yeah, right. All the years I've acted here, nobody's once recognized me outside the theater. No one gives a shit."

Ned unlocked the door to his unit.

"I'm afraid you're the first visitor to my sorry apartment."

He had rented the unit furnished. The sparse furnishings in the combined living room/dining room consisted of a blonde wood futon sofa-bed and matching low-slung coffee table, an oval dining table and four high-backed chairs in dirty maple, and a battered television stand. A ten-year old TV Ned had purchased at a second-hand store was perched on the stand. He'd bought very little to spruce the place up. He had to keep a close eye on his cash, and in any case Portland seemed like a way station to him.

"I've seen a helluva lot worse. I like the brick. And the floors look great."

"Authentic pseudo-warehouse condo. If you can't trick out a real old joint, then build a make-believe one from the ground up. Can I get you a glass of wine?"

He took her cheap black raincoat and folded it over one of the chairs.

"I never drink before rehearsal. Well, not since I was with Vox Unum."

"It doesn't get that actress blood pumping?"

"Robin didn't think so. She chewed me out one night when she smelled it on my breath. Her version of chewing out, anyway. She just said, very quietly, 'Let's save the drinks until after rehearsal, OK?' And that's what I've done ever since."

"I noticed." Ned grinned.

"Hey, when the work is done, it's time for fun."

"Amen. What sort of pizza do you want? Coming from Chicago, I have to put in a plug for deep dish, but I'll go along with that cheap, pathetic New York excuse for a crust if it's what you really want. No pressure, though."

"That's cool. How 'bout sausage, bacon, and onions?"

"Not into veggie, uh?"

"I'm Serbian. We like meat on our bones. That goes for animals – and women."

She cupped her palms along the back of her head and stuck out a hip.

"Meaty it is."

He phoned in the order, motioning her to take a seat on the sofa. He pulled a mineral water and a beer from the fridge and drew one of the chairs over from the table.

"I'm not rehearsing tonight," he said as he handed her the mineral water and opened the beer. "And I sweated bullets over a review today."

"For *Doll's House*?"

"Ordinarily I wouldn't say. But under the circumstances, I'll admit it was."

"I thought you loved it."

"I did. That doesn't necessarily make it easy to review. I wanted to do the play justice. I needed to do Robin justice."

"She blew you away, uh?"

She looked at him wistfully.

"Yes."

"That's why you need to know about Bergren?"

"Yes."

He leaned forward in his chair.

"How did you hear about them?" she asked.

"I saw them together."

"No way. They're incredibly careful. They never go out in public."

"They weren't in public."

"How did you know it was him?"

"He's got quite a reputation. Remember, I work for a newspaper."

"Have you told anyone?"

"No," he lied. "I'm not doing a story. I just need to know."

"For yourself?"

"Yes."

"OK."

She collected herself and gulped the mineral water. She did not sip her drinks.

"I told you about SoHo offering to share the theater they built. We'd only done one show. We couldn't believe they'd even consider us. We had no money. There was no way we could take on a lease. Plus SoHo wanted someone to sign the lease personally because the company had nothing.

We had all these meetings that basically came to the same place. It was a great space, but there was no way we could take the risk. Then all of a sudden Robin comes to us and says she's got the money lined up and she'll sign the lease herself. If it had been anyone else, we would have said, 'Yeah, right.' But with Robin, we knew it was for real.

Of course everyone was all over her to find out where she came up with the money. All she would say is she'd found an anonymous donor who liked our work. We couldn't get anything else out of her. Robin kept the checking account for the company, but somebody managed to fish out her file with the bank statements and canceled checks. He found big checks made out to the company by something or other LLC with a PO Box address. There was no way to trace it. And all Robin put in the program was 'Anonymous.'

I noticed some weekends after that she would just disappear. She was never much of a partier, but usually she would go out with us after a show and listen while the rest of yakked and drank. Part of the ensemble thing, you know. But now she would just vanish. I started to tease her about having a mystery boyfriend. She'd broken up with a guy she'd been pretty serious about right around the time we started Vox Unum and hadn't seen anyone since then as far as I knew. She just laughed and said her only boyfriend these days was the company.

Then one Saturday night after a show I was over at McMenamins with the rest of the gang. It turned out I'd left my purse in the dressing room. I had kind of a headache, so I took the long way back to the theater to get some air. I was coming down 22nd when I saw

Robin get into a huge, black Mercedes. It was real dark, but no question it was her. The inside light was on, and I saw her give the guy at the wheel a kiss. Then the car drove off like a bat out of hell.

After the next show I went over to her, grabbed her by the arm, and pretty much dragged her to a coffee place a couple of blocks from the theater. Just the two of us. I sat her down and basically said, 'Now you're going to tell me about the guy in the big, black Mercedes, or I'm gonna beat it out of you.'

She started to try and bullshit me, but I said, 'Robin, you're the best actress in Portland, but you're a lousy liar. I saw you get in the car, and I saw you kiss the guy. Are you gonna tell me it's a coincidence that you start hanging around with guys in fancy cars just when you come up with the money for our lease?'

Now I was going out on a little bit of a limb there, but I was pretty sure something like that was going on after I saw her in the car. I knew she didn't have any rich uncles or anything, and I knew she wouldn't sign a lease unless she was pretty damn sure about the money.

She took my hand and squeezed it – hard. She looked me straight in the eye, very steady.

'I can act anywhere, Elena,' she said. 'And you know the places I have. I've acted in a high school theater that was built after World War II and hasn't been touched since. I've acted in firetraps where we were as worried about the fire marshal closing us down as what the critics had to say. I've acted in dumps where the dressing room was forty-five degrees in January and I had to keep blowing on my fingers so I could put on my make-up. I've acted in concrete boxes where the sound bounced off the walls so hard I thought I was having a conversation with myself. I've acted in places with lighting so poor I would have been better off handing flashlights to people in the front row.'

'We put this company together. You know how long we'd tried to make it happen and how hard it was to get everyone committed. When SoHo showed us the plans for that theater – a real theater – and said we could be part of it, there was no way we were going to lose that chance. This was it. This was the way we were finally going to be able to make art, not just figure out how to get by. You know how often new theaters come around here. We'd be lucky if we got another chance like this in twenty years.' "

Ned noticed how Elena took on the elements of Nora as she spoke. Her eyes widened, her voice softened, and she seemed thinner, frailer. It was uncanny.

" 'I met this man maybe two years ago. He came backstage after a show. He said how impressed he was by my work. He said he'd love to get together sometime to talk about theater. He gave me his card. I thanked him but of course I never called. He came to a couple of other shows, and it was the same thing each time. He couldn't have been more charming.'

'I kept his card. I couldn't tell you why, but I did. When the SoHo chance came up, I took out the card and looked him up online. I could tell he was very successful. I called him up and said I would like to take him up on his offer. To talk about theater. He didn't act at all surprised. We went out to dinner at a restaurant a long way out of town. I told him what the company needed. He said how much he admired my work and that he would be glad to help. He asked for my number so we could stay in touch. I gave it to him. He called me the next week and asked me out to dinner again. We went to the same restaurant. He kissed me at the end of the evening. A few days later a check for the deposit SoHo wanted came in the mail.'

'You're a wonderful friend, Elena. I know how much you care about me and how much you'll want to protect me. I know you'll think I've sold myself. I know you'll want to gouge this man's eyes out. But I am completely at peace with what I've done. I know what matters to me most, and that's theater. Whatever I've given up, it's been well worth it. Now we can truly be artists, not just survivors jumping from one lousy space to another.'

I don't remember everything she said word for word, but I'll tell you it's stayed with me. She was so calm. The only way you could tell how intense this was for her was the way she was squeezing my hand."

"What did you say to her?"

"What could I say? It was a done deal. I hugged her and told her I understood. I did say she should never, ever feel she owed this to the rest of us. If this was something she felt she had to do for herself, OK then. It wasn't that we weren't incredibly grateful. But that sort of sacrifice – nobody owes that to anyone.

I dug in my purse for a pen and something to write on. I wrote a name down on the piece of paper and handed it to her. She looked at me like I was possessed.

'How did you know?' she said.

The name I'd put down was Jerry Bergren. He was pretty notorious for hitting on actresses. I had a couple of friends who'd had a tumble with the guy. Why not? He was rich, good-looking, and actually knew a thing or two about theater. He never hit on me, though. I guess I wasn't his type."

Her lip curled in contempt.

"Somebody told me he had a thing for blondes. I heard his wife is a big blonde who used to be an actress. Maybe she needs to go back onstage – that's how Bergren seems to get his jollies.

I told Robin to be careful and get away from the guy as soon as she could. She promised she would.

That was almost two years ago, and she's still with him. Our shows have been doing well, well enough to cover the rent from everything I hear. I've heard there's even something in the bank – which is pretty fucking amazing for a theater company that's only been around a couple of years. But he's her security blanket. As long as he's around, she can just be an artist. She doesn't have to worry about the rest of the crap.

You saw what it's done for her as an actress. Trust me – she was fantastic before this guy came along. But she's just taken it somewhere I've never seen somebody go before. And she's pulled the rest of the company along with her.

But it's poison to her as a human being. It's not the putting out to get ahead that bothers me. Hell, I'll fuck anybody I need to fuck to make it in LA. But this deal she made, she's somehow sealed off a part of herself to keep it going. It's sucked the life out of her as a person. She always had it together more than just about anyone I knew, but she would have her crying jags and her wild highs and her shitty break-ups and her madly in loves the same as anyone else. Now I feel like I'm dealing with Mother Fucking Teresa. It's like someone's drained her emotions totally dry and now without all that weight she's floating on some level where real human relationships don't matter a damn. She's in a cocoon with nothing but theater and Jerry Bergren, and I know she doesn't give a shit about Jerry Bergren. But she's not Jesus Christ or Joan of Arc. She can't just put her emotions in a deep freeze, not for month after month after month."

Ned, who had scarcely moved as she spoke, stirred in his chair.

"Maybe she gets it all out on stage."

"Are you kidding? That's work. That's not living. That's not who you are. And if it is all you are, you're in a heap of fucking trouble."

She sprang off the futon and began pacing.

"She's got to get away from that guy. She doesn't need him any more. But she's afraid of giving up the crutch. She's probably a little afraid of him. He's incredibly wired. Knows everyone in Portland. One word and he could probably wipe out Vox Unum."

"What could he do? He's not a theater critic, you know." Ned gave a sly grin.

She snorted. "I don't know. I don't know anything about the crowd he runs with. He's way out of my league. But what I do know about the guy is he plays the field. One of these days some other cuter, blonder actress is going to come along and he's going to dump Robin and all these feelings she's been penting up are going to blow past the dam and she'll burst. And all the great theater in the world won't be enough to pick up the pieces.

She won't listen to me, though. Every time I bring it up I just get that 'I'm totally at peace' look and the sweetest brush-off you could imagine. I've almost been tempted to tell off Bergren myself. One other time I saw his car near the theater. I'd had a few drinks, and it was all I could do not to go over and pound on his window and tell him to get the fuck out of my friend's life."

She stalked back around to the front of the futon and flopped back in to her seat.

"That's why it was so damned hard telling her I was leaving the company and going to LA. It wasn't just getting out of the company, it was ditching her, leaving her alone to face the music when it finally comes. Which it will."

"So no one else knows?"

"Not a soul. Not as far as I know anyway. That's why I couldn't believe it when you asked about them. They've stayed totally out of sight. They only hit places out of town where nobody knows them. He's got some fancy beach house they sometimes go to. I guess he makes up some pretty good cock-and-bull stories for his wife."

"And the checks keep coming?"

"I guess. She won't tell me, of course. And it would be pretty tacky – even for me – to keep asking how much she's sold herself for. But I know it's a helluva lot less than I would put out for a movie or a TV deal."

She drained the mineral water. Ned went to the kitchen to get her another.

"Just between us, we're keeping an eye on Jerry Bergren over at the paper. He's not a nice man, and some of his bad deeds are going to land him on the front page one of these days. Hopefully soon. Anything I can pick up about the bastard would be great. If you hear anything from Robin, let me know."

"Sure. But she doesn't let much slip. I doubt she knows that much about the guy anyway. Other than the size of his dick and his checkbook."

They sat in silence for a moment.

"So what's your next show?" Ned asked.

"We're doing *Blood Relations* – you know it?

"Isn't that the one about Lizzie Borden, the axe murderess?"

"Right. You know your shit."

"I'd hold my own in a theater trivia contest. The problem is that nearly everything about theater these days is trivia. Let me guess – you play Lizzie."

That hoarse laugh gurgled up from her throat.

"How did you know?"

"You just have that edge, I guess. And I figured you wouldn't stray too far from the spotlight."

The lobby buzzer rang.

Ned went to the door. "Sounds like the pizza man is here. You ready for some serious meat?"

"I'll sharpen my axe."

CHAPTER TWELVE

Ned drummed his fingers on the smooth wood of the restaurant table. After the neighborhood hang-out feel of the Tavern, it was strange to behold a more upscale member of the McMenamins family. Servers in pressed white shirts instead of rumpled tie-dye, tasteful wall sconce lighting rather than frat-house fixtures, starched cloths in place of battered table tops.

The Black Rabbit Restaurant was part of Edgefield, described in its brochure as a dilapidated former county poor farm converted to a hotel complex. It had been Karin's idea to come here, a half hour east of downtown Portland, for lunch.

He'd been expecting her to call. Not that she'd been uppermost in his mind. Nora had staked out that territory. But he couldn't help panning back to the motel room and that long, ripe body. He could certainly use some more of that, and he needed more on Jerry Bergren.

Her call came in on his cell phone the Wednesday after that weekend at the coast.

"Can you talk?"

"I'm at my desk. Let me take it outside."

He'd slalomed through the cubicles and dived past the reception desk, passing Bolden who had greeted him with a wave and a chortle.

"A fetching actress on the line?"

"I can't beat 'em off," he'd leered back, covering the mouthpiece section of the phone.

"Was that Roger?" she'd asked when he was safely outside.

"Oh yes. Living out his fantasies through my alleged Don Juaning with local starlets."

"Do you find the actresses of Portland appealing, Mr. Marlowe?"

It was clear she had regained her equilibrium.

"I do. But I prefer the more seasoned leading lady to the ingénue."

"You have experience reviewing both types, do you?"

"A gentleman never kisses and tells."

"I thought we were speaking of reviewing, not kissing."

"Pardon me. I mistook your meaning. We must have a bad connection."

"Perhaps it would be better to meet in person."

"Perhaps it would."

"Lunch next week?"

"I'll have to check my starlet schedule. Ah, it looks like I have a cancellation on Wednesday. A leisurely day for me. The paper comes out in the morning, and I usually have nothing to review until Thursday night."

"So how were you going to spend today?"

"Waiting for the phone to ring."

She'd suggested the Black Rabbit the following Wednesday.

"It's a little off the beaten path. If you get there before me, take a table in the corner," was her parting remark.

Over the past week he'd been hurtling ahead on the play. He'd been up most nights until two pounding on his laptop, sometimes later if he'd had a show to review that evening. After wandering without a compass on the novel, he was giddy as a flow of words coursed in a channel across his computer screen.

He was conscious as he wrote of a fierce protective urge. It wasn't just that he had to shield Nora from Jerry Bergren. After the session with Elena Devlin he saw that he needed to protect Nora from herself, from consuming herself in her own artistry.

His motives, he knew, were scarcely noble. He wanted to possess her as a collector would a rare hothouse flower. In her mastery of the art there was a spark of immortality, and to be in her presence was to catch a glimpse of the divine.

Following the play's initial monologue, the closing speech of the production the critic is reviewing, the critic approaches the actress for a post-show interview. He stumbles anxiously through a set of mundane personal questions, then finds himself braying about her magnificent performance. She deflects his praise, paying tribute to the strength of the ensemble. Irritated by this display of correctness, he challenges her, saying she is obviously superior to the rest of the cast. He has reviewed in other cities, major cities, he says, and surely she must know she is toiling in a provincial backwater. If she were truly committed to her art, she would seek out artists of her own caliber. She would push herself to perform at the highest level, be it in Chicago, or New York, or London.

Unruffled, she says she is a small-town girl who does not aspire to be a star. Stardom is a creation of the media and is alien to the ensemble artistry she embraces. She has forged in Portland a community of passionate artists who share her artistic values. There is no guarantee she would find that in the big city, no matter how deep the talent pool might be. Then she turns the tables. Gently, she asks, if this city is so mediocre, why is he reviewing here?

Ned had left off there in the early hours of that morning. He could have pushed on, but he wanted to save a little strength for the exertions of the afternoon ahead.

He saw Karin at the host's stand. The host pointed out Ned, who had asked for a table in the corner and said that a woman would be joining him. She spotted him and waved a wave of easy familiarity.

She was dressed in black. Tight-fitting slacks, a ribbed turtleneck, and low calfskin boots. She carried a black leather folio. The only touch of color was a scarf, draped over one shoulder, featuring intricate geometric patterns on a flaming red background. Though it was a cloudy day, she wore dark glasses which she removed just a few paces from the table. Ned rose to greet her.

"So gallant, Mr. Marlowe."

"We writers are the last bastion of chivalry. We're the last knights errant – we are constantly erring, almost always at night."

Her laugh was deep and warm as she took her seat.

"Then I'm glad to be seeing you by day."

"The pleasure is mine."

Her haggard look of that morning at the coast had vanished. She was startlingly radiant.

"Are you drinking?" he asked.

"We are theater people, are we not?" she replied.

"I do confess it."

"Then we must drink."

He motioned over a server. "An Aquavit for the lady, and a Turbo Pimms No. 1 Cup for me."

The server's eyes registered bafflement, but there was no trace of it in his voice.

"Very good, sir." He turned on his heel.

"I'm sorry I'm late."

"Is it because you were driving around, pondering whether this was a place for a married woman with two teenage children and a house in the West Hills?"

"No, no. West Hills women should be seen over lunch with promising young writers."

"But not at dive bars after hours in formalwear."

"Exactly. You're beginning to master our social code."

"Uh oh. Does that mean I have to join the MAC Club?"

"You'd have to find a sponsor first."

"You're not offering?"

"The membership is in my husband's name. I'm afraid I couldn't help you on that one."

A shadow flitted across her face, then was gone. He thought that something needed to be said, even if it were just for show.

"Karin, I want to apologize for telling you what I saw. At the beach, I mean. It was late and I was tired and I wasn't thinking clearly. You were asking me all these questions about the house and I had to tell you I wasn't there. And once I'd said that, I couldn't very well not say why. It was a terrible way for you to get the news."

She reached across the table and squeezed his hand.

"You did absolutely nothing wrong. I invited you to stay in my house. You drove all the way down to the coast late at night and found that somebody had checked in before you. I called you and asked if you'd settled in. I would never have expected you to lie. All you could do was tell the truth about what you saw. The truth was ugly, but it wasn't ugly because you saw it.

I have to say the next few days were awful. I'd never seen it coming. He was gone all the time, but I just thought that was his business. He has to wine and dine, take his clients out golfing or hunting or fishing or to some game. There was always some reason he wasn't around, but it was always a good reason. I sound like such a pathetic housewife, but I was wrapped up with the kids and all they've got going on and then the theater board and it just never occurred to me that something might be happening behind my back.

You know I'd come down there to confront him. I couldn't do it then, but I kept thinking I would – especially when he came back Sunday night, all smiles, saying what a wonderful time he'd had on the golf course in Astoria. I thought about leaving him, taking the kids and going to my parents.

The worst part was that there was no one I could talk to. All of our friends are <u>our</u> friends. Sure, they're my friends, too, but of all the women there wasn't one I could trust not to tell her husband. I never really know what he's got going on with the men, who owes who what to who.

My parents think he walks on water. They would just think I was over-reacting. They're at a stage in life when they don't want to hear it. They're done dealing with their kids' troubles."

Now Ned extended his hand across the table and returned the squeeze.

"I wish you'd called me."

"You'd done quite enough, thank you. I felt so guilty. Please don't get me wrong – it was wonderful. Fantastic. But I'd come down there as an avenging angel, and when I went back it was as if I'd sunk to his level. I couldn't call you, not then. Please don't be hurt."

"I would have been if you hadn't called. But you did."

Her face lit up.

"A couple of days later I was sitting in the breakfast room reading the newspaper. Not reading really, just scanning the pages out of habit. I was at a total loss. Then suddenly my eyes landed on the Call Board section. You know it? That listing of auditions they run every Tuesday. Everything from barbershop quartets to Shaw. I used to pore over every line when I was in college. I don't think I'd bothered to look at it in ten years.

I saw they had a notice for *Rosencrantz and Guildenstern Are Dead*. The name of the company didn't mean anything to me, but I love the play. *Hamlet* turned upside down. I saw it years ago with Jerry down at the Ashland Festival; it was the only time he ever took me down there with him. Of course when I was young I dreamed of playing Ophelia to some dreamboat Hamlet in the real thing. Now I knew at my age the only shot I had was Gertrude, the Queen, but all of a sudden it was clear to me I had to do it.

I called up the number they'd put in the paper. It was the Artistic Director's office number – he works a day job, of course. He said I was just in time. The last night of the auditions was that evening. I made an appointment.

He told me that they'd want to see a prepared monologue. I hadn't done an audition in twenty years. I was petrified. But it was time for me to go back on stage. I knew it was.

I thought I might as well do something from Shakespeare. We've had the *Riverside Shakespeare* for years. I dug it out of the library. It seemed too obvious to work up one of Gertrude's own speeches, but I couldn't think of what else to do. Then it dawned on me. I would do Portia's 'The quality of mercy is not strained' speech from *The Merchant of Venice*. You know: 'It droppeth as the gentle rain from heaven on the place beneath.' It just seemed to fit.

I made a copy in Jerry's office, then I worked it and worked it. I had a Willamette Stage committee meeting at noon, but I called in sick. It was great. I hadn't faked a cold in ages. I also did up a resumé. Of course I didn't put any dates by the plays I was in so that you wouldn't know I hadn't acted in two decades. By the time the kids came home from school, I was ready. I fixed an early dinner – Jerry was out, of course – then I told the kids I had an evening theater meeting. I don't like to lie to my children, but they don't always have to know the whole truth and nothing but the truth."

She flashed a single-dimpled smile.

"I decided to wear black. In fact, I wore exactly what I'm wearing now. I snuck down the back stairs so that the kids wouldn't start asking questions, and jumped in the car. The audition was in a tiny little theater behind some coffee house in Southeast. I'd never heard of the place, of course, but I found it. I knocked on the door, and a girl who didn't look any older than my daughter whispered to me to come in. I handed her my resumé. She had me sit in the house. They obviously didn't have a separate room to put the next person in. I watched the actor – some young guy who must have been going for Rosencrantz or Guildenstern, or Hamlet if he didn't get either of those. He wasn't very good, and I hate to say it, but watching him made me feel a little better about my chances.

The girl called my name. They had a single stage light on, and somehow I made it into the light. There were three or four people in the audience. I could barely make them out in the shadows. One of them – I could tell it was the Artistic Director by his voice – said to me, 'Whenever you're ready.' I wanted to say, 'That would be five years from now,' but I just went right into it. And I nailed it. I absolutely nailed it. Old Shylock would have been quivering before me."

The server arrived with the drinks.

"An Aquavit and a Turbo Pimms No. 1 Cup," he announced, as if he had been serving these his entire career. "Are you ready to order?"

"Give us a few minutes," Ned replied.

"Very good."

"The Artistic Director said they would be back to me in a day or two. I just about sailed out the door. The car almost drove itself to the Lowbrow. Mick was on that night, and he didn't miss a beat. He said, 'You're early,' and set up an Aquavit at the bar. I told him about the audition. He said, 'Tonight, the drinks are on the house.' Then it occurred to me: I did have someone to talk to.

The next morning I got a call from the Artistic Director. He told me I'd made the callbacks for Gertrude. I nearly jumped out of my slippers. Then I called you and made a date.

Jerry's having his adventure in theater. Now I'm going to have mine. And I'm going him one better. He's screwing an actress; I'm back to being an actress. He's building a theater; I'm going on stage."

Ned flinched.

"He's building a theater? Where?"

"Well, I probably shouldn't say. It's kind of hush-hush. I don't know if you've heard about this project he's doing east of the mountains. The Bhagwan place. It's crazy, but he thinks he can pull in thousands of people to this dusty old ranch that's miles from nowhere. He's putting in rides and restaurants and all the usual stuff. But he told me the center of it all is going to be an enormous theater. Like a Greek amphitheatre. I guess there's a valley on the ranch that's the perfect shape. It's supposed to hold something like fifteen or twenty thousand people in the round under a glass dome with one of those roofs that opens and closes, so you can run shows all year.

He came in one night maybe six months ago and showed me the plans. I was shocked, because he never says anything to me about his work. He'd had a few drinks. He told me they were going to put on shows from all over the world: from Shakespeare to *Jesus Christ Superstar* to Aristophanes. All quality material, none of this Disney garbage. The history plays in Shakespeare would have real battle scenes. When Richard III says, 'A horse, my kingdom for a horse,' he'd be in the middle of a battlefield, with real horses just out of reach.

Jerry said there would be nothing like it anywhere. It sounded marvelous. We sat there just talking about theater, almost like the first night we met after *Hedda*. He told me he couldn't go public with this yet; they were still working out some of the details. That was the last I heard of it."

"Wow."

"I didn't invite you here to be impressed with Jerry's plans. You're here to help me."

"Me?"

"Yes, you. My callback is tonight, and you're going to run lines with me. They gave me sides for the opening scene where Rosencrantz and Guildenstern get their instructions."

She pulled some stapled pages out of the black leather folio.

"You mean I don't get to play Hamlet?"

"Sorry."

"So we're going to sit here in the Black Rabbit dining room and run lines from *Rosencrantz and Guildenstern Are Dead*?"

He was not amused. He had counted on more. A lot more.

"No. We're going to have a nice lunch and drink like theater people, then we're going up to the room I've booked."

"You booked a room to run lines for your audition?"

"No. I booked a room for the reason an unmarried couple usually books a room. Once we're finished with that, then we'll run lines."

CHAPTER THIRTEEN

Ned crept up the darkened stairs of the *Columbian* office. A meager light from the street lamps filtered through the glass front doors and up the stairwell. At the top of the steps he paused, straining to catch any sound. He heard nothing.

He pulled black leather gloves out of one coat pocket and drew them on as he swung past the reception area and into the maze of cubicles. Out of the other pocket he produced a slender flashlight. He flicked it on as he crossed the threshold of Bolden's office.

Ned had bought the gloves and flashlight earlier that day. He'd come in to the office late after going full tilt on the play until almost four the night before. He was impressed with his staying power considering his Edgefield romp with Karin in the afternoon. They'd spent more time in bed than running lines from *Rosencrantz and Guildenstern* – a lot more. But then her character didn't have that much to say.

His first stop in the office that morning had been Selvaggio's desk. The reporter was hunched forward, peering intently at his computer screen.

"I've got something," Ned whispered. "On you know who."

"Pillow talk?" Selvaggio asked in a barely audible voice, still facing his computer.

"Fuck you," Ned hissed.

Selvaggio wheeled around in his chair. He kept his voice low.

"Now you're talkin'. Much better than 'asshole.' But if you were fuckin' me, you wouldn't have any pillow talk. But it doesn't matter any more what you got. Come on. Let's take a walk."

The afternoon had been clear and crisp. More like a Chicago fall day than the usual gray and damp of Portland, Ned had thought. They crossed the street and passed the imposing downtown library that stood across from the *Columbian*. Selvaggio waited until they were well clear of the office before berating Bolden with a fury that thickened his New Jersey accent.

Bolden's assistant had called him into the publisher's office that morning. Trustman, the editor-in-chief, was already there. Bolden told him they were putting a hold on the Bergren story. They didn't have enough to go on, at least not now. They had other stories, he said, more solid ones, that Selvaggio should move on. Trustman ticked off a list, but he was just going through the motions. Bolden had obviously told him how it was coming down. The reporter fought back, but he'd made no headway. The story was dead.

Selvaggio denounced Bolden for being gutless, spraying expletives into the chill air. They were running a goddamned newspaper, he'd raged, not a Good Person protection racket. Bolden was always afraid somebody would toss Chardonnay in his face at a West Hills wine and cheese.

Selvaggio said he had half a mind to ransack Bolden's office. Something must have come in to spook the publisher off the story. Maybe Bergren had photos of Bolden diddling little boys and had sent him copies by way of blackmail. Who the hell knew?

Selvaggio had finally left off bashing Bolden long enough to ask about Ned's news. He told the reporter about Bergren's mega-theater on the Bhagwan ranch. Selvaggio had been unimpressed.

"A theater? Who's he kidding? No one's going to truck all the way out to Bhagwan-ville to see a play, for Christ's sake. Not in this century. The wife's got to be off base anyway. Jerry's plans don't say anything about a theater, just a museum. If I were you, I'd leave off the pillow talk with Karin, big guy. Her information's no good, and Bolden's going to let Bergren off scot-free anyway. If you're shacked up with Mrs. Bergren, put the bed to its highest and best use. Which in her case sure as hell isn't talking."

He had left Selvaggio to pick up his second double espresso of the day. He'd needed a pick-me-up after the blow of Bolden killing the Bergren story. He had been counting on Selvaggio to reel Bergren in and destroy the bastard's reputation. Then Nora would have no choice but to turn down Bergren's tainted money and no reason to stay shackled to him any longer.

As he'd sat over his computer, setting out his review schedule for that weekend, he'd weighed his options. He could go straight to Nora and try to warn her off her sugar daddy. He could tell her of Bergren's shady deals and his serial womanizing. But she probably knew all that, or suspected it anyway, and still she stayed with the man.

He could try to use Karin as a lever – other than in bed, that was. But what leverage did she really give him? It wasn't as if he were going to confront Bergren and offer to stop sleeping with the guy's wife in return for cutting Nora loose. Women weren't chattels in this day and age and even if they were, Karin wasn't his yet. He could ply her for more inside dope on her husband, but she didn't look to be much of a source so far and anyway what use was her information if there would be no story?

Which brought him back to Bolden. Why had the publisher let Bergren go? Was it just that they ran in the same crowd? There had to be more to it than that. The *Columbian*'s stock in trade, other than kinky personal ads, was bringing down the high and mighty. That's why they'd hired a pit bull like Selvaggio. They didn't lightly drop the chance to hunt down big game like Bergren.

Bergren had to have something over Bolden. It wasn't pictures of little boys, not judging by Bolden's ogling of Karin or his leering patter about nubile actresses. Had Bolden run short of cash and turned to Bergren for one of those West Hills juice loans Selvaggio had mentioned? The publisher's appearance suggested he was comfortably off, but you could never tell. Maybe Jerry had agreed to write off a big debt if the story were deep-sixed.

The prospects weren't promising, but it looked as if the only quick route to Bergren went through Bolden. He had nothing on Bolden, however, and no useful tools for digging up dirt. He was a fiction writer, for Christ's sake, not a muckraker. At best, it would take him months before he sussed out any link between the two men. He was not prepared to leave Nora in Bergren's clutches for that long.

Selvaggio had said he was tempted to ransack Bolden's office. The reporter wouldn't do it, though. Despite all his bitching and moaning, he was still a company man and a lifer in journalism. He wouldn't risk his career over some stupid stunt.

Ned had no such scruples. He didn't really give a damn about the *Columbian* job. The estate would sort itself out soon enough and he'd be back to his old life. If he left a little unpleasantness behind, so be it.

Bolden's office was never locked. For a paper whose main line was prying out the secrets of others, they took scant care in protecting their own. After everyone had left for the day, he could waltz in unchecked. There was a security system outside the building, of course, but like any employee he had the code.

He'd decided to go for it. It was a long shot, but the best one he had. And if he were going to do it, it might as well be now. Selvaggio had said that Bergren was close to landing his environmental permit for the Bhagwan project. Once that came through, the reporter had made it sound as if the man would be untouchable.

Besides, Tucker Farr was due in town the following day. He'd called Ned earlier in the week to say he was coming to Portland on business. They were scheduled to have lunch. Farr and Bolden went way back. If Ned snared anything worthwhile in the office search, Farr might be able to fill in some blanks. Of course, there was no reason for Farr to know what he was up to. Nora was none of his affair.

Ned was scheduled to attend another show that evening, which would give him perfect cover to return to the office. If anyone turned up, he could always say he'd wanted to write up the review while the show was fresh in his mind – if that phrase could be applied to the stale fare on his reviewing plate.

He'd ducked out of the office and bought the flashlight and batteries at a convenience store near Pioneer Square, downtown

Portland's central plaza. He wouldn't want to draw attention to his presence in the office that night by turning on lights. It was a routine purchase, of course, but he felt the mournful eyes of the middle-aged Indian man at the register upon him. He paid cash.

Buying the gloves had been a bit of bravado on his part. He hardly thought they'd be dusting Bolden's office for fingerprints, but having on dark leather gloves would lend a little derring-do to the operation. He'd found a perfect pair at Meier & Frank, a middle-brow Portland retail institution that fronted on Pioneer Square. As it was a brisk December day, the made-up matron at the counter had paid little attention to his purchase, which he also made in cash.

He'd spent the rest of the afternoon lining up freelancers to review holiday shows he couldn't bear to see himself, then downed some noodles at a cheap Vietnamese joint where he was becoming a regular. He knew he should be saving money by cooking at home, but time at the grocery store was time away from his play.

The show that evening was a world premiere by a Portland playwright put on in a dingy dungeon of a venue in the city's outer reaches. If it weren't the hole in the wall where Karin had auditioned for *Rosencrantz and Guildenstern*, it could pass for it. The script had its moments early on, and the actors were earnest and committed, but Ned preferred the company of his own play's characters and took refuge with them for most of the second act.

He'd sped in the Navigator back to his apartment and leapt to his laptop. He had already wrapped up the first act – where the critic takes on the actress – and was well into the second act rendezvous between the businessman and the actress. He surged ahead until midnight, the time he'd figured it would be safe to return to the *Columbian*. On the few nights he'd worked late the cleaning crew had finished up around ten thirty, and even the most nocturnal of reporters should have gone home by eleven. He decided to walk, both to stretch out in the bracing night air and to make sure nothing that could be traced to him would be spotted near the office.

Bolden's office was by far the largest at the paper. This wasn't saying much, as only a handful of the *Columbian* brass had been liberated from cubicles and granted the privilege of a private space. The other offices had barely enough room for a modest desk and a few chairs, though Trustman had managed to squeeze in a sagging sofa where he occasionally napped. Bolden's, however, featured a complete suite of blonde wood furniture, including an imposing desk on the left side of the room and a round conference table in the far right corner. As Ned trained the flashlight around the room, the light played off the glass of framed photographs on the walls featuring the publisher and various notables. Bolden liked visitors to know he was on speaking terms with those worth hearing.

There was little clutter on the desk, which was bathed in the dull glow of the publisher's desktop computer. Bolden kept the only assistant at the paper, and she was known as a ruthless filer. There were a few neat stacks of what looked to be invoices and display ads, but nothing more. Ned was not discouraged. The man would hardly leave smoking guns in plain view.

He stole behind the desk, the Converse All Stars he usually just wore for basketball treading lightly on the thin carpet. He thought the combination of black leather gloves and green basketball shoes cut a nice dash. There was a long credenza behind the desk along the wall that featured family photos and a stuffed bulldog sporting a "Y"-emblazoned sweater. Bolden was a Yale man through and through.

While the credenza contained several cabinets, Ned thought the drawers on the left-hand side of the desk to be a better bet. The top drawer was a mishmash of paper clips, business cards, and Altoids tins. Breath freshening was something of a fetish with Bolden.

Ned rummaged in the rear of the drawer. He was unaccustomed to wearing gloves, and everything he touched felt undefined. He pulled out a deck of playing cards tucked in a small manila envelope. The backs of the cards were unremarkable, but the fronts featured Playboy centerfolds in differing poses based on the card. The image for the jacks was particularly diverting. Bolden must play a mean hand at solitaire.

He put the cards back and tried the middle drawer. It was a model of organization, with office supplies meticulously arrayed throughout. It looked as if the assistant had set this up, and it had barely been touched since. No doubt Bolden just went to her when he needed something.

He couldn't open the bottom (and largest) drawer. There was no lock on the drawer, so there had to be some mechanism in the desk that sprung it loose. He re-opened the top drawer and pressed his fingers along the sides, trying to find the catch. He had no luck. He tried again inside the middle drawer, without success.

The air in the office felt stale and close. He undid the top few buttons on his coat. He might as well have a look at the credenza before he gave it all up as a bad job. He crouched down, pulled open the center of three cabinets, and raked the narrow beam of the flashlight across the shelves. There was an ancient boom box, its black electric cord tightly coiled beside it. On the shelf above it was a bundle of old issues of the *Columbian*, saved for no apparent reason.

Ned shut the door and started to scuttle to the cabinet on the right when he heard the sound of footsteps in the paper's front entry downstairs. His head jerked toward the office door and as he did his shoulder hit the side of the desk. The impact knocked the flashlight out of his hand. It rolled beneath the desk, its light shooting feeble rays across the carpet. He rolled Bolden's sleek leather office chair out of the way and scurried under the desk to retrieve the flashlight. As he reached for the light, the round of his back hit something on the underside of the desk.

He backed out and saw that the bottom drawer of the desk had sprung open. He heard someone ascending the stairs. Light from the stairwell trickled into the office.

He cast a frantic look into the opened drawer. There was a CD case sitting atop a stack of files. To his amazement, the case was labeled "Bergren" in neat block letters. He grabbed the case, stuffed it into his coat pocket, slammed the drawer shut, spun the desk chair back into place, and hurtled toward the office door. He pivoted at the threshold, his eyes darting around the room to make sure he had forgotten nothing. As he turned to leave he noticed that the flashlight was still flickering in his hand. He switched it off and dropped it into his other pocket.

He hurled himself through the office doorway, making it into the corridor just as a figure rounded the corner from the reception area.

It was Argent, the rock music writer. He was a gaunt, soul-patched man who sported a grunge-style wardrobe despite being a decade too old for the trend.

"Dirk, man, what are you doing here in the dark?"

Ned decided to stick to his alibi.

"I had a show tonight. It was hideous. I thought I might as well get the review out of the way so I would never have to think about it again. Believe me, if you'd had to sit through that abomination, you'd want to write it up in the dark as well."

Christ! He was still wearing the gloves. He tried to hide his hands behind his back.

"It's the same thing with me. But just the opposite. I just got back from a gig. Amazing. Wicked. These guys could be the next Crazy 8s. I had to get it down right away."

Argent was a booster. He was forever discovering groups that would take the world by storm and casting them in the mold of once-promising bands Ned had never heard of.

"You're a lucky man. Since I've been here I've only once come out of a show feeling more alive than when I went in."

Argent shook his head. He gave off a faint odor of beer and cigarettes.

"You can't just look at what's on stage, man. That's not the half of it. These people are young. Really young. They're raw and they're stoned and they're horny. They're all over the goddamned place. You've got to tear all that down and get to down to the nub. Then you'll know what you've got."

Ned had heard tell of epic debates in the newsroom between Argent and Milson on the essence of criticism. He had no time for that now.

"I know what I saw tonight, and with all due allowance for youth, it was still a piece of shit. Well, I'll leave you to writing up the next Everclear. What's the name of the group?"

"The Slam. Check 'em out."

"Will do. Good night."

"See ya."

The music critic extended his fist, expecting a return bump from Ned. It was part of Argent's hipster schtick. Ned hesitated, then in a spasm shot his fist out and back. He looked for signs of suspicion on Argent's face about the black glove, but none were apparent. The man saw more outrageous accessories on a nightly basis.

Ned quick-stepped past the reception area, then bolted down the stairs, the flashlight bouncing in his coat pocket. He punched the touchpad that unlocked the front door and pushed through on to the sidewalk. The post-midnight chill was welcome after the stifling air of Bolden's office. He scanned the street for suspicious types. It occurred to him he was the only one in sight who fit that description.

CHAPTER FOURTEEN

Ned chucked his coat on the sofa and hustled into the high-backed chair. He kept his laptop on the dining table. He hadn't seen the need for a desk. He was content to do his eating and writing on the same surface, having only himself to impress.

He extracted the disk from its case and slid it into the drive. He had only a few hours to find out what was on the disk and get it back to Bolden's office. Hopefully Argent would not be laboring all night over his ode to The Slam.

The file contained only two e-mail folders, one marked "Inbox" and the other "Sent Items." Ned felt a mild voyeuristic thrill as he clicked to open the inbox. He'd scanned a few open e-mails of his friends when checking webmail on their computers, but this was the first time he'd actually set out to read someone else's correspondence. Gentlemen might do otherwise, but he couldn't afford to be gentlemanly.

There were some three dozen e-mails in the inbox, all from Bergren. He opened the first, which was dated May 25 of last year. It began "Dear Brooks." Ned looked at the e-mail address of the recipient: "CBP@comcast.net." "CBP" were his father's initials: Curtis Brooks Prince.

Ned had never sent an e-mail to his father, nor ever received one. As far as he knew, his father had never opened an e-mail account.

His sister Celia had bought Brooks Prince a computer two Christmases ago, but Ned thought it had just sat in the former library that had become his father's office. But as he began clicking back and forth between the two folders, the disembodied voice of his father was unmistakable.

It was evident, as Ned scrolled urgently through the e-mails, that Bergren was making a sales pitch to Brooks Prince. The first few notes were transparent efforts to get a foot in the door. The tone was light and breezy. The two had apparently had lunch together with a mutual friend named Foster, who was the butt of several in-jokes.

Then, in August, Bergren shifted gears. He began to sketch out the contours of the amphitheatre on the Bhagwan ranch. Bergren made a masterful case. This would be a theater to top all theaters. One for the ages. It would be like ancient times, when theater was an event for the masses and a spectacle that brought the entire community together. Not like now, Bergren suggested, with tiny audiences packed into cramped boxes. There would be cutting edge sound and light systems and room enough to do Shakespeare with real battle scenes. All as part of a theme park dedicated to world peace and understanding.

Bergren's biggest selling point was bringing kids back to theater. This amphitheatre would get them off of the couch, out of their headphones and video games, and into a place so huge, so wired, it could compete with anything – even movies.

Subtly, gradually, Bergren started working the need for funds into the e-mails. He had the connections and the architects and the planners, he said, but he needed a partner who could help him tie up the land, get drawings made, and hire consultants. Bergren never actually asked for money in the e-mails, though. It appeared he'd saved the asks for meetings and phone calls that were mentioned in passing.

His father took the bait. Soon Brooks Prince's e-mails rose to a fevered pitch that surpassed even Bergren's zeal. He raved about making over a culture in decline. He became hands-on in shaping the project. He offered ideas for shows, even color schemes. The two went back and forth about building a string of amphitheatres all over the world.

As Ned pored over the e-mails, Brooks Prince took on an unfamiliar dimension. Ned had never witnessed the joy that sang through his father's writing about the theater. There was a pride of creation that Brooks Prince had never shown in all the charity projects he had chaired on the Ingram family's behalf. There was practically nothing in the e-mails about the investment, about the deal itself. That seemed almost an afterthought. His father was completely, obsessively, focused on the design of the theater, on its mission and audience. Particularly on kids, how the project would restore their faith and wonder in live performance.

Then, for over six weeks starting this past June, there were no e-mails from Bergren. His father's mood plunged. Brooks Prince complained that Bergren wouldn't return calls. The e-mails started to turn panicky. At last, a note from Bergren surfaced in the inbox. He said he'd been talking to lenders and they weren't buying the theater concept. "Nobody goes to the theater anymore," they were saying.

Bergren said he'd gone to all the funding sources he knew, but he couldn't find anyone who would sign on to the whole project.

Several more weeks went by without word from Bergren. His father sent off a stream of frenzied e-mails. Finally, Bergren replied. He said he'd found a way to get the lenders to do the deal. They'd have to replace the theater with a museum, however.

Would it be a theater museum, his father demanded? After some hemming and hawing, Bergren admitted that it would have nothing to do with theater: the museum would be devoted to Rolls Royce.

Bergren explained that a Rolls Royce museum made sense on the site of the Bhagwan's notorious collection. Tourists would flock to anything having to do with the lifestyles of the rich and famous, he said, so the lenders were upbeat about an ultra-luxury car attraction. Bergren had spoken with Portland's Rolls Royce dealer, who thought they could pull the concept off. The change in plan had to be kept confidential, Bergren said, because they needed a sign-off on their environmental impact statement. He had been pitching the project to politicians and bureaucrats as a theme park for world peace and understanding and did not want word about a Rolls Royce museum getting out until the approval came through.

The swing in his father's mood was ghastly. The mania of hatching this spectacular plan gave way to a wild desperation. Bergren's e-mail announcing the Rolls Royce museum came in mid-September. Ned checked the date. His father had shot himself two days later.

Before Ned had had only contempt for Bergren, for his unworthiness to possess Nora and for his shabby treatment of Karin.

Now, as he traced Bergren's seduction and abandonment of his father, he was consumed by hatred of the man.

Ned had pulled out the box full of dog-eared playbills and faded cast photos a time or two since he'd arrived in Portland, but he could not bring his father into focus. Hazy specters of the college leading man, the black tie socialite, and the stricken suicide flitted by in a numbing jumble. But Bergren's despicable bait-and-switch – promising some pie-in-the-sky theater, conning millions to get his hands on the Bhagwan's ranch, then blaming bankers as he surfaced the tawdry Rolls Royce scheme he'd obviously had up his sleeve all along – fired the image of Brooks Prince with a searing clarity. Ned pictured his father alone in the grand old mansion on the lake, walled off in the Ingram library amidst the rows of unread books, hunched over the unplayed upright piano, helpless as Bergren snuffed out the blaze of his vision.

Ned fantasized confrontations with Bergren, calling him out at his office or his beach house or his fancy downtown club and beating him to a pulp. He knew, however, that revenge should be meted out through channels. He knew he should call Tucker Farr and lay out everything he had discovered. Farr would be impressed. The man had put a squadron of high-priced suits to work tracing his father's funds and come up with nothing. Through an extraordinary convergence of circumstances, Ned had cracked the case all on his own – courtesy of a CD that must have been turned over to the paper by some disgruntled Bergren employee.

It was clear what Farr would do. He would hand the matter over to the lawyers and the accountants. They would take the mess and transform it into an orderly array of claims against that bastard Bergren.

But Ned needed to deal with Bergren now. He couldn't wait years for some dreary lawsuit to work its way through the courts. Bergren could probably manage to bury a lawsuit in Portland. Not to mention Chicago, where everyone knew justice was for sale.

He stood up from the table and in the pre-dawn stillness began to pace the room. Until this morning he'd been depending on Selvaggio and the *Columbian* to bring down Bergren. He had planned to help, of course, but only in a supporting role, unearthing such nuggets of information as he could mine from Karin.

But that plan was dead. Bergren must have the fix in with Bolden. The publisher had killed the story even though he had a smoking gun on the disk. If the *Columbian* wouldn't touch the story, no one else in town would either. Portland's daily paper was notorious for its gutless fawning on the city's establishment. TV and radio didn't have the attention span.

So short of buying a handgun and bumping off the man in broad daylight, how could he get to Bergren? He knew next to no one in Portland. He had no money and no influence, except the power he wielded as a critic over hapless theater people.

It flashed on him that what he had was his play. He had never thought of it as a weapon until now. The script was intensely private. He'd given no thought to producing it once it was finished.

But there was no other way he could take on Bergren. All that lay within his power was the shape of his script. He could write the part of the businessman so that it was unmistakably Bergren to a Portland audience. He could expose the man and his schemes through the play. He could avenge his father and redeem Nora.

He would have to find a way to put the play on. The prospect was daunting. He had never been involved in producing theater. Production to him was an exercise in deal-making, and he was no wheeler-dealer. He'd left money-grubbing to his buddies who'd gone the business school route.

As he made the circuit of his cramped living room, he sensed the futility of an assault through theater. If he ran the play for two weeks, he could manage maybe eight to ten performances. There was no use in this town trying to bring in an audience on Tuesday or Wednesday. He was limited to Thursday through Sunday, maybe with matinees on the two weekend days. If he were lucky, he might average a three-quarter full house. If he rented out a hundred-seat theater, the best case was an audience of seven hundred fifty people.

And who came to theater these days? A motley collection of tottering pensioners, wispy-chinned students, and loner losers. As a reviewer scanning the seats around him, he saw precious few power brokers in sleek suits – the sort of insiders whose opinion could sway Bergren's fate. The audience was mostly fringe players, whose righteous indignation would be comforting but meaningless.

It was a far cry from the halcyon days of ancient Greece or Elizabethan England or even robber baron America, where a well-wrought play could sway rulers and humble the mighty. Christ, John Wilkes Booth almost brought down a nation from inside Ford's Theatre. Nowadays, theater in this country was a cultural artifact, a lost rite preserved by a dwindling band of cultists.

And yet, art was mercurial. You never knew how its particles, once unleashed, might collide. A popular magazine might have millions of subscribers but its articles were disposable, consumed and instantly forgotten. A play could move the minds of its audience over decades, even centuries, and work strange wonders.

He was likely firing blanks, he knew, but it was his best and only shot. He would put on the play. In time he would act responsibly and deliver the matter up to Farr and his team. But for now he had a score to settle as his father's son.

CHAPTER FIFTEEN

Farr ordered his lunch with authority. As he did, Ned observed, in just about everything.

They were seated in the restaurant of the Heathman, one of Portland's tonier hotels. Their choice corner table overlooked Broadway, where pedestrians braced against the chill December drizzle.

Tucker Farr was a rugged, powerful man. Ned heard that Farr had been a standout linebacker at Yale and a fierce club rugby player in his Harvard MBA and early investment banking days. He had the tanned, lined face of an avid sailor. Farr was a fixture in Lake Michigan regatta circles and always a contender in the annual Chicago to Mackinac Island race. This morning he was dressed in a faintly pinstriped dark blue suit. His thick neck pressed against the white collar of an otherwise powder blue shirt, elegantly offset by a wine-colored tie.

"So how was your Thanksgiving?"

"Somebody at the paper took pity on me and invited me over."

"With a date?"

"Sadly solo."

"No prospects?"

"Well, I have been seeing someone. But she had her own family plans."

"Which didn't include you."

"No. It's a bit complicated, I'm afraid."

"An actress?"

"Yes."

"It'll only get more complicated. Actresses have a lot of moving parts – so to speak. How's the reviewing business?"

"Hit and miss. Lately, the misses have the upper hand."

"It's not Chicago, uh?"

"No. And it never will be. But I have to say there's a certain provincial charm. Things are more laid back. Not everyone wants to be a star, not everybody is going for the big time. Real life makes room for theater – not the other way around."

"I don't head back until tomorrow morning. Anything I should see tonight?"

"Absolutely. It's the last weekend of an amazing production of *A Doll's House*. The lead actress could go anywhere, and I mean top companies in London or New York. But for some reason she's decided to stay here."

"Sounds to me like she's turned your head, Ned. Is she your complication?"

Ned reddened.

"No, no. I'm just a distant admirer."

"Whatever you say. Where is this place?"

"It's playing at the SoHo Theater. I'll get you directions. Let's see – it's Friday. Tomorrow night is almost certainly sold out, but you might be able to get a single ticket tonight."

"You won't join me?"

"I'm keeping my nose to the grindstone just like you wanted. No, I've got other shows, other reviews."

"Any time left over for the novel?"

Ned hesitated. He'd been looking for an opening, but the subject had come up earlier in the conversation than he had planned. He decided to plunge ahead.

"Well, actually, I've put the novel aside for a while."

"So you can spend more time on that complication?"

"No. So I can spend more time on theater. I'm writing a play. In fact, the script is just about done. I need your help to produce it."

Ned had not slept that night. After burning a copy of the disk, he'd scurried back to the paper at four in the morning to return it to Bolden's desk drawer. Thankfully Argent was nowhere to be seen. Then he'd gone home and plunged into his script, pausing only for a quick shower and a stale bagel.

Just after ten he'd called SoHo Productions, the company that ran the SoHo Theater, and asked whether the venue was available to rent for a few weeks. The company's manager had offered three weeks next August, but that was long after Bergren's environmental impact statement would come up for decision. He'd asked if they had anything earlier in the year. She'd said it was probably too soon to be of any use, but they'd just had a cancellation for a two-week slot at the beginning of February. She'd given him a quote of two thousand dollars, which included rehearsal time on off nights during the run of SoHo's winter show. She'd agreed to hold the slot open until that afternoon.

He'd then called Elena Devlin on her cell phone. Her lunch shift at the deli was just getting under way. He'd asked if she would have time to meet him before rehearsal that afternoon. It was about Robin and Bergren, he'd said. He'd sensed her impulsive need to know more, right then, but she'd had to attend to her customers. She had agreed to come to his place at four thirty.

He'd rolled into the office at quarter to eleven. No one at the *Columbian* took notice. They were accustomed to his odd hours. He'd placed a few calls to stringers to confirm their coverage of shows that weekend and mulled over whether to take Selvaggio into his confidence about the play. He'd decided against it. Selvaggio was a top-rank reporter, but brought nothing to the table when it came to producing a show. He would disclose his plans for the play on only a strict "need to know" basis.

Ned wondered whether Selvaggio had been aware of the disk and not told him. He doubted it, but he couldn't be sure. Selvaggio had blasted Bolden's cowardice, but that might be because the reporter had read the e-mails and was appalled the publisher wouldn't green-light the story. If Selvaggio had seen the e-mails, he would have no way of connecting Ned – whom the reporter knew as Dirk Marlowe – to Brooks Prince.

Ned had headed to the Heathman shortly before noon. He'd resolved not to tell Farr about the substance of the play. If he did, he might as well just get out of the way and let the JDs and the CPAs paper Bergren into oblivion. There would be plenty of time after the show was over to route this through the proper channels.

"You want to put on a play?" Farr sounded as if Ned had taken up an unfathomable hobby.

"I do. I've been hanging around theaters for years now, you know. I have some idea of how it's done."

"I'm sure you do. I just wasn't expecting a sudden change from reviewer to producer."

"Don't worry, I'm not quitting my day job. This is just moonlighting. But it's a play, so I can't moonlight without stage light. Which is why I need your help."

"How much do you need?" Farr was one to get to the point.

"Fifteen thousand."

Ned had done some back of the envelope figuring that morning. He thought twelve or thirteen thousand would probably do it, but it was wise to have a cushion. Farr didn't blink.

"That's all you need to put on a play?"

"No one's in it for the money, so it doesn't take much. The ego budget is high, but I've got that line item covered."

"What's the play about?"

"I know this will sound strange, but I'd rather not say."

"You want me to back a play you won't tell me about?"

Ned glanced down at the table for effect before delivering the little speech he'd briefly rehearsed.

"I needed to write this play to deal with Dad's death. I didn't think it would be so hard. We writers, after all, are supposed to have an inside track on the human condition. We deal with pain and trauma and loss, at least the best of us do, and you'd think we would display a certain grace when life treats us as we treat our own creations. But we're really just pathetic creatures of habit, addicted to our daily ritual of coffee and calculated time-wasting and gossip and those few hours of intense communion with a computer screen that we despise but can't manage without. We love our petty little routine, and we're pretty damned hopeless when something or someone comes along and just rips it all to shreds.

Dad's death knocked me completely out of whack. Everything I knew, everything I counted on, was just kicked out from under me. The only way I could get my footing back was to write something new. The new thing turned out to be this play. I need to put it on because it's not enough just to have written it. It's not complete if it just sits on my computer."

Farr eyed him closely.

"I wouldn't have guessed it would come out in a play, but I'm not surprised to hear it. It's only natural you would write about your father. Just like the story collection after your mother died."

Ned gave him a sardonic look.

"Are you saying I can't write unless I have a parent die?"

"Hardly. I'm no authority on the creative process. But from what I've heard, a writer deals with pain by writing – just like a money man deals with pain by making more money. Just ask my ex-wife. I'm delighted to hear the news. Don't worry about the money. I'll put it together."

Ned straightened in his chair.

"Thank you. I really need this."

"I can tell. We'll consider it an advance on your share of the estate. Which, I'm afraid, is still up in the air. We haven't found much more since the last time we spoke. Except this."

He leaned down and picked up a rolled blueprint that had apparently been lying at his feet. He swept the table settings to the side, removed the rubber band, and unrolled the print.

"The maid found this inside your father's office. Inside the piano, to be exact. We'd gone over the office with a fine-toothed comb, but we never thought to look in there. How she ended up digging through the piano I have no idea, but she'd dust the inside of your mouth if you'd let her. We can't be sure, but we think this must have been the project your father was funding. Amazing, isn't it?"

The theater was just as Karin had described it. A colossal Greek amphitheatre, shown from overhead and in cross-section. The performance area was immense. Actors were arrayed in a battle scene like toy soldiers, complete with horses and artillery. A note in the lower right hand corner read: '*Richard III* – Battle of Bosworth.' Ringing the stage were ascending rows of seats packed with miniature patrons. The cross-section showed the retractable roof set atop a façade of Ionic columns. It was breathtaking.

Ned did his best to feign surprise.

"You think he was investing in some sort of mega-theater, where you could do real battle scenes from *Richard III*?"

"In a strange way it all makes sense. Your father loved the theater. His heart would never have been in a real estate deal or a new factory. That's what the Ingrams did, and he thought they had no soul. If he wanted to make a mark, he would do it in a way they couldn't possibly imagine. You couldn't do a much better job of that than backing a theater. Your grandfather Ingram would have spun right out of the Christ Church graveyard. Which I'm sure is why your father kept all this from the family wise men.

We've tried to trace this, but no luck. You see at the top it says 'Project World Stage.' We've searched all over the country trying to find a project under that name or that looks anything like this, but we've come up with nothing. The architects who drew the plans are out of Los Angeles, but of course they won't say anything. Client confidentiality."

Ned played along.

"So this theater was never built?"

"As far as we know, no."

"Do you think that's why Dad killed himself?"

Farr pursed his lips.

"It would certainly explain it. It would have been devastating if he poured all this money into a project that never got off the ground. But I honestly can't say."

"But if it was never built, where did all the money go?"

"We don't know. Obviously they would have had to pay the architects for this design, but that would have only been a small fraction of what your father spent."

The server arrived with their lunch. Farr rolled up the blueprint and put it back under the table.

"We need to keep this, but would you like me to have a copy made?"

"That would be great."

"I thought you would want to see the plan. It says a lot about your father. What really made him tick."

"Thank you. Have you shown this to my sisters?"

"I thought I would start with you, Ned. You're the theater person in the family. Even more now, seeing that you're going to be a producer. When does the play go on?"

"The first part of February. I'm doing it at the theater you're going to tonight. The SoHo. Which reminds me – I need to get you directions."

After they finished lunch, Farr told Ned to call when he needed a check for the play.

"You think I've been hard on you cutting off your allowance."

"That's what I thought at first. But you did what you had to do."

"I appreciate your saying that. But I want you to know I will support anything that helps you with your father's death. Anything. Even a play, for Christ's sake."

CHAPTER SIXTEEN

The theater was his. Right after his lunch with Farr, Ned called SoHo and booked the two weeks in February. He asked SoHo's manager to keep the booking confidential. He knew theater tongues would wag on word that the *Columbian*'s critic was producing a show. He considered reserving the space in his own name, instead of Dirk Marlowe, but he needed to avoid any move that might help Bergren connect him to his father. The play had to be kept under wraps until it opened. If Bergren got wind of what was coming, who knew what strings he could pull to shut it down?

After a tedious afternoon plowing through holiday show press packets, Ned walked through the late afternoon gloom back to his apartment. Once again, Elena was there before him. She was wearing the same cheap black raincoat despite the chill.

"So what did you find out?"

The lobby was empty, but he saw no reason to take any chances. "Let's wait until we get up to my place."

"You're right. Sorry."

"Don't be. I'd want to know why I got a sudden summons from this nosy critic. Well, at least you'll get a pizza out of it. I put in an order for our usual."

Once inside his unit, Ned offered Elena a seat at the dining table and a mineral water.

"OK," she said. "But I may need something stronger depending on what you have to say about Robin."

"It's nothing so sinister," he said from the kitchen as he pulled a beer from the fridge for himself.

"When you mentioned her with Jerry Bergren, I was thinking the worst."

He took a seat next to her at the table and looked her in the eye.

"I've written a play. I've decided to produce and direct it. And I want you to play the lead."

Her wide-set eyes stared at him in confusion.

"What the fuck does that have to do with Robin?"

"The play is how we're going to get her away from Bergren. We're going to expose him, in public. We're going to bring him down."

"How the hell are you going to do that?"

"You remember I told you the paper was keeping an eye on Bergren? Well, they've come up with a scoop on a huge project of his. If it gets out, the deal is toast. We're going to put it out there, in the play."

"Not in the paper?"

"They won't touch it. Bergren's got even the *Columbian* wired. He managed to kill the story."

"Won't this get you fired?"

"Maybe. I don't care. It'll be worth it. Well worth it."

She sat quietly for a moment, her fingernails working loose the label on her mineral water bottle.

"She won't go for it."

"Robin? What do you mean?"

"She's too loyal. Even to the worst pricks. If Bergren's going to hell, she'll ride down the elevator with him."

"I don't think so. My bet is she'll do whatever it takes to save her company. If Bergren can't deliver the checks, she'll move on. But even if you're right, I'm not counting just on bursting Bergren's bubble to bring her around. We'll force her to look at herself in the mirror."

"How?"

"She's in the play. In fact, she's the heart of it. I want you to play her."

"You want me to play my best friend?"

"That's right."

"In a play that exposes the most private parts of her life?"

"Yep. Her character has a different name, of course. So does Bergren's, but just barely. Nobody who knows anything about Bergren will be able to mistake him. I doubt anyone outside of Vox Unum and some real theater junkies will figure out your part is Robin. It's more likely people will recognize the third character – the play has only three roles."

"Is this someone I know?"

"It is. It's me."

At this she rocked back in her chair and gave a snort.

"You put yourself in the play?"

"I did. As the theater critic for a local weekly."

Ned recounted the first scene, describing the opening monologue and the awkward encounter between the actress and the critic after her performance.

"Then the critic feels he's hitting his stride. He senses the actress is peering into his soul, just as she touched his soul on stage. They exchange visions and aspirations. The actress has a way of revealing the personal while remaining utterly impersonal. The critic doesn't notice this, though. He thinks he's forging a real bond. He feels momentum building. He's about to make another date to get together when she apologizes. Someone is coming by to meet her, she says. She is as gracious as can be, but he feels defeated. He babbles a goodbye and slinks off.

On his way out he passes a man coming in. The man is the picture of success – well-dressed and well-tanned. He seems a strange person to be coming into a theater like that an hour after a performance. The critic recognizes the man as a local tycoon."

The lobby buzzer sounded. Elena started in her chair. Ned got up from the table and went to the intercom. The pizza delivery man had arrived. Ned rang him up.

"When did you start writing this?"

"Just after I saw the two of them together."

"You've blasted out a whole play since then?"

"Most of it. I'm still working out some of the kinks. But it's all framed out."

"Sounds pretty damned intense."

"It has been. But that's how I do my best work."

"You've done this kind of thing before?"

"Never a play. I had a collection of short stories published. I'm supposed to be working on a novel."

"Cool. You couldn't work all this into the novel?"

"No, this had to be a play."

"Because it's about theater people?"

"Bergren's no theater person. Well, maybe he is. Theater's always had rich patrons preying on vulnerable performers. He's part of a long and sordid tradition. But no, I didn't write it as a play just because it has an actress and a critic. I can't tell you why, but I needed to tell the story in one time and one place, like an ancient Greek drama. That's not a novel, or at least not any novel I could write. That's a play."

There was a knock at the door.

"And that's a pizza."

Ned paid the delivery man and set the meat-laden pie out in the center of the table.

"Do you want a plate?" he asked.

"Nah. Too classy for me."

They chewed in silence for a few moments.

"So?"

Ned resumed his account.

"The man comes into the theater and asks the actress who the hell that was. She tells him it was a critic from the weekly. He wanted to talk about the show, she says. The man looks suspicious. The actress soothes him.

While she's doing this, the critic comes out on the theater mezzanine. The actress had given the opening monologue from that level, and the critic has somehow figured out how to get up there. The audience can see him, but the actress and the man down below do not.

She asks where they're going that night. He says it turns out his wife has scheduled some sort of parent-teacher conference first thing the next morning, so he has to get home.

She turns away. It's clear this is not the first time he's made a wife-and-kids excuse. He apologizes, stroking her hair and her shoulders. He says things still look good for the beach house next weekend.

He kisses her hair, then turns to go. As he starts to head out of the theater, he stops and turns back. He pulls a check out of his wallet and holds it out to her.

She has to come to him to get the check. She does not thank him. As he starts to leave again, she tells him that the rent on the theater is going up next month.

He asks why she is still paying rent, why she doesn't get her own theater. She asks him how they're supposed to manage that when the company can barely make ends meet as it is. Besides, she says, there aren't any other theaters available in town. The man says well, then, he'll just have to build her a new one.

She's incredulous, then giddy. He tells her to make a list of everything she'd want in a new space. She's almost skipping around the stage in excitement. She begins to reel off her wish list.

At first he takes in this virtual shopping spree with a benevolent smile. Then we see in his face that he's getting turned on. He catches her from behind and begins to kiss her neck. Soon he starts to stroke her breasts. She plays along, but the audience can tell she's not into it. He gets rougher. Finally he pulls her down to the stage floor.

When he begins to undo her pants, she pleads with him to wait until they're out of the theater. But he's used to having his way. His face turns ugly. He sneers and asks her if this is some sort of sacred place.

She gives him a look of infinite wounding. She picks herself up off the floor, smoothes her rumpled clothing, and crumples into a chair.

The critic has taken all of this in from above. We can tell by his expression that he's about ready to leap from the mezzanine and beat the man bloody. But he does nothing.

The man tries to make light of it all. He says in the new theater they'll put in a deluxe bedroom for stars and their special guests. She is not amused."

Elena broke in. "No shit."

"The actress turns toward the man and in a voice that's eerily quiet tells him just what this theater means to her. To her, it is a temple, a place of communion between artists and audience. She is eloquent, moving, powerful yet vulnerable. At the end she apologizes for being so sensitive. She says she would gladly go to bed with him anywhere else but here.

This is the man's chance to be gracious. He does not take it.

He doesn't appreciate being told he's committing some sin making love in a theater, he says. He might not be an artist, but he respects the magic of theater. He sees as many shows as anyone in town. That's how he met her, he reminds her, at some hole in the wall. But a theater is magical, he says, only when a play is on. Now, after everyone's packed up and gone home, it's just another empty space. It's not a church, for Christ's sake, where God is supposed to be on duty twenty-four/seven.

'Don't forget,' he says, 'the only reason you and your friends are putting on plays here is I pay your rent. I don't ask for anything when you're on stage. But when you come off, you might show a little more hospitality.'

With that, he turns and stalks out of the theater.

The critic, up in the mezzanine, looks like he's going to say something to comfort the actress, who sits slumped in her chair. But he says nothing. Slowly the lights fade to black. End of Act I."

"Wow," said Elena. She had been listening intently, but had also managed to go through three slices of pizza. "That's intense."

"Thank you. Assuming that's a compliment."

"Yeah, it is. I think you've laid a lot of yourself out there. But you've laid out even more of Robin."

"Have I?"

"Oh yeah. You've hit what makes her so special, but also what's so totally screwing her up. And you've made Bergren a bastard, but not a total bastard. If he were completely evil, then it would make it easy for Robin to say 'That's not Jerry' and just blow the whole thing off."

"You mean, if she saw the play."

"That's the point, isn't it?"

Ned hesitated. He'd debated on and off that afternoon whether to tell Elena about Bergren and his father and the ranch. On his way home from work, he'd decided against it. He saw no mileage in letting her know. Better she should think of him as dedicated only to her friend. But now, as she sat there in front of him, he was tempted to open up.

"Yeah. That, and bringing down Bergren."

"But that's to help get Robin away from him, right?"

"Right."

"So how do you bring down Jerry?"

"That's in Act II. The critic confronts Bergren."

"Where?"

"In the theater. The whole play takes place in the theater."

"Oh right. You said it was all in one place. How does he get Jerry back into the theater?"

"The critic calls up Bergren the next morning and tells him he has some urgent information about one of Bergren's deals. He says to meet him at the theater that afternoon. The critic had already called the theater with some phony excuse about wanting to see the space again to help him with his review. That's how he gets access. None of this happens on stage, of course; we find out about it as the critic and Bergren get into it."

"So the two of them go at it?"

"Right. The critic tells Bergren he has him nailed. He spells it all out. He threatens to expose Bergren unless he stays away from the actress.

At first Bergren tries to bully him. He says the critic can't touch him, he's got the paper locked up, they wouldn't dare run the story. He tells the critic he'll lose his job and his reputation, or worse. He just hints at worse, which makes it even more menacing.

When Bergren sees the critic won't give in to threats, he tries another tack. He asks why the critic cares so much about the actress. Is he jealous? Is he trying blackmail because he can't win the girl fair and square? If he wants a sporting chance, says Bergren, that's fine. He'll call up the actress right then and have her come over. They can both take their best shot at her and may the best man win."

"So this is where I come back in?"

Elena scooped up a piece of sausage that had fallen off the pizza into the open box.

"No. This scene is just between the critic and Bergren. The critic doesn't take Bergren up on his offer. He knows he'd lose. Which leads Bergren to try and bribe the critic."

"So I'm not in the scene at all?"

"No. The three characters each go head to head with one another in a single scene. They're never on stage at the same time. It's who's offstage that creates the tension. You know that. Put everyone on stage together and you expose everything to the light. You lose your shadows."

"So I don't go back on at all?"

"You get the last word. The play ends just as it started, with the actress doing a monologue from the play the critic reviewed. But this time it's the opening monologue."

"Cool. It seems kind of short, though."

"I'm still working it, but I would guess it'll run about eighty-five to ninety minutes. There's no intermission. So you want to hear the rest of Act II?"

"Nah. I'm not in it. I'll just read the script. When are you looking to put this up? Next season?"

"February."

"February a year from now?"

"No. February six weeks from now."

"What?! You gotta be fucking kidding me."

"I'm not. It's the only time I could get the SoHo Theater. They had a two-week slot open at the beginning of February."

"You got the SoHo?"

"Can you think of a better space to bring everything home to Robin?"

"No. Putting it on there is pretty fucking brutal when it comes to laying things bare. But I can't do it. *Blood Relations* runs into early February."

"Then you'll have to put down your axe, Lizzie."

"You're asking me to quit?"

"Absolutely."

This brought Ned out of his chair. He started circling the table.

"I'll give you five reasons why. Number one, you need to do this for your friend. You said it yourself: Bergren is sucking the life out of her. You haven't come up with any other way to pry her away from him. This is your best shot. Number two, this is not about ensemble. You want to make a big splash and get out of this town. Trust me, this show is going to get attention. A lot of attention. And you'll be the star of the show. This is your ticket out of Portland and off to LA. Number three, I'm risking my job and my career to do this. You said it – I've laid a lot of myself out in that script. I've got some serious skin in the game. I don't think it's asking too much for you to quit one show. Number four, as long as you quit now, they'll have plenty of time to recast the part. They'll piss and moan, sure, but you know they can find someone else. Nowhere near as good as you, of course, but good enough. And number five, I'll pay you $2,500 to play the lead and help me put together the best team in town to do the show. My guess is that's three times what they're paying you for *Blood Relations*. And we'll only be doing a two-week run."

He ended up directly behind her. Without turning around, she said "Three thousand."

"Sold."

She got out of her chair and faced him, hands on her ample hips.

"You got a name for this play, partner?"

"*Pay to Play*."

"Cool."

CHAPTER SEVENTEEN

The buzz around the table was the self-conscious chatter of those who know a meeting is about to begin, but won't let go of their conversations until told they must. A school lunchroom-style table, two of its corners chipped, was set up in the middle of the theater floor, surrounded by battered folding chairs. The theater's work lights were on, bathing the stage in a warm glow but casting shadows across the empty audience seats.

The group was gathered for the first read-through of *Pay to Play*. Around the table sat seven copies of the script, each bound in a powder blue folder. Ned had picked these up cheap at the copy store where he'd had the play run off after pulling a string of near all-nighters pounding out the last scene.

He and Elena had decided not to hold open auditions. The lower the profile of the show before it opened, they had agreed, the better. Cattle calls were an invitation for gossip and backstabbing by those not cast.

She had quit the Lizzie Borden play the night he'd offered her the role. She'd quit without even reading the script, which had impressed him with her commitment, or at least her sense of adventure. The next day they'd met again at his apartment to plot their strategy. They would really have to scramble, she told him, to cast a show just before the holidays that was due to open in February. They weren't likely to land any big-name Portland actors – other than Elena Devlin, she'd noted – as most top people were already booked through the end of the season. Still, she said, there was talent to be had if you knew where to look for it – even in this shithole town.

She'd drawn up a short list of actors for the critic and Bergren and started making calls immediately. They'd managed to get the SoHo for three hours that Sunday morning. Actors loathed anything before noon on a Sunday, which was why the time was available. Several of her top choices were out of town or already booked, so she'd had to be a little less choosy on whom she invited to read.

Ned had tried to appear nonchalant, but it had been a rush to sit in the center row, sheathed in darkness, pad of paper purloined from the *Columbian* in hand, listening to anxious actors try to win him over literally in his own language. They'd asked each actor to do a prepared monologue, then had each of them do a cold reading of two passages from the script with Elena.

Afterwards the two of them had driven back to his apartment to thrash out the cast. They'd stopped off at a breakfast spot downtown called Lorn& Dottie's, whose Greek eggs and banana nut bread Elena had raved about. They'd ordered their food to go, though Elena had said the café was not the sort of see and be seen place where they might run into Bergren's crowd.

They had reached quick agreement on the actor playing Bergren. Calvin Anderson had blown away the field. He was a former Foreign Service officer who had served thirty years in Africa. His wife was an Oregonian from an old West Hills family. According to the rumor mill, they'd retired to Portland to be near a sister whose husband had gone heavily into debt and then died of a heart attack. Anderson had done a few plays in embassies where he'd been posted, then kept busy on stage in Portland after retiring thanks to a chronic shortage of older men. Elena had growled that old white guys may not run local theater the way they did everything else in life, but they sure the fuck got cast.

Ned had been concerned when told of Anderson's diplomatic background that he'd be a preppy, bow-tie type, too suave to show a mean streak. But there had been none of that in the audition. Anderson had been tough, arrogant, and domineering with Elena, yet tender in the right places. He was an imposing presence, a few inches over six feet and a solid two hundred pounds. And he had all his hair. Ned was surprised that he'd never made ambassador.

The role of the critic had been a much tougher call. Elena had reluctantly conceded that an actor named Trent Davis had given the best reading. He had been her last call for the part and had made the list only after several of her top choices turned out to be unavailable.

She'd never worked with Davis, but had seen him in a few shows. She allowed that he had talent as an actor, enough to take over a stage at times. Physically he bore a strong resemblance to Ned: long and lean, with dark, flowing hair. He'd worked in most of the top theaters around town.

But from what she'd heard, he was more devoted to the good life than to good acting. He'd grown up on the wrong side of the chair lift in Ketchum, Idaho, the town that serviced the Sun Valley ski resort. From an early age he'd hankered for the glamour of the beautiful people who wintered in Sun Valley. He'd done everything he could to be around the jet set, from washing windows at the toniest mansions to busing tables in the trendiest watering holes. He'd discovered a flair for acting in high school and after a few years of theater at community college had made his way to Portland. He was a waiter who had bounced around the top rank of local restaurants.

He had looks, almost pretty rather than handsome, that got him noticed. There were rumors of affairs with matrons in the West Hills. From what Elena had picked up, his aim was to milk whatever connections he could make among the Portland upper crust for film and television opportunities in Hollywood.

"In other words," Ned had said, "he has the same game plan as you. So you resent him."

"No. My game plan was to become one fucking good actress, then get rich and famous. The actress part came first. With this guy, I think it's always been about fame and fortune."

"But somewhere along the way he learned to act."

"Yeah, but it's not the same."

"It may not be if he were auditioning for Vox Unum, but right now we're looking for the best guy to do this part. Is that Trent Davis?"

"He gave the best reading. But I also think he's bad news."

"Is the news bad enough to go to the next guy on the list? It's a big drop-off."

"I don't know."

Elena had started to lobby for another round of auditions, but they agreed the timeline was too tight. It was just before Christmas, and they wouldn't be able to start rehearsal until after the holidays. Calvin Anderson and his wife had already booked a trip to visit family and wouldn't be back until New Year's. He was too perfect for the

Bergren part to pass up. And Ned had promised his sisters he would be back in Chicago for Christmas.

Ned and Elena had wrangled for over an hour before finally going with Davis.

"He's you," she'd said. "You're going to have to get him to remember that he's you and that he has to forget him. If you can do that, we'll have one helluva show."

He had left the choice of technical people to Elena. He hadn't seen enough shows in Portland to get a feel for local designers. They'd decided that with the show's barebones staging, they could manage using a single technical director who would handle lighting, sound, set design, and set construction.

Elena had recruited David Blevins for the job. Blevins had worked as technical director on several shows she'd been in around town, though none with Vox Unum. He had a part-time job managing the theater shop at one of the area colleges and moonlighted doing freelance work. The three of them had met at a tiny coffee house near Elena's apartment that looked like someone's disordered living room.

Blevins was reserved to the point of morose. He had the pallor of a nocturnal creature and a scruffy soul patch on a bony chin. He wore jeans and a black T-shirt that somehow fit tightly around a concave chest. During an hour-long session, he'd stepped outside twice for a cigarette, not bothering with a coat despite the biting cold.

Yet Blevins had listened intently to Ned's account of the play. He'd asked a few terse but pointed questions. Then he'd abruptly said, "I got it" and slipped out the door.

The stage manager, Marty Michaels, had asked to meet the two of them at the theater, rather than at a nearby café suggested by Elena. She had insisted on getting a copy of the script before their meeting and came armed with a long list of questions printed neatly on the first page of a spiral notebook that Ned noticed had already been labeled *Pay to Play*.

Michaels was a massive woman, of middle height but pushing two hundred fifty pounds. Her hair was buzzed close to her scalp. She wore thick, black glasses, a flannel work shirt, and heavy-soled boots. Her voice was deep and booming. She was the butchest lesbian Ned had ever met.

They had all agreed Michaels would serve as both stage manager and assistant director. Ned had never directed before and needed someone seasoned and disciplined who could keep track of his directions as well as the schedule. Michaels had worked both jobs for over ten years in Portland and was close to qualifying as a union stage manager – no mean feat in a town where union productions were limited to a handful of companies.

Michaels was obsessed with her craft, but still couldn't earn enough to make a living at it. Elena said that the stage manager's significant other was a successful downtown lawyer who indulged her partner's theater habit. Elena also told Ned that Marty was short for Martha. The last person who had called Michaels "Martha," however, had been made to regret it.

Midway through their meeting with Marty, a swirl of scarlet had suddenly surged into the semi-dark of the theater and spun toward the front row seats where the three of them were speaking. As the splash of red had whirled closer, Ned could see that it was a woman and remembered that Elena had invited the costumer to drop by. She was clad in what might have been a flamenco dancer's outfit had Ned ever seen flamenco. An exotic ensemble of folds and bustles were wrapped around taut olive skin. She went by the name of Gia, just Gia, and had been introduced as such by Elena. Michaels had lumbered out of her seat and engulfed the costumer's lithe frame in a bear hug. They had apparently worked together on many shows. Wordlessly, Gia had grasped the script handed to her by Elena and swirled back out of the theater.

Now the seven of them were arrayed around the table's chipped Formica. Ned had debated whether to be a man of the people and take a seat on one of the sides, but had decided on the father's place at the stage right end of the table. To his left was Gia – almost floating rather than seated – this evening's costume a confection of silken turquoise. Beside her was Trent Davis, chin on hand, showing off his impressive profile. Marty Michaels, notebook open and pen poised, had taken the other seat of authority opposite Ned. At the corner, his chair several feet removed from the table and shrouded in shadow, was David Blevins, who had taken no part in the pre-meeting conversation. In the middle on that side of the table sat Calvin Anderson, erect against the back of the folding chair in a starched Oxford shirt, hands folded neatly in front of him. To Ned's right was Elena, her area a jumble of already dog-eared script, beaded purse, cell phone, and housekey ring.

Ned had rehearsed a welcoming speech.

"Thank you all for signing on to make *Pay to Play* a reality. Just a few months ago I had no thought of ever writing, directing, or producing a play. It's one of the wonders of this strange line of work we're in that you can have a sudden brainstorm in the privacy of your crappy little apartment, bat it around in the addled confines of your mind, feverishly punch out a script in deepest isolation, and then in a matter of months dare to present your monster to the general public. We can do a nice job cutting out the middleman in the theater when we choose. Take that, Hollywood.

I know I have cut to the front of the line. I know I should have done reading after rewrite after reading after rewrite. I know I should have submitted my script to august festivals to be judged by a jury of those far too wise to be my peers. I know I should have prostrated myself on bended knee before eminent artistic directors and craved the privilege of placing my work upon their nightstands, to be read weeks or months or years later – if ever.

But I don't have time for all that. What I have to say needs to be said now. There are deeply personal reasons for this, and with apologies for the mystery, I just ask you to accept that this is so. I hope that over a glass or three of something potent at our cast party after opening I can lay it all out for you, but for now I would appreciate it if you could keep your focus on Oz, not on the wizard behind the curtain.

I expect the chattering classes to call this a critic's vanity project. This is their chance to take a shot at a disarmed gunslinger, and I have no doubt they will. For that reason, and because of the other personal matters I mentioned, I'm very sensitive to how this play is marketed. As much as you can trust someone that reviews theater for a living, please trust me that people are going to hear about this show. There will be butts in those seats. But I want to be the one who decides how and when word gets out. I need you to keep this play under wraps until it opens. Of course your friends and family will know you're in a play, and it's no problem for them to know the name and very generally what it's about. But let's allow the plot to unfold when the curtain goes up, and not before.

A playwright who directs his own work is a bit like the lawyer who represents himself: he has a fool for a client. There will be plenty of times when you want to ask Dirk the director what the hell Dirk the playwright had in his unhinged mind when he wrote such and such a line. Dirk the director will give you the best direction he can. Dirk the playwright may never make an appearance here – partly because he may not have a clue what he meant when he wrote the line and partly because even if he does have a clue, he may not want to share it with you. Feel free to abuse Dirk the director as much as you want until he runs screaming from the theater and cries for Marty to take over. Please leave Dirk the playwright in peace if you can.

This is going to be an intense process. That's because I'm intense and you're all intense and the whole wacky notion of seven strangers sitting down in an empty theater with nothing more than a jumble of words jotted on a few pages and daring to presume that in a month's time they will present a finished product ready for prime time is as intense as it gets. For those of you who are into that sort of thing, you'll see that I've borrowed a little from Greek tragedy in structuring this play. What we're doing is on the edge of hubris, pulling on the beards of the gods. The gods may choose to punish us, but only if we let audacity become arrogance and fearlessness become folly. It's my job as a director to drive all of us until we're stretched taut along that line, but no further.

I know we've got the team to pull this off. I asked Elena to get the best in town, and she has. Each of you is just who Dirk the director and Dirk the playwright would have wanted in this show, and who Dirk the critic would be raving about if he were allowed to review it, which sadly is not permitted under my paper's oppressive ethical rules. We'll be ripping out the fourth wall in one of the best black boxes I've ever seen, and that includes just about every small theater in Chicago.

So before we strap on our armor and go charging into battle, is there anything you'd like to say or ask? Believe me, if you don't speak now it will not mean you will be forever holding your peace."

Elena did not hesitate. She leaned out across the table, her flashing gray eyes fixing each person in the theater.

"This show means more to me than any show I've ever done. I don't care if that sounds like some Oscar speech load of crap. It's the truth. Dirk talked about some heavy personal stuff behind all this. I've got a few reasons of my own. But I guess we all do in this nuthouse life.

I've never done anything like this before: get a script from some guy I barely know and drop everything to do it, under insane time pressures. It's crazy. But I'm doing it, and I'm going to work my ass off to make this show incredible. I've got a big ass, so that's a helluva lot of work. But I know it's going to be worth it. For all of us."

Ned murmured his thanks. The rest of the group cast glances around the table, other than Blevins, who sat barely visible in the shadows.

Calvin Anderson gave a little cough. It was clear he was accustomed to breaking the ice, doubtless from years of diplomatic receptions.

"It takes great courage to do what you've done, Dirk. I don't know what led you to write this play, but most of us would never have made the effort, let alone pulled together the resources to put it on stage. It's a fine script, and I am privileged to be included in the cast. I do hope Dirk the playwright will make an appearance from time to time, because he's a talent all of us could learn from. And when this is all over, I also hope Dirk the critic will not forget our loyal service the next time he reviews our work."

This line brought mild chuckles around the table.

"Bribes are cheerfully accepted," quipped Ned.

The display of good humor seemed to be the cue for Marty Michaels to weigh in. She produced a sheaf of stapled pages, which she divided with her thick hands into two stacks and began passing in both directions around the table.

"This is the rehearsal schedule. As Elena said, our timeline is tight, so that's why you won't see many off days. Please get here fifteen minutes before the scheduled rehearsal time. If for some reason, like death, you can't make a rehearsal, call me as far in advance as possible, so Dirk and I can plan to work other scenes. I've attached a contact sheet that shows everyone's phone numbers and e-mail addresses. You're welcome to change your phone or e-mail at any time, just as long as you do it the day after we close. Tomorrow you'll get your contracts. We open in less than four weeks, so we need everyone off book in two weeks tops. If you've worked with me before, you know what happens if you're not off book when you're supposed to be. Don't go there. They say I have no sense of humor, but that's not true. I'll laugh my fat little head off at your funeral if you screw up this show. Any questions?"

"No, ma'am," said Trent Davis, in deadpan earnest. Gia tittered beside him.

"Actually, I do have one question," said Davis. "But this one's for Dirk. Why *Pay to Play*?"

"Ask me again in four weeks. Somehow, I don't think you'll need to."

CHAPTER EIGHTEEN

The Navigator rolled through the deserted industrial district near the theater. As he passed under the dark hulk of an overhead freeway, Ned noticed telltale signs that the Pearl District was at hand. Functional but fashionless boxes gave way to sleek high rises. In place of scattered storefronts came retail armadas, anchored in tight formation to achieve maximum mercantile force.

He found a parking place a block from the Lowbrow. The red neon of the tavern window glowed through the cold drizzle as he stepped out of the SUV and looked down the street. An older man, back hunched against the elements, passed him on the sidewalk, leading a tiny dog on a slender leash.

It was a Monday night, and the crowd in the bar was thin. Ned knew that Karin would not have arrived before him, but he gave a cursory glance around the place just to make sure. He caught the eye of the bartender, who had looked up from his newspaper.

"What, no tuxedo?" he hailed.

"It's my valet's night to brush it."

"Valet, eh? The critic business must be paying well these days."

"It's those payoffs I've been raking in from actors. They know all it takes is a word from me and they're on their way."

"On their way to where?"

"I haven't the heart to tell them."

The bartender gave a low chuckle.

"Turbo Pimms No. 1 Cup?"

"You don't miss a drink."

"I'm serious about my work. Though not about anything else, as both my exes will tell you."

"I won't ask."

"Oh, they'll still tell you. So are you meeting a certain leading lady?"

"Actually, she has a supporting role."

"I thought she was the queen."

"She is, but this play's all about the common man, I'm afraid. The court's been turned upside down."

The bartender gave him a searching look.

"But they still honor the queen?"

"After a fashion."

"Because you know someone will cut your head off if you don't. Or draw and quarter you. Or put your nuts in a vise."

"Even though it's set in those nasty Middle Ages, it's really more of a modern play."

"Times haven't changed that much. Ah, the queen has arrived. Grab a booth and I'll bring your drinks over."

Karin had called him over the weekend. After that first lunch at Edgefield they'd made Wednesday afternoons there a regular thing. They would finish off a bottle of wine over a leisurely meal, always at the same table, then take the same room, always booked by Karin in the name of Ibsen. Karin would work her lines with him and then, at a point he could never predict, she would abruptly stop and pull him into bed. The sex was charged and potent.

They had not seen each other since the week before Christmas. Her kids had been out of school, and he had gone back to Chicago to spend the holiday with his sisters. She had asked that he not call, as she never knew who might be around or whether the kids might answer her cell phone.

Her play opened on Friday. She had called following their final technical rehearsal on Sunday and asked to meet at eleven on Monday, after her show's first dress rehearsal. And, as it happened, after the read-through of *Pay to Play*.

Her wardrobe had been all variations on black since she'd taken the part, and the look was unchanged tonight. Her face was streaked with hastily removed make-up. Her hair was a tangle, an elaborate hairstyle let down without repair.

"Hey, we run a respectable operation here," said the bartender. "Vagrants, derelicts, and out-of-costume actresses need not apply."

"Screw you, Mick, and pour me an Aquavit."

"I'm already on it, your highness."

She dropped into the booth.

"God, I'm exhausted."

"Heavy sits the crown?"

"Heavy sits my costume, bright shines the lights, and old is my body."

"Oh, I think it has a few shows left, judging from the performances I've seen."

She squeezed his hand.

"You're sweet. Is that a review?"

"Nope. I'm off duty. Just an eyewitness account. How's the show?"

"Awful. Rosencrantz is a mess."

"He's supposed to be. Or is it Guildenstern? I can never remember."

"I don't think Stoppard expected him to be constantly stoned. The last few weeks he's smelled like a bong at every rehearsal."

"How would you know? I thought you went to a good Lutheran college."

"It wasn't exactly a nunnery, dear Hamlet. And kids in Astoria learned about pot long before college. How do you think we got through all those dark and stormy nights?"

"So how's the director managing?"

"The usual – ranting and raving. He sounded like a football coach tonight. I thought he was going to start breaking up the set and making us do push-ups. He and Ophelia are at each other's throats."

"They've got a thing going?"

"Didn't I tell you? But he gave her a few pissy notes after one of the rehearsals last week and now they're not speaking."

"Watch out – they might find her floating in the river."

"No, if life were to imitate art, our whole cast would be put on a boat down the Willamette with a note to the governor asking that we all be put to death."

"Oh, come on, one of your leads is on drugs, the director's in a lover's tiff with an actress – you've got a sure-fire hit on your hands."

"Particularly since the *Columbian* is going to give us a great review."

"Do I detect undue influence being exercised here?"

"Oh yes."

The bartender arrived with the drinks.

"Your royal potion, majesty. And a Pimms for your vassal."

"Give it a rest, Mick."

"Yes, m'lady."

With a mincing bow, he withdrew.

"So how was your holiday?" asked Ned.

"Exhausting. We had rehearsal just about every day except Christmas and New Year's. It's crazy, opening a show this time of year, but I guess it's the only slot they could get. Jerry insisted that we make the rounds to all the usual holiday parties, even though I could barely stand up. He was in a jolly mood."

"How come?"

"Oh, it's that ranch. He's got some big government approval coming up and seems to think everything's in the bag. He was worried for a while, but something must have happened."

"Really? I don't remember seeing anything in the paper."

He tried to keep a casual tone.

"You wouldn't. He makes sure nothing gets into the press 'til he's good and ready. He's a little scary that way. Anyway, the strange thing at the parties is how he would show me off. His wife the actress, you know. He used to do the same thing when we first met. How was your Christmas?"

"Eerie. Just four of us in that huge house. It was the first Christmas without my father. We were never exactly close as a family, but we always got together for Christmas dinner. It was the only time since my mother died that I would see Dad sit down at the grand piano and just play. None of us kids could carry a tune, but he would bang out Christmas carols and we would sing and drink. We were better at the drinking part.

Anyway, my older sister asked me to make a toast before we sat down to eat. She's a designer. She's always liked to set a scene."

"So what did you say?"

"She gave me about two minutes' notice, so I was scrambling. Then it came to me. I stood up and toasted Dad's passion for the arts. I said he'd married into a business family, but at heart he was an artist and a romantic. He'd had music in his soul. Artists and romantics aren't made to live in the world of money and society, and Dad had never really been at home there. The music in his soul had played but little; then it had finally died away. But we who lived on after him needed to honor his memory by not betraying the art and romance in ourselves. That was his gift to us, I said. Then I sat down and had a good belt."

"That's lovely, Dirk."

"Thank you."

He sat silent for a moment, weighing whether to let Karin know about the play. He would have to tell her before it opened, but he hadn't done it yet. She was still married to the man, after all. No matter how bitter she might be over his cheating, she might just go to him and spill it all out. That would give Bergren the chance to destroy the show. Not to mention it would mean the end of the fling with Karin. He wasn't ready to give up those Edgefield afternoons just yet.

"So are we on for Wednesday?" he asked.

She cast her eyes down at the table.

"That's why I wanted to see you. I think we should take a break until after the play closes."

"What are you, a boxer? Practicing abstinence before the big fight?"

"No. Not hardly. But I am a mother. I still have two kids at home, and this Christmas I was gone all the time, running off to rehearsals and parties. I've decided I can only one manage self-indulgence at a time, and for now that has to be this crazy play."

"So I'm an indulgence?"

She wrapped her fingers around his clenched fist.

"The best – no, make that the only – I've had for a very long time."

"Why did you feel the need to tell me this at the Lowbrow?"

"I didn't think I would have had the courage at Edgefield. You know how much this place means to me. It's where I can be honest with someone who also means a great deal to me."

He pulled his hand away.

"The place where you met your husband."

"That's cruel."

"Or there's a certain symmetry to having your last date with me at the same place you had your first."

"That was not a date."

"This isn't much of one, either."

"I knew you'd be angry. You've never been a parent, so you can't understand the guilt you feel when you don't put your children first. Especially at Christmas, which is the No. 1 kids first time of year. I knew you'd want some sort of a sign from me."

She reached into her purse and pulled out a folded piece of copy paper.

"This is an e-mail confirmation for a room reservation at Edgefield the Wednesday after our show closes. I'll be there. I hope you will."

"Reservations can be cancelled."

She reached under the table and stroked his crotch.

"Consider that a non-refundable deposit. Oh, and undue influence on that glowing review I know you're going to write for us. I trust you're enough of a professional not to let this personal matter get in the way of your critical judgment. Now, I need to get home to bed. Unlike Rosencrantz, I don't have pot to get me through these rehearsals."

She rose to go. Even with the streaks of make-up and the unkempt hair, she was lovely.

"Break a leg, Karin."

"If you're not there the Wednesday after we close, I'll break yours."

CHAPTER NINETEEN

The cast was scattered in the semi-gloom of the theater. Elena was reclining on the landing of the carpeted stairs that ran between the center and stage left sections of the house. Calvin Anderson was seated, upright and respectful, in the front row. Trent Davis was stretched out over three seats in the back row, arms akimbo, legs propped on an armrest.

Ned sat facing them in a dented folding chair centered on the stage floor. Marty Michaels was installed in a chair to his left, notebook at the ready. He was giving notes following a lurching dress rehearsal. This was their fourth and final week of rehearsing. There were two more dress rehearsals on Wednesday and Thursday evening, then they opened on Friday.

There had been no shortage of spats and mishaps. Several times Elena had gone off on Trent Davis in the middle of rehearsal, spraying expletives over his effort and attitude. Ned had quickly calmed her down. Her tirades didn't appear to bother Davis, who just stood there sporting a faint grin as she raged.

David Blevins, the technical director, had disappeared for the first three weeks of rehearsal. Ned's phone calls to his cell phone – he had no home phone – went unreturned. Ned, Elena, and Marty had huddled and pulled together a list of possible replacements. Then, the next day, he'd materialized – offering no explanation or apology – with carefully crafted set, sound, and lighting designs in hand.

One evening in the middle of rehearsal the sound of snapping whips came from next door. This was followed by the rattle of chains, then low moaning. It turned out that SoHo's neighbor was a sado-masochistic porn producer who did video shoots at all hours. SoHo's manager claimed to have given their performance and rehearsal schedule to the neighbor, but she couldn't promise it would always be respected.

During a fitting, Gia the costumer had mistaken Calvin Anderson's embassy-honed charm for flirting. Without hesitation, she threw her arms around his neck, jumped into his grasp, and kissed him full on the lips, her vaguely Elizabethan garment billowing around him. The astonished ex-diplomat gasped and staggered as the other cast members howled.

Ned the director had cautioned the cast that Ned the playwright might not be much in evidence. He was badly mistaken. Ned found himself in a constant state of re-write. Of the notes he scribbled furiously during rehearsal from a favored seat along one aisle, well over half were to himself, as lines of sheer brilliance on the printed page fizzled on stage. He would leave the theater around eleven and often work past two at his apartment, returning to rehearsal the following evening clutching a sheaf of replacement pages. At first the actors enjoyed the novelty of a living, breathing playwright in their midst. But after weeks of manic revision, he could see his crazed writer act was wearing thin.

His greatest struggle was the final scene, in which the critic confronts the businessman. The challenge was partly his as playwright, as the critic seemed to lose his bearings in places despite what seemed an unshakable position at the start of the scene.

But the problem was as much the performance of Trent Davis. Davis was smooth and facile, but his acting lacked conviction. He made a show of confrontation, but there was a resolve missing. Ned would give him note after note, but they did not seem to register.

Many of his notes after this rehearsal were for that same scene. He had given most of his direction with a light touch. Unaccustomed to exercising authority over actors other than by a critic's distant dominion, Ned preferred to wear the mantle casually.

But tonight, with only two rehearsals left, he came down hard. He goaded and prodded Davis, calling him out to match the intensity of the rest of the cast. Smug though the actor could be, he'd usually made a semblance of respectful attention when Ned gave notes. Tonight, however, he remained slouched in the back of the theater, barely acknowledging the comments. Ned wished that Elena would rise up and curse Davis out again, but she was spent like the rest of them - and besides, she wasn't in that scene.

Before letting them go, he announced one more change to the script. There were groans all around. He raised his hands for calm.

"No, this is not my thirty-ninth rewrite of the last scene. I've just decided to change the name of Cal's character to Borgren. Don't ask me why. The guy just felt like a Borgren to me. His last name only appears three times in the whole show, so I don't think this will throw you off too much."

He and Elena had decided not to surface the name "Borgren" in the script until the very end of rehearsal; he had changed it to "Bailey" in the copies he had given everyone else. It was unlikely that anyone in the show would recognize the character as Jerry Bergren – removed as they all were from the Portland business scene – but there had been no reason to take a chance.

"But," Anderson protested, "I've built my whole character around the name 'Bailey.'"

"Well, you are now officially in rebuilding mode. You've managed tangled foreign names at embassies around the world. I think you can handle 'Borgren.'"

"Yes, boss."

He had asked Marty Michaels to stay after rehearsal so they could talk about publicity. Elena would probably be more knowledgeable about theater PR, but he couldn't own up to her how little he'd done. He had promised Elena that the show would be a media sensation, but all he'd found time to do was send out calendar listings to the *Oregonian* and of course the *Columbian*. The listing notice had given only the name of the play, the performance times and place, ticket prices, the reservation line number (he'd rented a voicemail box out of the Yellow Pages), and a brief teaser: "A new play of deception, betrayal, and the price of a place of your own." Not exactly a killer tag line, he acknowledged, but he was used to having more than one sentence to get his point across.

His name appeared nowhere on the notice. The playwright was not identified, and he had put no contact person. Whatever publicity value there might be in letting Portland know the *Columbian* critic had written a play was outweighed, he thought, by letting the cat out of the bag too soon. At a minimum, Bolden and Selvaggio would be all over him to find out what the play was about. He would need to have those conversations before the show opened, but he intended to wait until the last possible moment.

He'd reviewed countless shows put on by tiny troupes where the company had obviously invested all of its energy and money in the production itself and had nothing left over for PR. He'd sat in many a near empty theater and clucked his tongue as another fine play had managed to avoid an audience. He'd vowed it wasn't going to happen to this show.

But it had. He had proven no better than any other theater upstart: too consumed by the play itself to get the word out. Between rehearsing and rewriting and poring over Blevins' designs and calming Elena's ever-jangled nerves over watery drinks at McMenamins and cutting checks for costumes and set pieces and light rentals (Blevins wanted some looks he claimed he couldn't pull off with SoHo's own lights) and voicemail boxes and graphics for a poster (designed by Calvin Anderson's art student daughter) and tickets and programs (desktop-published by a friend of Elena's) and theater rental and a box office manager (someone Marty knew who would check the voicemail box and man the ticket booth at the theater) and, oh yes, working his daytime job, he was a shell of the man who had set out to take down Jerry Bergren.

Bergren in the meantime had become an abstraction to him, super-imposed on the Bailey/Borgren character but without a separate reality. At times during his late night revisions of the script, the image of Bergren and Nora nestled on the beach house sofa would give him a momentary spur. But mostly the flesh-and-blood Bergren hovered on the fringes of his consciousness, pushed to the periphery by the monomania of putting on a play.

He had planned to have a set of explosive press releases all cued up, promising startling revelations made through the medium of theater. He was going to drop these bombs two days before the show was set to open – enough time to stoke the media but hopefully too late to derail the production. But two days from opening was tomorrow and he had nothing written and frankly no clue where to send it if he had. He knew the theater press in Portland, but they were next to useless for this sort of story line. He'd intended to make a study of the reporters in town besides Selvaggio who would run with something like this, but he hadn't had the time.

In fact the only media contact he'd made – and it was hardly that – was to get in touch with the former *Columbian* critic Milson and ask him to review the play. Ned couldn't review the show himself, of course, and he didn't much value the views of the stringers he used. He wanted candor and weight in the review; he knew Milson would deliver those in spades. He had said nothing to Milson about his connection with the play.

His best hope as far as publicity went was his old Chicago friend Linda. She was a true PR pro. He'd told Linda and her husband Scott about the play over Christmas, and they'd promised to make opening night. They were due in tomorrow afternoon. They had never been to Portland and had decided to come in a few days early to sightsee. He could coax a little help out of her once she arrived. He hadn't given her a head's up, though, and of course she knew nothing about the press in Portland.

In the meantime, he'd decided to pick Marty's brain about newspaper connections. She might be more media savvy than most theater people because of her downtown lawyer partner. Plus, she was a stage manager and not as obsessed with butts in the seats as the actors. She would be less likely to freak out at being asked about PR three days before they opened.

As nonchalantly as he could, he probed Marty for press contacts. He tried to leave the impression that he had the theater bases covered, but wanted to see if someone off the performance beat might take an interest in the show's convergence of business and art. She wasn't much help. Marty could build a box with impeccable craftsmanship, but thinking outside of one was not her forte.

She changed the subject to the last act. She hadn't made many suggestions during rehearsal – partly, he thought, because she was more comfortable making the trains run on time and partly because she didn't quite know how to deal with an all-in-one playwright/producer/director. But she knew they were struggling and thought she had a way to get through to Trent Davis.

"You can't bully this guy in front of the cast," she said. "He doesn't care enough about the rest of us for that to change what he's doing. You need to take him aside, one-on-one, and tell him your life is in his hands. You need to say how much you have riding on this play and that it all comes down to him. Maybe you need to tell him now what you said you'd tell all of us at the cast party – you know, a little of the wizard behind the curtain. If he sees he has that sort of power over you, I think he'll kick it into a different gear. But not if you try to beat it out of him."

"OK. Good point. I'll talk to him before rehearsal tomorrow. Thanks, Marty."

He told her to head on out. He needed to use the bathroom and would take care of locking things up.

He trudged from the dim shadows of the theater into the welcoming glow of the lobby. The whitewashed walls embraced the light. SoHo had hung a set of tall, thin paintings at wide intervals around the lobby that were supposed to tie thematically to their production. He hadn't seen the connection when he'd reviewed their show, and he still didn't.

One of the fluorescent lights in the men's room was flickering wildly. Marty had complained to SoHo's manager, who had promised to have it fixed by opening night. Ned used the urinal, then stepped in front of the bathroom mirror. The gyrations of the light over and behind him played havoc with the image of his face. He thought he looked haggard and beaten.

He shuffled wearily back into the lobby. The name of some donor was posted over the double doors to the theater in silver block letters. Ned noticed for the first time that the letters were slightly askew.

Ned pushed through the black curtain that separated the entry vestibule from the theater proper. There was a man seated in the first row, in the very center seat. His arms were crossed, and his legs were stretched out before him.

"I always take this seat. Best in the house. Front row center."

The man wore one of those multi-stranded, multi-hued sweaters so popular among Selvaggio's Good Person set. Corduroy slacks and tasseled loafers completed the ensemble.

"The upper rows in here don't have enough leg room. I don't like to feel cramped when I'm in a theater."

The man had a full head of thick gray/blonde hair. The jut of his chin was remarkable. His icy blue eyes pierced through the gloom. Jerry Bergren was in the house.

CHAPTER TWENTY

The voice was even, but carried a quiet menace.

"I guess you know who I am. It seems you've taken an interest in my affairs. I've seen hundreds of plays over the years, but never one about me. I suppose I should be flattered. No, I am flattered. How many people ever get to see a play about them? See their own life on stage? Get to be part of the art, not just sitting in the audience?

I'm honored. I really am. This could be my ticket to greatness. People might be talking about me for decades to come. People thousands of miles away. Children not yet born.

But this play of yours, you want to put it on here in Portland. Where I live. In my backyard. In front of people I know. While I'm still alive. And tell my business to every Tom, Dick, and Harry.

I'm one of the biggest supporters of theater in this town. I know you don't think I've got much of a soul, but whatever I've got, it's because of theater. That's why I've always liked to be around actresses. It keeps a little stage light shining on me, wherever I am.

I'll do just about anything to get a play put on. Write a check, get friends to a benefit, spread the word. And I do it myself, in person. Other causes I farm out. Never theater.

That's why I've come here myself to tell you this play will not happen. Your actors and your tech people will get paid. I'll cover your tab to SoHo for the theater and whatever you've laid out for your set.

I haven't seen any advertising around, but if you've booked ad space, I'll pay for it. Hell, I'll even throw in a royalty for the script. Writers never get the credit they deserve.

But you just finished your last rehearsal. And come Friday, this theater will be dark."

Ned stood, a few feet stage right of center, blinking.

"How did you find out about us?"

"Never put your trust in theater people. Best folks in the world for a party. Stay up with you 'til dawn, tell you stories 'til the cows come home, hug you 'til your ribs ache.

Their hearts are all in the right place. No nukes, no land mines, no clear cuts, no child labor, no wars – true blue, all the way.

And Christ, what a work ethic. They'll knock themselves silly for a month, pull all nighters, run on fumes – just to put on a show that maybe two or three hundred people will see. Total."

Bergren shook his head in a show of wonder.

"But they're usually a little short of cash. It comes with working for the love of it all. And in their world, the more lines you have, the bigger the person you are. That's a system that rewards opening your mouth, not keeping it shut."

"So someone in the show sold us out? Who?"

"What does it matter? I would have found out anyway. There aren't a lot of secrets in this town I don't know, and trying to keep something secret in the theater is like trying to hide a four-foot spotlight under a six-inch bushel.

Besides, I wouldn't want you retaliating against a whistle-blower. We're all about protecting whistle-blowers these days, aren't we? I read your reviews. They're good. You've got a nice way of putting things. You could finish off someone's career if they wound up on your bad side."

"So it was one of the actors?"

"You don't just review the acting, do you? You usually say something about the lights, or the costumes, or the set. No, all I'll say is that it was somebody you might review.

They were good enough to give me a copy of the script. Like I said, I'm a big fan of your writing. I have to say, I haven't read a lot of plays. I never saw the use of reading something that wasn't written to be read. But yours I couldn't get enough of. The pages just kept turning. Of course, it helped that I could identify with the characters. Except the theater critic, who came across as a self-righteous little prick. No offense.

I think you've got something there. In a different time and a different place, you might have yourself a hit. People always love threesomes – the Holy Trinity, the Three Stooges, you name it. A patron, an actress, and a critic: it's a great set-up. Lots of possibilities.

So don't be discouraged. If you were willing to do a little rewrite, I'm sure somebody would put this up. You wouldn't need to produce it yourself, which is a nasty business. Particularly when you're the chief cook and bottle-washer. Playwright/director/producer – that's a mouthful. Robin's told me how tough it was being director and actress. Your gig sounds even worse."

Ned's stomach tensed.

"Does she know?"

"About the play? No. Why get her stirred up about something that isn't going to happen? She's not the excitable type, you know, at least not for an actress, but she might get just a little worked up about a play that puts her whole life on parade. In her own theater, for Christ's sake. And starring her best friend. Or her soon to be ex-best friend. I am going to tell her Elena Devlin is a snake in the grass."

"Elena had nothing to do with my finding out about the two of you."

"Really? Now you've surprised me there. We've been very discreet. I could've sworn nobody knew about us other than Elena.

Which reminds me. Elena's a pretty fair actress, but she's no Robin Story. You're the critic, not me, but for my money nobody can touch Robin in this town. If you wanted to do her justice, you should have gone to New York and found someone major league. Just like you say in the play. Come to think of it, you should have asked me. I go to New York every year. I could have given you a damned good list. But a New York actress probably would have busted your budget. Which is always the problem in a minor league town. Not enough money to keep the really good people. They all go off to chase the rainbow. Except Robin, of course."

"Because you pay to keep her here."

"So what are you saying – that artists can't have patrons? That's what I am. A patron. I find talent, and I support it. I don't just see these traveling Broadway shows. I go to piece-of-shit, hole-in-the-wall dumps because that's where the young talent is. Busting their ass to get noticed. Rolling the dice. That's how I found Robin. I may not have some fancy-pants education, but I know when someone's good. I went backstage the first show I saw her in and told her she was fantastic. Then I kept tabs on her to see if I could give her a leg up."

"Or get her legs spread."

"Jesus, you ride a helluva high horse for a theater guy. There was never any tit for tat, pardon the expression. Maybe Robin saw it that way at first. These young actresses, they're used to assholes hanging around the stage door, promising them the moon and the stars for a roll in the hay. She probably thought that was my game too. But we've been together now for what, two years? If I was just in it to get laid, she'd have seen through that a long time ago. She knows what I'm about."

"What she knows is your checks keep coming."

"I keep writing checks because her company keeps doing great work. They're the best thing going in this town. You know that. I read your review of *Doll's House*. That's what it means to be a patron. You find something good, you support it. If more people wrote checks like me, we wouldn't have our best people running off to LA. Not that Robin would. But I don't want her to even be tempted."

"Tempted to leave you."

"You ever hear of consenting adults? She could leave me tomorrow. Just ask her. Hey, that's an idea. Let's give her a call and ask her to come down here. Then you could test all your theories in person. Instead of acting them out in a play. While you're at it, you could have her read a few scenes. Then you'd really know what you've got. You could do the critic's part. You'd have to leave out the scenes with my guy, though. I know my limitations. I'm no actor. Just a born audience member."

He pulled a cell phone out of the pocket of his slacks and thrust it toward Ned.

"Here you go. Give her a call. I'll give you the number – in case you didn't get it from Elena."

Ned eyed the phone, but did not take it.

"A little braver on the printed page, are we? Well, that's all right. She should save her energy for her own show, not waste it in on one nobody's going to see."

Ned tried to get his edge back.

"If she did come, I doubt she'd want talk about what number she is on your actress-mistress list. Or who's going to take over her part in a year or two. She's probably already got an understudy."

Bergren snorted.

"You think it's news to her that I have a thing for actresses? Hell, I married one. Though I married her because frankly, she wasn't that good. Robin knows I'd never rob the theater of someone with talent. The other ones, they were all comers. Not like Robin, but good. Good enough that almost all of them left Portland."

"And you."

"Sure. But I like to think I gave them a boost. With me, they got a little comfort and a little encouragement. Not much of that in theater, I can tell you."

"Not enough patrons."

"No. And too many asshole critics. The guy before you, Milson, he was a piece of work."

"They all hated him because he called it like he saw it."

"I've got no problem with that. A critic's not supposed to be out there leading cheers. But he's got to know when to say, 'Here's somebody young and raw and green who's maybe stuck with a lousy director in this show but is worth helping along.' These actors are so shaky, one nasty review when they're starting out can just destroy them. Milson drove some people right out of theater."

"Which was probably a good career move on their part."

"Maybe. But his job was to spot talent."

"Like you."

"Yeah, and I don't get paid to do it."

"Oh, I think you've gotten a pretty fair return on your money."

"You're a sanctimonious bastard, aren't you?"

"No, I've had a long night, and I've got a show that opens in three days."

Bergren sprang out of his seat and stalked toward Ned.

"Have you been listening to me? I told you your show is not going to happen. Do I need to spell it out for you?"

"What are you going to do – get me fired? You'd be doing me a favor. Let someone else spend their nights in those piece-of-shit, hole-in-the-wall dumps. Are you going to get me blacklisted in Portland? I don't care. I'm not from around here. We don't scare so easy where I'm from."

Ned was astonished at his show of bravado. He'd almost said something about how they did things in Chicago, but he wasn't ready to tip his hand about who he was and where he was from. Bergren would find out whose son he was soon enough.

Bergren's scowl turned to an ominous grin.

"Tough guy, uh? Good for you. Stick by your guns. Well, it's true I didn't make you much of an offer. If I were you, I'd have held out for a better deal too. Though I really shouldn't offer you much. You have almost no publicity out there, so hardly anyone would see your show anyway."

"So if no one's going to see it, why do you care if we put it on?"

"Because I take no chances. You never know with theater. Every once in a while a play throws a spark. Next thing you know, there's a blaze. I've seen it happen. Which I guess is why all these theater people keep coming back, groping around in the dark for peanuts. You never can tell when lighting's going to strike. So I tell you what – I'll make your royalty $25,000. Cash on the barrel. Do we have a deal?"

Ned sat quiet for a moment. He was broke. $25,000 would carry him for a year, long enough to finish the novel and get himself back on track. By that time Farr should have straightened out the estate; there had to be something left he could live off of. Bergren could probably afford to pay more, but he'd already tried the man's patience plenty.

"Elena's my partner in this. I can't just call it off without talking to her. She gets off work tomorrow around four. I'll talk to her then and call you. You're supposed to give me twenty-four hours to make a decision anyway, aren't you? That's how the plot usually goes."

Bergren gave a thin-lipped smile.

"Sure. You go ahead and talk to Elena. You have to respect your partner. I know you two will make the right decision. You know what,

I'll even throw in an extra $5,000 for Elena – just to show there's no hard feelings.

Here's my card. If I'm out, just tell my office you need to get a hold of me. They can track me down.

Well, I've got to get home to the wife and kids. Speaking of my wife, did you know she had a small part in *Rosencrantz and Guildenstern Are Dead*? Played the Queen. She was a little miffed you didn't mention her in your review."

"I remember her. I thought she looked very much a queen. But it's a small part. She would have to have been amazing, or amazingly awful, to get a mention. As I recall, she wasn't either."

"As I said, she was never much of an actress."

"She's no Robin Story."

Bergren sneered.

"Not hardly. Good night, Dirk. Tell Elena she'll get other chances to break a leg. I'd hate to break hers if the two of you go the wrong way on this."

CHAPTER TWENTY-ONE

Ned floored the Navigator past the "No Trespassing" signs flanking the entry, snapping the slender chain that barred access. The road twisted and climbed past mounds of close-cropped yellow-gray scrub dotted with stunted evergreens. The blaring sunlight was harsh on eyes accustomed to Portland's muted drizzle.

He drew the SUV on to the narrow shoulder and studied the plan once more. The site marked "Museum" was supposed to be three miles into the ranch. It was closer if you went through the main entrance, but that had been padlocked. The plan had shown this side road just a few hundred yards from the main gate.

He took a sharp curve past a withered stump and there it was. There could be no doubt. The earth sloped below the road down to a magnificent natural amphitheatre.

There was a stretch of gravel past the curve that formed an overlook. Ned pulled over and parked. He grabbed the blueprint rolled beside him on the passenger seat. It had arrived in the mail from Tucker Farr several weeks before.

The chill morning air stung Ned's face as he clambered across the gravel to the valley rim. Gone was the leaden damp that weighed down winter days in Portland. A thin veil of clouds shimmered on the horizon.

Ned unfurled the blueprint and held it before him, centering the amphitheatre in his field of vision. He was seized by the grandeur that had captivated his father. He could picture the towering Ionic columns rising from the valley floor. He imagined the thundering hooves of horses galloping through Shakespearean battle scenes. He saw legions of cheering patrons rising in unison from row upon row of stadium seats ringing the gently sloping walls of the vast expanse. The scene was intoxicating.

The braying of his cell phone had been the first sound he'd heard that morning. The past few days he had left the phone on at all hours in case calls came in from the cast or crew. Selvaggio's staccato voice had jarred him awake.

"What the hell you doing up? I thought I'd go right to voicemail. You vampires in theater are usually hitting the hay about now."

"I left my phone on. In case someone important should call. Meaning someone other than you. What's going on?"

"I just got off the phone with one of my Bergren sources. I circle back to these people when I get a chance to see if we can come up with a new angle. This guy, Ted Sorenson, runs a diner out in Wasco, north of Bhagwan-land. I always call him early, before his breakfast rush. They guy's got a thing against Jerry. His brother was the caretaker for some West Hill types who had a nice spread out east. They had to sell it off when Jerry squeezed them on one of his juice loans. The brother ended up losing his job.

Jerry sometimes stops into this diner for a meal. Sorenson's picked up a few scraps of conversation he's sent my way. Jerry's less on guard out in the sticks than he is in some chi-chi restaurant downtown. Anyway, Sorenson says Jerry was in the place after Thanksgiving with some big shot in a fancy suit. He said he'd fill me in if I came on out there. He doesn't like to talk over the phone. The guy's seen too many movies – thinks his phone might be tapped. With everything else I've got going, I can't get out there any time soon. It's a good two-hour drive. If you want, I thought you could check it out."

Selvaggio had called at around 5:30 that morning. Ned was due to meet Karin at 1:00. It was the Wednesday after her show closed, the day she'd made the reservation for the two of them at Edgefield. He'd figured if he left right away, he could talk to Sorenson and still have plenty of time to get back for Karin. Edgefield was just off the highway on his way back to Portland, so it should all work out.

It had occurred to him as he'd scurried to get ready that he might have time to visit the ranch. He had thought about making the drive out there before, but he'd been overwhelmed by the show. Besides, it had seemed easier to write about the place if it were just some remote image. He had nothing more to say about the ranch now, though, so just in case he had time he tossed the blueprint and the site plan Selvaggio had given him into the Navigator.

The diner had been humming when he'd arrived. Sorenson, a lean, hollow-cheeked man with mournful eyes, had greeted him cordially, but had asked if he could come back in a few hours after the breakfast crowd had thinned. Ned had decided then to set out for the ranch. He'd have to move quickly, but it looked from the map like he could make it to Antelope and back in time.

As he took in the panorama from the overlook, a hawk arced into view at the far end of the valley. It glided effortlessly toward him, scanning the ground below for prey.

His father had traveled here once, according to the e-mail traffic on Bolden's disk. Bergren had surely known that this scene would seal the deal. Brooks Prince had probably stood where he was now, surveying the site of spectacles to come, as Bergren hovered beside him and gave his well-practiced patter about reinventing theater and redeeming America's youth.

It was time to head back. Ned rolled up the blueprint, climbed into the SUV, and reversed course down the road.

He was leaning toward calling off the show. Bergren's bribe was chump change in the overall deal, but it could buy him time until things returned to the way they used to be. Back to the days when work was a sideline, not a lifeline.

It would be degrading, after a fashion, to let this tawdry Rolls Royce scheme go ahead. But his father's vision, the grand amphitheatre, was dead. Why not recoup at least a little of that misplaced investment?

It's true he would be leaving Nora in Bergren's clutches. But who could say whether the play would actually be her salvation? She might stay with him, for all he knew. They had been together for two years. She'd hardly looked miserable on the sofa at the man's beach house. She was in a sort of captivity, of course, but the cage was one of her choosing. If she wanted to be a kept woman in a black box, who was he to interfere?

Elena would feel otherwise, of course. And Elena had a real claim on him, for her devotion to his play. She was in a class apart from the rest of the cast and crew, as far as he was concerned. The others might be disappointed if the play were called off, but they would be paid in full for their pains. They had no emotional capital invested.

But Elena was in this as much to advance her own career as to liberate her friend. She wanted to get to LA as soon as possible. Bergren's payoff would give her a cushion for the move. He could throw in a little extra for her, if need be.

But even if Ned called it off, Bergren was wrong about the play. It was a damned good script. It was the best writing he'd done in years. He had written out of conviction, and it showed.

The production was strong. Elena was terrific, and Calvin Anderson was very solid. David Blevins had come through with a first-rate design. The only question mark was Trent Davis in the final act, and he'd planned to put Marty's advice about motivating Davis to work. At least he had before Bergren showed up in the theater.

But *Pay to Play* didn't have to be performed now. If it were a worthy piece of writing, it would be just as worthy three years from now in Chicago or New York – where a competent publicist would get the word out. Of course the impact of the work would not be the same, but so be it. He was not some journalist or social activist, obsessed with the here and now.

Only a few stray cars were left in the diner's pockmarked parking lot. An aroma of greasy bacon wafted toward him as he strode toward the entrance. A tattered sign perched on a listing stand invited him to seat himself. He folded himself into a red naugahyde booth, giving a slight wave to the owner at the counter as he did. He ordered two eggs over easy and a side of toast from a chirpy waitress.

A few minutes later Sorenson settled into the opposite seat of the booth, wielding a glass pot of steaming black coffee. Without bothering to ask first, he poured Ned a cup to the brim. Sorenson spoke in a low, husky voice that at times verged on a whisper.

"Sorry to put you off. Always busy around eight."

"It's no problem. I got to do a little sightseeing."

The diner owner expressed no interest in the sights Ned had seen.

"So Mr. Selvaggio says you're helping him nail Jerry Bergren."

"That's right. We appreciate your help."

"Glad to do it. I was surprised you came out here so fast. I hadn't heard from Mr. Selvaggio in a couple of months. I thought you'd dropped the whole thing."

"No, we're still on it. It's not easy, though. Bergren covers his tracks pretty well."

"Yeah, he's a shifty sonofagun. From what I hear, one day's he's smiling at you, all friendly and everything. Next day, you're on your can and never knew what hit you."

"So you see a lot of him in here?"

"Never laid eyes on the man until he started in on that ranch down by Antelope. You know, the one with that nutty guru and all his Rolls Royces. Then he'd be in here like once a month. Always with a car full of flunkies. Architects, consultants, I don't know who. Plans spread out all over the table. Bergren did most of the talking. The rest of them mostly just chewed their food and nodded their heads. A bunch of yes men, if you ask me."

Sorenson's voice dripped with disgust. He freshened Ned's cup. The perky waitress arrived with Ned's food. He tucked in with relish.

"He always talked in a real loud voice. So everyone knew he was top dog. He didn't care who heard what he had to say. Thought we were a bunch of yokels, I guess. So I picked up some of what he was up to. I didn't go looking for someone to tell it to, but when Mr. Selvaggio came in asking questions I told him what I knew."

"That's great. Thanks. I know it's been really helpful."

"Sure. I want to see him go down. I'll do what I can to help. How's the food?"

"Terrific. Now I know why Jerry keeps coming back."

"Yeah, I guess. Thanks. Anyway, I hadn't seen him for a couple of months. I was beginning to wonder whether he'd given up on the whole ranch thing. Then right after Thanksgiving, he shows up with a guy I'd never seen before. A big guy in a sharp suit. Just the two of them. This guy wasn't like the other ones, with their noses up Bergren's butt. He did most of the talking. You could tell Bergren wasn't too happy about what he was hearing.

I always refill the coffee at Bergren's table. He thinks it's so I can suck up to him, but it lets me pick up what's going on. I can see that there's a big contract on the table. I can tell it's a contract because of the way it's laid out and because it has those stickies stuck to the page where you're supposed to sign.

This guy's not like Bergren. He keeps his voice down. But he has his back to me when I come up with the coffee, so he doesn't see me coming. When I went over for like their third refill, I hear him say, 'That's the deal. We get forty percent, plus a million five now. We're out of time.' Maybe not exactly those words, but pretty close. A little later I see Bergren sign the contract and hand the guy an envelope. Then off they go."

Ned had been listening intently, but had also polished off his eggs and toast.

"Has the other man been back?"

"Nope. Bergren and his flunkies have, but not this guy."

"I don't suppose you caught his name."

Sorenson gave a lopsided grin. It was the only time he'd cracked a smile that morning.

"He picked up the check. First time in here Bergren didn't pay himself. Paid by credit card. I made a copy of the slip for Mr. Selvaggio."

He triumphantly pulled a well-creased piece of paper out of his shirt pocket and handed it across the table. Ned unfolded it and squinted at the faint block lettering.

Tucker Farr had paid the bill.

CHAPTER TWENTY-TWO

Ned brushed a stray strand of hair off of Karin's forehead, then gently ran his fingers over her cheeks and chin and down her neck to her breasts. The bronze glow of her skin had faded little during the oppressive overcast of a Northwest winter. She gave a little shiver as his fingertips brushed her nipples.

He glanced over at the digital clock on the nightstand of their room at Edgefield. It was already past three thirty. They usually brought things to a close before four so that Ned could make an appearance in the *Columbian* newsroom by the end of the business day. If he were going to tell her about the play, he needed to do it now.

He'd had the opportunity over lunch. He had waited for her at their usual table for half an hour. He'd begun to doubt whether she would come. He hadn't heard from her since that brush off at the Lowbrow after the holidays. He'd thought she would at least call after his review of her show came out – a review, as Bergren had said the night before, that hadn't even mentioned her.

Those he had mentioned had not benefited from the attention. Karin had been right. Rosencrantz was a mess, and the rest of the cast had sunk to his level. Ned had wished as he came out of the cramped and dirty theater that he'd sent a stringer to handle the review, but he knew she would have never forgiven him that.

Just as he was about to give it up and leave the Black Rabbit, she had made a dramatic entrance, sweeping into the dining room wearing a low-cut black dress and three-inch heels. Her honey-blonde hair was dressed in the same elegant plait she'd worn the night he'd met her at the black tie gala downtown; the same jeweled pendant disappeared into her cleavage. She'd turned every head in the place.

"Remember me?" she'd asked coyly as she eased into her seat.

She'd teased and flirted throughout lunch. It was as if they had never left off. She regaled him with stories of her dysfunctional cast. One night Guildenstern hadn't shown up for a performance, in protest at the sorry work of Rosencrantz. The Player King had reached him on his cell phone, and several other cast members - herself included - had taken turns pleading. Guildenstern had finally arrived at the theater five minutes before curtain, and the show had gone on. She harbored no grudges over Ned's review, which she'd actually considered an exercise in restraint.

The actor who'd played Polonius was recruiting her for a new play he was directing over the summer. It wasn't a lead, but a lot closer to one than the part of Gertrude.

"Jerry doesn't know about it yet. He came to one performance, you know. I could tell he didn't think much of my work. He was never much of an actor and never thought I was much of one either. He'll be shocked if I start working steadily around town. Which is just what I plan to do."

She gave a conspiratorial grin and drank deeply from her wineglass. It was as good a moment as he'd get to come clean with her about his own theater plans. Yet he'd said nothing - in part because he'd felt the imminence of the bed upstairs and in part because his plans were in tumult after the morning's revelation about Tucker Farr.

On leaving the diner, he'd immediately called his father's executor. According to his assistant, Farr was out of the country and not reachable by phone. Ned now recalled Farr apologizing for being unable to make the opening weekend, but promising to come to closing. At the time this news had come as a relief to Ned, as it would give him another week to polish his explanation for the true purpose of the play. But now it was he who was looking for answers from Farr.

Farr had said he knew nothing about Brooks Prince's mystery investment, but it was plain that was a lie. He was clearly in bed with Bergren. He claimed the estate had nothing when he had pocketed a million and a half dollars and taken a forty percent stake in the ranch deal.

Ned had been fighting what seemed a losing battle against Bergren. Now, as he had cruised along I-84 toward Edgefield, it looked as if a key ally had turned on him, forcing him to wage war on two fronts. The tandem of Bergren and Farr was too much for him. He was outgunned and overmatched.

He was in no position to put on the play. He would speak to Elena and call it off. He'd called her as he neared the Black Rabbit and left a message asking her to meet him at McMenamins before the evening's scheduled dress rehearsal.

He didn't look forward to coming clean with Elena, but a conversation he relished even less would be leveling with Karin. She might cut him some slack because of his father's death, but he doubted she would forgive his concealing a play aimed at bringing down her own husband. Better to say nothing, he thought, as he straddled her on the crisp Edgefield sheets. If the show did not go on, she need be none the wiser. They could carry on as before.

The bellowing of his cell phone jerked him out of his rhythm. He was tempted to let it go, but it might be Elena about their meeting. With a whispered apology, he rolled to the nightstand and grabbed the phone.

He recognized the number as the SoHo office line. He sprang off the bed and made quickly for the bathroom, shutting the door before he answered. SoHo's manager was hysterical.

"Someone's wrecked the theater. It's a total mess. The walls are smashed, there are huge holes in the floor, the glass in the booth is shattered, the seats are all ripped up. It must have happened last night. I've been in the office all morning and didn't hear a thing. I just went into the dressing room to check on something and this is what I found. What happened?"

"I'll be right over. I'm about a half hour away. Just sit tight."

He threw open the bathroom door and scrambled across the room to the chair where he'd draped his clothes.

"I'm sorry, Karin. There's an emergency I've got to deal with," he said as he pulled on his pants.

"An emergency? For a theater critic? On a Wednesday afternoon?"

She smiled wryly from the bed.

"It is a theater emergency, actually. I'll explain later."

He leaned over the bed and kissed her.

"You're fit for a queen, Gertrude."

"Why thank you, Hamlet."

"You should go for that part Polonius is pushing. 'Though this be madness, yet there is method in it,' and all that."

"If he casts me, I'll take it. I don't care what Jerry says."

"I don't either," he said without smiling. Then he dashed out the door.

He sprinted through the Edgefield hallways, painted in primitive folk art tableaux, down the hotel's front stairs, and out to the parking lot. He gunned the Navigator's engine and shot out of the driveway. In a few minutes he was on the Interstate heading into Portland.

He deliberated for a few minutes as sped down the freeway. Then, with a look of resolve, he pulled out his cell phone and punched Elena on his speed dial. This time she answered.

"Yeah? What's up?"

"Are you off work?"

"I'm just cleaning up."

"Meet me at the theater as soon as you can get there."

"Why? What's going on? I thought you wanted to meet tonight, before rehearsal."

"That was then. Now we've got other issues."

"OK. I'll see you then."

Next he called Scott's cell phone. He knew it would go to voicemail, as their plane from Chicago was still in the air. They were due in late that afternoon. He had hoped to meet them at the airport, but that wasn't going to happen now. He left a message telling them to rent a car and go straight to their hotel. He left brief directions.

His last call was to Selvaggio. The reporter spat out his usual phone greeting.

"Selvaggio here."

"It's Dirk. Listen, there's some heavy shit coming down with Bergren. I can't explain it all now, but I'm going to need to get a hold of you tonight. Will you be on your cell?"

"Yeah."

"I'll call you. Sorry to leave you hanging."

"They call that theater, don't they?"

"Yeah, they do."

He hurtled west across the Fremont Bridge. Bright sunshine glittered off the ripples of the Willamette River. The paper had called for several days of fair weather, a rare occurrence in Portland during the winter months.

He pulled up in front of the theater. SoHo's manager, a moon-faced, pink-cheeked woman in her thirties, was hunkered down in her office. With an unsteady gait, she led him through the lobby into the theater.

The wreckage was staggering. It looked as if a barbarian horde had swept through with axes and picks and laid waste to the place. They had apparently found the venue's ladders and climbed up them to pull down the stage lights, which lay dented and twisted amidst the splinters of the stage floor. There were gaping holes in the back wall, exposing the dressing room. Bits of upholstery and foam cushion from the ravaged seats were scattered all about. The railings lining the catwalks above each wing had been hammered loose and now hung precariously over the wings.

Ned turned and hugged the manager. As he did, he heard a low moaning coming from the corner of the theater, under the lighting booth. The two of them picked their way through the debris. Their shoes crunched shards of glass from the shattered booth window as they mounted the steps bisecting the center and stage left sections of the house. Ned pushed through the curtained doorway at the top of the stairs. In the faint light of the passageway under the booth, he could make out the shape of a body huddled against the far wall.

"There's a flashlight on the wall for the actors," said the manager. She found it and flicked it on, training the light on the body with a shaking hand.

It was Trent Davis, although Ned could barely tell. His face had been beaten to a pulp. His nose looked broken, and dried blood was caked along his mouth. One eye was swollen shut. His shirt had been ripped open, revealing ugly purple bruises and red welts across his chest. When he saw Ned, he tried to speak.

"Just stay quiet, Trent," Ned said. "We'll get help."

He pulled out his cell phone and called 911. The operator promised an ambulance.

"Hello?!" Elena's voice rang out from the lobby.

"We're in here. Be careful."

After a few beats, he heard her gasp. "Jesus fucking Christ!"

"Will you stay with him for a few minutes?" Ned asked the manager. She nodded.

He went back into the theater. Elena stood, stock still, at the mouth of the vestibule. Ned put his arm around her shoulders and led her into the lobby. Its order was comforting after the chaos of the theater.

"This was Bergren. He came here last night after rehearsal and told me to close down the show. I told him I wouldn't do anything without talking to you. I said I'd call him tonight. I guess he decided he couldn't wait. He must have hired some thugs to trash the theater. They also beat the crap out of Trent, then left him under the booth. He doesn't look good."

"Holy shit. How did he find out about the show?"

"I don't know. He said someone in the cast or crew tipped him off, but wouldn't say who. Whoever it was gave him the script. He'd read the whole thing."

A look of panic crossed her square face.

"Did he tell Robin?"

"He said he hadn't. He actually made a joke out of it. He said he ought to get her down to the theater to do a few scenes. She could play the actress and I could do the critic."

"Jesus. So why did he think you would shut down the show? Did he threaten you?"

He saw no choice but to lay it all out. He told her about the suicide, about Bergren's seduction of his father and the failed amphitheatre. He left out Farr's collusion on the deal, as that didn't really concern her.

"This is what I was going to tell all of you after opening. I didn't want it to get in the way of putting on the play. I thought it would be a distraction."

"You could have trusted me."

"I know I could have. I do. But I wanted you to deal with your character's motivation. Not mine. Anyway, Bergren offered me $25,000 to call off the show. He said he would throw in an extra $5,000 for you."

"What a fucking prince of a guy."

The shrill piercing of a siren sounded behind them. An ambulance screeched to a halt at the base of the theater walkway. Two paramedics in dark uniforms scrambled out and hurried into the lobby.

"I'll take you to him," said Ned.

He led them through the carnage of the theater, which didn't seem to faze them. As they examined Davis, he guided the manager back into the lobby, where Elena was pacing. She came over beside them.

"I'm so sorry about all this," he said to the manager. "You need to know this was not some random act of vandalism. This was about our play. About stopping it from going on."

"How do you know?"

"I know. Someone came to the theater last night after rehearsal and told me to put a stop to it."

"Who?"

"It's best for now that you don't know. It'll all come out soon enough. But Elena and I need to get away from here. I don't know what else they might do."

One of the paramedics hustled through the lobby to the ambulance. He pulled out a stretcher and carried it back into the theater.

"So what should I do?" Her high-pitched voice quavered.

"You should call your insurance company. And the police. When they ask you what you know, tell them the truth. Tell them that you rented the theater to me, that we were scheduled to open a play in two days, and that I told you this was an attempt to sabotage the show. They're going to want to get in touch with us, of course. Go ahead and give them my number. We'll be a little hard to find, though. At this point I don't trust anyone. Not even the police. Not with the guy who's behind this."

Elena took the hands of the manager.

"Do what Dirk says. This is a bad guy, but he's not after your company. Just play it straight."

"OK."

The paramedics emerged with Davis laid out on the stretcher. In the light of the lobby his battered face looked even more disfigured. Ned and Elena followed the stretcher out to the ambulance. As Davis was loaded in through the back doors, he spotted Ned through his one open eye and feebly gestured to him to come closer.

"It's my fault," he managed to croak through blood-stained teeth.

"No, Trent. We know who's behind this."

"I know. Jerry Bergren. I told him about the show."

"It was you? Why?"

"I figured out he was your businessman. I was at some cocktail party. They were talking about his Bhagwan ranch thing. I must have seen it in the paper, but it never registered. I finally put it all together. I figured I'd get a nice payday if I tipped him off. He promised me

$5,000, plus he said he would line me up with all the right people in LA."

"So what happened?"

"He told me to meet him at the theater at midnight last night. He'd already paid me a thousand. He said he would bring the rest of the money with him. A few minutes after I got there a car pulls up. Two guys jump out and grab me. One of them had a key to the theater. They drag me inside and start beating the hell out of me. That's the last thing I remember."

One of the paramedics tapped Ned on the shoulder.

"We need to get this guy to the hospital."

"OK. Where are you taking him?"

"St. Vincent's."

"Thanks." He turned back to Davis. "Trent, what's done is done. Is there someone we can call? I'm sorry, but we can't come to the hospital with you."

"Call Anthony, my housemate. The number's on the contact sheet."

Part of Marty's ruthless protocol as stage manager had been getting an emergency contact number for everyone.

"I'll call him. Take care of yourself."

Davis slumped back against the frame of the stretcher as the paramedics finished loading him in. The rear doors slammed, the siren blared, and the ambulance took off, lights flashing.

Ned turned to Elena. "Let's grab the costumes and get out of here."

She stared at him, incredulous. "The costumes?"

"Yes."

They hurried back into the theater, through the lobby and into the dressing room. The costumes were hanging on an iron rack in the far corner. Ned draped them over his arm.

"Take your make-up box, and Calvin's."

Elena did as she was told.

They passed the manager on their way out.

"Things are going to get a little wild," he told her in as soothing a voice as he could muster. "Stay cool. And don't leave the theater tonight until I call you. OK? Just leave a message on my cell if you need to get a hold of me."

"I think I've got it," she squeaked.

They loaded the costumes and make-up kits into the back seat of the Navigator, then jumped in.

"Where are we going?" Elena's tone was bewildered.

"We're booking a room in a hotel. Don't worry. My intentions are honorable."

CHAPTER TWENTY-THREE

The Inn at Northrup Station was a sleek, stylish building perched along the tram line that gave it its name. It sported a tony brick façade that recalled more an upscale rowhouse than a hotel. The lobby was a garish collage of lime green and lemon yellow.

Ned approached the front desk clerk, a lithe blonde in a burgundy coat stationed behind a tangerine counter.

"Has Scott Ashburne checked in?"

She scanned her computer screen with a winsome frown.

"Not yet."

"Do you have a couple of rooms next to each other for three nights?"

"Yes, we do. There's a connecting door."

"We'll take them both. The name is Clyde Barrow. Mr. and Mrs. Clyde Barrow."

The clerk registered the information without batting an eyelash. Ned filled in a registration card with totally erroneous information. The clerk ran his credit card without noticing the discrepancy.

"Would you please send Mr. Ashburne to my room when he gets in?"

"Certainly, sir."

Ned led Elena back to the Navigator to retrieve the costumes and make-up boxes. Arms laden, they negotiated the hotel's narrow hallway lined with angular art to their room.

"What the fuck are you doing?" Elena thundered as soon as they were inside the door.

"Patience, dear. I have a few calls to make. Why don't you go powder your nose."

She shot him a dirty look.

He reached both Calvin and Marty on his cell phone. He told them to come to his room at the Inn instead of meeting at the theater for rehearsal. He suggested they pack a change of clothes and asked them both to bring a toothbrush.

"Whatever you do, don't go to the theater," he cautioned each of them. "I'm sorry to be so mysterious. I'll fill you in when I see you."

Just as he was wrapping up the call to Marty, there was a knock at the door. Ned went to the peephole and spotted Scott and Linda in the hallway. He opened the door and waved them in with a grin. He glanced at Elena across the room and caught a flicker of disdain as she took in their blonde suburban good looks. He signed off with Marty.

"Welcome to the provinces," he said to Scott and Linda, motioning them to take a seat on the loveseat – a study in eggplant beneath a jagged urbanscape. "I just couldn't bear to be apart from you two, so I took a room in your hotel. Two rooms in fact, as a man of my station deserves a suite. Allow me to introduce my leading lady, Ms. Elena Devlin."

Elena gave a curt nod.

"Elena, Scott here is my oldest friend. At this point, in fact, he may be the only person who would cop to being my friend. Scott is a glorified bank teller. The real talent in the family is Linda, the future mother of his children. When she's not fantasizing about redecorating a four-bedroom colonial with a white picket fence, she's a public relations ace for a big-time firm."

"It's not a fantasy any more, Neddy," said Linda. "We closed on the house three weeks ago. And it's five bedrooms, thank you very much."

"Congratulations. Your capitulation to bourgeois living is now complete. But I have to keep my gratuitous insults to a minimum, as I'm about to ask you to take on a pro bono assignment. You might have thought you were coming out here to the backwoods for some R&R, but no – it's really so you could be an apprentice theater publicist."

"Isn't it a little late to be getting the word out about your show? I thought it opened on Friday," said Linda.

"It was supposed to. We've had a few adverse developments, however."

He briefed them on his encounter with Bergren the night before, the trashing of the theater, and the assault on Trent Davis.

"If I had any common sense at all, I would just fold up my tent and go home." He turned towards Elena, who sat, arms crossed, on a chair with a triangular wooden back in a corner of the room. "Which I'm sorry to say is what I'd planned to do until I heard what that bastard did to the theater."

"You were going to sell out the show?" she snarled.

"I was going to talk it over with you first, but yes, I'd decided it didn't make sense to be a hero."

"And now that you have no theater, a cast member in the hospital, and one of Portland's heaviest hitters after you, you're thinking different?"

"This is Ned's version of logic, Elena," put in Scott. "He's never just marched to a different drummer. He's always had to build his own damned drum kit."

"And what's this Ned/Neddy stuff? That's a helluva strange nickname for Dirk."

"My real name is Ned Prince, Elena. Dirk Marlowe is a pen name. Sort of an alter ego."

"You've got no shortage of fucking ego. Enough to cover at least a couple of alters, I'd say."

Scott and Linda both tittered on the love seat.

"OK. Touché. But all that ego is now going to be put to good use. Here's what we're going to do. Linda, you're going to bang out a killer press release. You've got your laptop with you?"

She nodded.

"I knew I could count on you to be a pathetically workaholic yuppie. You're going to say that the SoHo Theater was destroyed by dark forces bent on suppressing the eagerly awaited new show, *Pay to Play*. These same evil elements put one of the stars of the show in St. Vincent's Hospital. They will stop at nothing to torpedo a brave new play that tells the truth about one of Oregon's most shameless scams. You won't mention Jerry Bergren by name, of course. We'll want to keep 'em guessing.

You'll say that show will go on. On Friday, as scheduled. You'll say that Lazarus Productions – that's the name of our new company, Elena – will make an announcement tomorrow at five p.m. about the time and the place. You'll send the release out to all the major media around here. I can give you a list for the print people. Maybe your buddies in Chicago can help you on the TV and radio side. They don't usually give a damn about theater, of course, so I don't know who any of them are. The key is to get on the phone to the TV people and get them over to the theater. When they get their cameras on all that mayhem, their lenses will pop. I've got SoHo's manager over there to let 'em in. And make sure you repeat that Trent is at St. Vincent's. If one of their paparazzi can get his face on tape, that's a bleed-and-lead on the evening news. I know I should be concerned for his privacy, but he didn't seem to care much about mine, now did he?

We won't do interviews. You'll tell them we're worried about our safety because of what's happened. We're in hiding, rehearsing and regrouping.

On the subject of rehearsing, Elena, we're now in our new studio. The other room is for Calvin and Marty. I don't know if Calvin's wife has ever had a look at Marty, but maybe we should e-mail her a digital photo if she's worried about him straying. This is our stage manager, Scotty, who's the encyclopedia entry under 'bull dyke.' Calvin's retired and Marty's unemployed, so we shouldn't have any time issues with them. Can you get off work, Elena?"

"Tomorrow's my day off, and I'd already planned to take off Friday because of opening."

"Great."

"Yeah. But aren't we missing someone?"

"What do you mean?"

"There's no way Trent's coming back by Friday. Who are we going to get to play the critic?"

"Me."

"You? Have you ever acted before?"

Scott piped up. "He played The Nutcracker in our fourth grade play. Knocked those rats right on their tails. All the parents, too."

"No," Ned said, "I'm not an actor. But I think I'm supposed to play this part."

"Well, at least you know the lines."

"They'll probably ring a bell."

Linda jumped up from the loveseat. "We have to put this out to the media."

"Put out what?" said Ned.

"That the director slash playwright is going to take the place of the guy in the hospital. We should dribble it out, though. Let the drama build. Tonight we'll just say that we're searching for a replacement for the wounded actor. 'Wounded' is the way we want to put it – makes it sound like a war zone."

"Believe me, that's exactly what it fucking looks like," said Elena.

"Tomorrow, when we announce the location, that's when we'll say that Ned is going to step up to the part."

"When Dirk Marlowe takes the role," Ned corrected. "That's my identity here."

"So, Mr. Ultra Ego, where are we going to put on the show?" Elena was still caustic.

"I don't know."

"Just a minor detail that slipped your mind?"

"Christ, Elena, give me a break. I didn't end up selling us out, did I? I'm sorry I didn't tell you about the whole family angle, but I really didn't see what good it would do. Look, we've got Jerry Bergren and his goons after us, and who the hell knows what other strings he'll pull to stop us. We've got about forty-eight hours to totally rework this play. We don't have the luxury of bickering and badmouthing and all those other grand theater traditions. If you don't want to go on with this, just tell me now and we'll have done with it. I can take Trent's part, but I can't play yours."

Scott shifted awkwardly on the loveseat. Linda caught his eye and mock-grimaced.

Elena rose from her chair and crossed the room to where Ned stood. She put her hands on his shoulders and looked up at him.

"We were partners, Ned a.k.a. Dirk. We decided to put this damned show on together. We put all the pieces together, and we just watched them get blown apart together. It would be one of the ballsiest things I've ever seen if we go on with it. One of the dumbest, but definitely one of the ballsiest. No question, I'm up for it. That asshole may have brainwashed my best friend, but he's not running my fucking life. But I'm in only if we're still partners. Which means we call the shots together. Got it?"

"Got it. So where do you think we should put this on, partner?"

"I thought you'd never ask. I think we've got to do it outside. There's just no way we'd be able to line up a new space, reblock the show, figure out the lights, all in forty-eight hours. There're so few spaces around anyway that Bergren would know where to look for us. If we do it outside, we don't have to ask anyone's permission, we don't have to sign a lease. We just show up and go. It's like, you know, guerrilla warfare. We'd have to get Blevins to lay his hands on some light trees, so we're not running around in the dark, but he could pull that off."

"If we can find him," put in Ned.

"We'll find him. He has a weird way of popping up just when you need him. Look, I know it's February, I know it's cold, but the weather's supposed to stay clear through the weekend. As long as it doesn't pour, we should be able to hold our audience for eighty-five minutes. Whaddaya think?"

"I think it's brilliant," said Ned. "I had Greek tragedy in mind when I started on the play, and Greek tragedy was performed outdoors. It sort of brings us full circle."

"I love it," said Linda. "It'll make it a lot easier for the TV people. Plus it'll give you more room if you draw any sort of a crowd. But you're probably wrong about having to ask permission, Elena. If Portland's anything like Chicago, you'd have to get a permit to put on a public performance."

"The only way Portland's like Chicago is that someone like Bergren can put the fix in on a permit if he's given the chance," said Ned. "So we don't give him the chance. We announce that people who want to see the show should be at such and such a place at such and such a time. Then we lead them through the streets to where we're actually putting on the play. When everyone's in place, we just pop up from out of the shadows and roll. The police could try to break it up then, but I don't think they'd dare."

Linda headed toward the door.

"I've got to get cracking on the release. We won't make the five o'clock news, but ten is definitely doable."

"That's another way Portland's not like Chicago, Linda. The news here comes on at eleven. They drink too much cappuccino around here to go to bed at the same time as those Midwest soybean farmers."

"Great. Gives me another hour. I'll be back with a draft as soon as it's ready."

Scott made a plaintive face as his wife charged out the door.

"Thanks, Ned. Our room is now command and control HQ. I can tell you she'll kick me out of there as soon as I come in. Your room is now Rehearsal Studio A, and I know you're not going to want me around. So what am I supposed to do?"

"We'll list you in the credits as 'assistant to the producer,' old buddy. Which basically means you do take-out, errands, and laundry. No windows though. I know that would be too demeaning for an MBA."

He flipped his car keys to Scott.

"My dad's old Navigator is out in the parking lot. Why don't you park it on the street about seven or eight blocks away. You can't be too careful about letting on where we are. Then take your rental car and pick up dinner at Typhoon over on 23rd. The best Southeast Asian you'll ever have. They can give you directions at the front desk. Get enough for six: three of us in the cast, plus Marty, plus you two guys. The laundry we'll need tomorrow. Elena and I don't have a change of clothes other than our costumes, and I don't even know if I can fit into Trent Davis's clothes. We're not going to get anything out of our apartments, because we don't know who's watching them. Oh, and on your way out, hang the 'Do Not Disturb Sign' on the door, would you?"

"Jawohl, Herr Kommandant."

CHAPTER TWENTY-FOUR

A muffled bell sounded as the elevator doors opened. Selvaggio was the first out.

"This way," he said.

He turned left and led Ned and Scott in his rolling gait down a hallway carpeted in earth tones. The reporter pushed through glass double doors at the end of the corridor into a plush reception area. He barely paused as he angled past tufted leather chairs and *Wall Street Journal*-lined end tables into a massive room dominated by a mahogany conference table.

The conference room commanded a sweeping view of the moon-lit river through floor to ceiling windows that ran the length of the room. The three of them rounded the table and made straight for the windows.

The scene unfolding beneath them was frenetic. At the base of Salmon Street below was a plaza bordered on its far end by a promenade running along the Willamette River. Pouring into the plaza and spilling on to the grass on either side was a huge crowd. They streamed in from all directions, down Salmon or along Martin Luther King (which ran parallel to the river) or from the promenade itself. They arrayed themselves around the fountain, dry in winter, which stood at the center of the plaza.

Snaking through the crowd were the glaring lights of television cameras. Ned counted at least three, possibly four crews. Reporters could be seen corralling members of the crowd for interviews.

Selvaggio nudged Ned and pointed.

"See them up on horses?"

Ned squinted and made out a squad of mounted police massed on the grassy area to the right of the plaza. They appeared to be wearing riot helmets.

"Jesus."

He glanced at his watch. It was seven twenty. They had announced seven thirty as the time for the audience to gather.

Linda had executed the PR plan to perfection. She had sent out a searing press release around this time Wednesday evening, then started working the phones. By nine thirty that night she'd had two television stations over to the theater. SoHo's manager was there to let them in. Both of them ran stories on the eleven o'clock news, one as the lead. The images of the devastated theater were so chilling that they managed to overcome the inane commentary of the on-scene reporters.

By Thursday, yesterday, all of the local network affiliates had gone with the story. One of them had contrived to get into St. Vincent's Hospital and snap a shot of Trent Davis's swollen, discolored face before they were shooed away. The photo stayed on screen for most of their coverage that night.

Linda had fielded all calls from the media. She'd told each of them that the director and cast were not available for interviews due to the intensity of the rehearsal process. The stations had turned to various local arts luminaries for on-camera comment, rounding up scathing denunciations from the artistic director of Willamette Stage and the head of the regional arts agency, among others. One of them had likened the intimidation of Lazarus Productions to the Spanish Inquisition.

The police had left a message on Ned's cell phone Thursday morning. They'd gotten his cell number from SoHo's manager. He'd called back and politely told the answering officer that he would be pleased to answer all of their questions just as soon as the show was over. Then he'd abruptly hung up. The police had called back several times, but he'd ignored their messages.

Selvaggio had been with them at the hotel most of the last two days. Ned had called him after dinner on Wednesday and invited him over to the room. Once the reporter arrived, Ned had laid it all out for him. He'd apologized for keeping Selvaggio in the dark about the play and his father's identity as Bergren's investor. Once Bolden had killed the *Columbian* story, he'd said, he had to keep the show under wraps. It was his only chance to get Bergren.

"Hey, join the club. He didn't tell me a fucking thing either," Elena said to Selvaggio.

"Did you think I'd go to Bolden?"

"Hey, we're friends, but you're a journalist. The story's the thing, and there was no way you could run your story without his sign-off. And it looked to me like telling Bolden was as good as telling Bergren."

"One card-carrying Good Person to another," sneered Selvaggio.

"Exactly."

Ned had offered to make it up to Selvaggio by giving him an exclusive on the show's backstage. He would have access to everyone and see everything at the hotel. The *Columbian* didn't publish until the following Wednesday. Ned agreed they would do no other interviews until the paper went to press next week.

"And Linda here won't return any phone calls from the *Oregonian* until then?"

"You drive a hard bargain, but OK. That should piss them off pretty good."

"You got that right."

Selvaggio was too bulky to be a fly on the wall, but he'd kept a low profile through the hours of rehearsal, the PR skull sessions with Linda, the crazed efforts to track down Blevins and get lighting, and the late-night wrangling over where to perform. His presence had been audible only when Scott went to order in deep-dish pizza.

"Hey, if you want dough for dinner, why don't you just order some bread?"

"Jersey born and bred, Scotty," Ned laughed. "Can't shake the habit of eating cardboard."

When they'd finally decided on where to assemble the audience, Selvaggio had mentioned a contact of his at a law firm whose office overlooked the plaza.

"Might be a good place to size up the scene before you commit yourself."

"Can you set it up without telling them what it's for?"

"Sure. I'll just say I want to use their conference room to meet with someone. I know this guy pretty well."

Ned, Scott, and Selvaggio had driven over from the hotel in the reporter's old Chevy. The tree-shaped air freshener dangling from the driver's mirror was sickeningly sweet. They'd parked in the building's underground garage. Ned wore Trent Davis's costume under his overcoat. The fit wasn't perfect, but Ned felt he had to step out of his own clothes to do the part. Elena had put light make-up on his face before they'd left the hotel room.

"Christ knows whether we'll need it with Blevins's lighting, but let's be ready just in case," she'd said.

The guard at the building's front desk had looked slightly askance at Ned's made-up face when Selvaggio signed them in, but he was apparently accustomed to stranger sights in Portland. He'd sent them over to the elevators without comment.

The moon glistened in a cloudless night sky over the river. Scott motioned to his left.

"Look at all those cruisers. You'd think this was a riot, not a theater outing."

Ned looked up Martin Luther King and saw five or six police cars parked in a row. A knot of police officers huddled on the curb opposite the middle car.

Ned pulled out his cell phone and dialed Linda. She had taken Elena and Calvin in their rental car and was circling downtown.

"Mobile green room here," she answered.

"The place is crawling with cops."

"That's what you expected. What do you want to do?"

"We're about to head down there. I'll call you back."

"OK."

Next he called Marty. She was with Blevins in the technical director's weathered van.

Blevins had suddenly turned up at the hotel around noon on Thursday. He'd expressed no surprise at the turn of events, nor apologized for failing to return Ned's calls. Ned had sketched out on hotel stationery where they intended to put on the show and how they planned to stage it, with Elena chiming in. After studying the sketch, Blevins had matter-of-factly listed the equipment they would need.

"Can you get it by tomorrow?"

"No problem. I used to work at Broadway Lights. They've got everything. I'll need to go over to the place first, though, and check out the power."

"Great. Just call me while you're over at Broadway. I'll give them my credit card over the phone."

"Yeah. Bye."

Then he was gone.

They'd heard nothing from him for the rest of the day. In a panic, Ned finally tracked him down Thursday night around ten.

"Did you get the equipment?"

"Yeah. No problem. I just put it on my account. It's all in my van."

"How much time will it take you to set up?"

"About fifteen minutes if I've got someone to help me."

"Marty will do it. Why don't you plan to meet us at the hotel with your van at six tomorrow night."

"Yeah. Bye."

After hanging up with Blevins, Ned had left the hotel for the first time since they'd checked in. He'd told Marty and the cast to take a break and found out from Scott where the Navigator was parked. Then he'd driven to the Lowbrow.

The crowd was thick. The bartender was a dervish, whirling to fill orders. Ned waited for a lull, then pushed his way through to the bar. The bartender gave a snort of recognition.

"You meeting the queen?"

"No. Not tonight."

"Been sent into exile? I read your review. Queens like to be noticed. Even when her subjects are being slain all around her."

"I'm still in good standing at court. At least for now. But I need to get a message to her. Could you call the number on the back of this envelope and tell her I've given you a note? I need her to read it before tomorrow night."

"Someone steal your cell phone?"

"It's a little complicated."

"Would a Turbo Pimms No. 1 Cup make things simpler?"

"I can't, Mick. I'm in the middle of a show."

"You came over here at intermission?"

"Something like that. Can you get her the note?"

"Sure. I'll just put the messenger charge on your tab. Hey, did you see about that theater that got trashed? Ugly stuff. Who knew putting on a play could be so hazardous?"

After Ned had driven back to the hotel, they'd rehearsed until two in the morning. They'd had a few hours' sleep, then had gone full tilt all day, fueled by a steady stream of coffee funneled in by Scott. The only interruptions had been occasional media updates from Linda.

Blevins had arrived twenty minutes late. After a quick check of the equipment, Ned had packed him and Marty off. Now the van was parked about a block from the place.

"You guys OK?" Ned asked Marty.

"Fine. David's over there doing reconnaissance. Which means he's not smoking in the van. Which is good."

Despite years of stage managing cigarette-fiend theater people, Marty was sensitive to smoke.

"I wish you hadn't let him out of your sight. I never know when he leaves if it's the last time I'll see him again."

"He'll be back. Are we still looking at an eight o'clock go?"

"Yes. I'll call you at seven forty with the final word."

"Got it."

Selvaggio had moved away from the window and was seated in one of the black leather conference room chairs, writing notes. Scott stood solemnly by the window.

"You still up for this, Scotty? Now that you're a responsible suburban homeowner and all?"

"It beats doing your laundry."

"With the two point five children you have coming once you hit the 'burbs, you better get used to it."

"Fuck you, Ned."

"That's what I wanted to hear. Let's go."

Ned led the way out of the conference room. Selvaggio scooped up his notebook and followed.

The guard gave them all a quizzical look as Selvaggio signed them out.

"Quick visit."

"They charge by the tenth of an hour up there, you know. Every six minutes, ka-ching. Gotta talk fast," said Ned.

"I hear you."

The chill night air knifed through Ned's overcoat as they left the office building. He turned up his collar, then put on a Sherlock Holmes-style cap that Calvin had worn to the hotel and donned reading glasses he'd borrowed from Scott. It wasn't much of a disguise, but it wouldn't need to last long. Scott picked up a folding chair he'd left leaning against the building.

They joined the throng on Salmon Street. Ned tried to gauge those around him. It was not the typical theater audience, not the predictable assortment of old-age pensioners and scruffy students. These people looked vital, stylish, and hip. It was the sort of crowd you sometimes saw on the closing weekend of a hit show, when the theater was a place to see and be seen. He saw a handful of perpetual protest types – bearded, bereted, or becaped – but that was not the evening's profile.

The mass that surrounded them was seething with anticipation. As the three of them crossed Martin Luther King (where none of the assembled police was directing traffic) and reached the plaza, they found the crowd in high-spirited clusters, gossiping, glancing around to see where the action might be coming from. The harsh lights of the television crews cast spectral shadows across the fountain.

Ned saw that most of the crowd held unlit candles in their gloved hands. That had been Elena's inspiration. When they'd gone over Linda's second press release yesterday afternoon – the one announcing the gathering place – she'd suddenly clapped her hands and in a voice even huskier from fatigue proclaimed:

"A candlelight procession!"

She explained that it would be in honor of the desecrated theater. Everyone was in favor, and Linda revised the release.

Ned spotted a local actor across the plaza. He had reviewed two forgettable productions where this guy had been in the cast. In both plays the actor had been feeble comic relief. Ned was surprised there weren't more actors out, but remembered that it was Friday night and theater people had work to do.

They jostled their way through to the center of the crowd. A television reporter, her helmet of golden hair unruffled by the windless night, was interviewing a thirtyish man in a dark leather jacket some ten feet away.

"You ready?" Ned asked Scott.

"Just a little stage fright."

"You'll be great. Remember, Linda will kill you if you fuck it up. And I'll help her."

"Thanks, asshole."

They did a restrained fist-bump. Ned and Selvaggio then melted into the crowd, leaving Scott alone by the fountain.

Scott brought the fore and middle fingers of both hands to his lips and let out a series of piercing wolf whistles. He then unfolded the chair and climbed atop it. The television crews scrambled to train their lights on him.

"Ladies and gentlemen, Lazarus Productions thanks you for joining us here tonight. As you know, our theater was savagely attacked two days ago in a vicious and misguided attempt to silence our voice. Well, we may have no theater, but we sure as hell have an audience!"

A wave of applause swept through the crowd.

"Our show will go on. We will not be intimidated by these cowardly and brutal acts. We will perform as generations of actors have performed before us, in the open air, our theater bounded only by the evening sky and by the arc of your imagination.

The play is about to begin. So if you please, light your candles and follow me!"

CHAPTER TWENTY-FIVE

Ned had intended to deliver these lines himself. He had written the speech during a break between rehearsal sessions. But the rest of them, Elena in particular, had argued against it.

"Who the hell knows what they might do out on the street?" she'd said. "We need you for the play. Besides, actors don't give curtain speeches."

Scott had promptly volunteered for the job. He hadn't done much public speaking, he conceded, but he could be plenty loud.

"I'll vouch for that," Linda had said, dryly.

Ned had insisted on going along with him, in case anything should happen, but he agreed to stay on the fringes of the crowd.

Scott pulled a candle from the pocket of his parka, lit it, and strode toward Martin Luther King. All around him was a percussive unison of matches striking and lighters clicking. Then a firmament of candlelight suddenly blazed along the plaza, casting flickering shadows across the eager faces of the audience as they began to march behind Scott.

Scott had driven over with Selvaggio in the morning to go over the route, rehearsing the speech in his head as they drove. Now he crossed over Martin Luther King and headed west up Salmon, staying in the middle of the road as he did. The crowd poured into the street behind him. Eastbound cars on the one-way street screeched to a halt. A few drivers sounded their horns, but most just gave bewildered stares through their windshields as their cars were engulfed by the candle-toting mass.

Ned and Selvaggio stayed on the sidewalk on the north side of Salmon. Ned saw the mounted police guide their horses off the grass beside the plaza, towering menacingly behind the crowd. The police cruisers along Martin Luther King fired up their lights and sirens and sped off.

Ned checked his watch. It was seven thirty-nine. He veered toward one of the office buildings that lined the sidewalk and pulled out his cell phone. Selvaggio stayed with him.

He called Marty first.

"It's a go. We're on our way. Go ahead and set up."

"All right."

"Is Blevins back?"

"Yeah, he's here."

"Great. See you there."

Then he called Linda.

"Scott was perfect. The crowd is huge, but it didn't bother him a bit. Now he's playing the Pied Piper. It's all working, Linda."

"That's wonderful, Neddy."

"We're right on schedule. I've just given Marty the word to set up. You should drop off Elena and Calvin just as we'd planned."

"OK. Be careful, Neddy."

"We're fine."

He rang off and made his way back toward the crowd. The television crews had raced up from the plaza. Cameramen trotted along the curb, capturing the procession on video as it rolled along. Many of the marchers had a hand cupped around their candle to keep it from guttering, although the winter air was still.

Selvaggio surveyed the scene.

“This is way more than I was expecting. How many people do you think showed up?”

“I have no clue. I’m a theater critic. What do I know about crowds?”

“Hmm.” Selvaggio started chewing on a candy bar that just materialized.

“Let’s catch up with Scott.”

They wound their way forward. There was a hum pulsing through the crowd as it surged past cars stranded along Salmon. No one heeded the traffic lights changing overhead.

The street tilted upward as it passed a park on the left several blocks west of the plaza. Ned made out Scott in the lead about three quarters of a block ahead of him. Several police cruisers had positioned themselves at the next intersection above Scott, red and blue lights flashing.

Suddenly, a figure darted out of the murky darkness of the park and bore down on Scott from behind. Ned saw an upraised arm and the glint of candlelight on a dark object held aloft. It swung down swiftly on the side of Scott’s head. He crumpled to the street. The figure stole back through the crowd into the gloom of the park.

Ned and Selvaggio sprinted up the street. The vanguard of the procession lurched to a halt as the lead marchers huddled around Scott. Ned frantically pushed his way through. Scott lay on the pavement, an ugly ooze of blood seeping from his blonde scalp. Ned dropped to his knees, cradling Scott, who managed to raise himself into a sitting position. His head swiveled gingerly towards Ned.

"So much for breaking a leg," he said with a rueful grin.

A television crew muscled its way on to the scene. The dim flicker of candles clutched by the onlookers was powered into a dazzle of camera light.

Scott's eyes locked in on Ned's.

"Go," he said. "Take these people to their show."

"I'm not leaving you here."

"Yes, you are. I'm fine. I'll call Linda to come and get me. Go."

Selvaggio squatted alongside them.

"Get going. I'll stay with him. I didn't want to see the frigging play any way. That's for guys like Milson."

Scott steadied his weight on one arm and shoved Ned in the solar plexus with the other.

"Get the hell out of here. Or I'm going to give another speech."

Ned hesitated, then got to his feet. He looked behind him. The marchers had broken formation, straggling off to the sides of the street. A few emboldened drivers were starting to weave their cars through the scattering throng.

Ned yanked off his glasses and Holmes cap.

"The show goes on!" he bellowed. "Follow me!"

He turned and set off down the middle of Salmon, his feet pounding the centerline. Thirty yards in front of him, the police cars waited, bathed in a wash of gyrating colored light.

The original plan had been to go two more blocks before turning, but from where Ned stood it looked as if the police had blocked off Salmon. He angled quickly to his right on to the sidewalk, turning sharply on to Fifth Avenue as he took the corner. Several police standing beside their cruisers took threatening steps toward the marchers. The police froze, however, when they saw that television cameras were trained directly on them.

The crowd streamed into Fifth. Buses were stacked up in a line of seven or more, stymied by the police blockade. Weary commuters stared open-mouthed from the bus windows as the procession poured past on either side. Ned heard a knocking as he passed the last of the stalled buses and saw a wispy young woman in a down vest rapping on the window. She gave a thumb's up sign. He saluted in return.

Two blocks down Fifth, he turned left on to Yamhill. Cobblestones dug into the soles of his shoes. He made for the light rail tracks that ran down the center of the street.

A breathless voice just behind him asked, "So where are you taking us?"

The voice sounded familiar, but he had no time for questions. Without breaking stride said, "To the center of town."

Some fifty feet further, at the corner of Sixth and Yamhill, Ned took a diagonal path across the intersection into Pioneer Courthouse Square. The square was an entire city block lined with rust-colored brick. On fair days it was swarming when he would wander down from the *Columbian* office for a burrito stand lunch. Now it was desolate but for a clutch of bystanders staring at the light trees

Blevins had set up on the eastern and western flanks of the square. Looking over the easterly light tree across Sixth, Ned could see the squat old namesake courthouse shrouded in shadow.

Pioneer Courthouse Square was an amphitheatre. From the crest along Yamhill Street, descending terraces of brick formed bench seats facing north toward the central floor of the square. The rows were arrayed in a gentle curve.

Marty stood on the top level, a flashlight in her hand.

"I'll take it from here," she said. "They're in the coffee shop. I'll give you places on the cell phone."

"They went after Scott."

"I heard. Selvaggio called Linda to say he's doing fine. They're taking him to the hospital just to be sure. Now get out of the audience."

Ned started down the widely spaced rows. He spotted the spare figure of Blevins scurrying to make adjustments to the stage lights. The tech director had done one hell of a job considering what little he'd had at his disposal. The light in the center of the square was heightened, clearly defining a stage, but not harsh. The side-lit bricks cast an ochre glow.

A few paces away, he heard the same voice, no longer breathless, that had questioned him on the street.

"So where's the best seat in the house?"

It was Karin. Her hair was down, falling in blonde tresses on the shoulders of a long black coat.

"Wherever you're sitting."

"I got your note. Mick insisted I come by the bar. He said he had something for me that looked to be a show-stopper. I'm sorry about your father. What happened to him was awful. But we've all been conned at least a little, haven't we?"

"Karin, I know I should have …."

She interrupted.

"You have a show to do. We can go over the program notes and my review after the curtain goes down. Shall we say the Lowbrow an hour after your last curtain call?"

"The Aquavit's on me."

"It's all on you."

She turned away. He completed his descent and crossed through the square, skirting the uneven edges of the stage light. The coffee shop, a sleek chain outlet, was perched atop a bank of stairs in the square's far corner, across from where Ned had entered at the head of the crowd.

He looked back and saw the audience flowing into the amphitheatre, candles still glimmering in the hands of many. They filled all the seats and spilled on to the floor of the square. The buzz of the march from the river had given way to an expectant hush.

Elena and Calvin were seated at a boulevard café-style table just to the right of the door. Their faces, features sharpened by make-up, turned toward him as he came in. Elena squeezed Ned's hand.

"I can't believe what happened to Scott."

"That was meant for me."

"I know. How's the audience?"

"Phenomenal. Come out and look."

"I'll wait until Marty calls places."

"You don't want me to point out where Milson is sitting? I thought you always wanted to know where the critics were."

"Don't worry. I'll spot the bastard."

"Hey, take it easy on the guy. He's reviewing tonight as a favor to us."

"To you. I would have taken any old stringer."

"He'll tell us how we really did."

"I think we'll know."

Ned's cell phone rang.

"Places," said Marty.

"We're up."

They filed out the door and down the stairs. On the right side of the square as they headed toward the audience was a footbridge that crossed over a silent water feature to a transit information office. They had decided at the hotel that the far side of the bridge would serve as their backstage area.

As they passed over the bridge, they heard Marty's booming voice behind them and turned toward the stage. She stood along the downstage arc of the light.

"Lazarus Productions welcomes you to the opening, and perhaps our only performance, of *Pay to Play*. We are honored that you have braved the elements to join us this evening. We would have preferred to perform for you indoors, but as you all know by now, some people who didn't want our show to have an audience destroyed our theater. They thought that by wrecking our space, they could crush our spirit and our play. Thank you all for helping us to prove them wrong.

Please turn off all beepers, pagers, and cell phones - unless you are expecting a call from the theater critic for the *New York Times*. There will be no intermission. At the end of the play we will pass the hat. Please contribute as much as you feel you can.

Pay to Play is dedicated to the queen, who graces any stage on which she appears. This play is fictitious, but any resemblance of the characters to actual individuals, living or dead, is entirely intentional.

At the count of three, I would ask that you extinguish your candles, and the play will begin. One. Two. Three."

A collective whoosh of exhaled breath swept through the crowd, and the rows of the amphitheatre went dark. Only the lights of the television crews, stationed on the wings of the audience, still shone.

Elena waited for Marty to lumber offstage right. Then she strode to a place just to the left of center stage and began the lines from Chekhov:

"Why do you say you kiss the ground I walk on? I ought to be done away with. I'm so tired. If only I could rest ... rest! I'm a seagull ... No, that's not right. I'm an actress. Yes, that's it. So he's here too ... Yes, that's it ... Well, it doesn't matter ... Yes ... He never believed in the theater - he always laughed at my dreams - and little by little I stopped believing too and lost heart ... I was afraid he didn't love me, I was jealous, I worried all the time about the baby ... And I started being mean and petty. My acting made no sense ... I didn't know what to do with my hands, how to stand, I couldn't control my voice. You can't imagine what it's like to know you're acting badly. I'm a seagull. No, that's not right ... Remember when you shot the seagull? You left it at my feet, he came to me and said, 'I had an idea. A subject for a short story. A girl, like yourself, lives all her life on the shores of a lake. She loves the lake, like a seagull ... But a man comes along, by chance, and because he has nothing better to do, destroys her ...' What was I saying? ... I was talking about the stage. That's not the way I am now ... I'm a real actress now. I enjoy acting, I adore it. I feel exhilarated onstage, I feel beautiful ... I've been walking a lot since I've been back, walking and thinking, thinking that my soul grows stronger every day ... Now I know, Kostya, now I understand that what really counts in our work – acting or writing – is neither fame nor glory, the things I dreamed of; what really counts is learning how to endure. I must bear my cross and have faith. I have faith, and I don't suffer so much anymore. And when I think of my calling, I'm not afraid of life."

CHAPTER TWENTY-SIX

Tucker Farr hailed Ned as Farr neared the corner table in the Heathman dining room.

"Good morning. Sorry I'm late. Did you already get coffee?"

Farr was not dressed for business. He sported a casual ensemble: blue blazer, pleated gray corduroys, and open-necked Oxford shirt, striped and heavily starched. He smelled of strong cologne, which Ned did not recall noticing on him before. His hair looked hurriedly brushed.

"My apologies for the short notice on this, Ned. I didn't get back in the country until yesterday morning and decided to come straight to Portland. Word has it you've had an eventful week."

"How did you hear?"

Farr gave his usual self-assured grin.

"I have my sources. But if I'd been in the country, I wouldn't have needed them. I understand you made the news in Chicago. 'Theater troupe rises from ruins.' I heard those shots of the theater looked pretty awful on television."

"It looked a lot worse in person."

"I'm sure. How's that actor?"

"Still in the hospital. He won't be on stage any time soon, but he'll be fine."

The waiter arrived to take their order. Farr ordered a Western omelet with customary aplomb. Ned said he'd have the same.

"Is there some reason you couldn't tell me what was really behind the play?"

"Is there some reason you couldn't tell me about the deal you cut with Jerry Bergren?"

Farr balled the white cloth napkin in his fist.

"What are you suggesting?"

"I'm not suggesting anything. I heard from a reliable source that you and Bergren signed a contract for forty percent of the ranch deal and that he paid you a million and a half dollars. I'd like to know whether that's true or not."

"It's true."

"So when were you planning to tell us what was really going on?"

"Today. After his ranch project was approved."

"What?!"

"I just got the word before I came down to breakfast. Jerry got his approval."

"But Selvaggio's article absolutely crucified him. Have you seen this?"

Ned pulled out yesterday's edition of the *Columbian*, which carried a front-page story with the blaring headline: *JERRY RIGGED.*

"I sure have. He won't able to hold his head up in Portland for a good long while. But you forget we have an economy in rural Oregon that's desperate for development and a Republican administration in DC that isn't too bothered by environmental regulations. The feds and the locals loved the project. The PC crowd in Portland might think it's tacky to put a Rolls Royce museum on the Bhagwan's ranch, but Portland's not calling the shots on this one. Of course, it may have helped that the minority partner sent a letter to the bureaucrats in DC saying it had a solid development team in place in case the majority partner could not continue."

"Minority partner – do you mean you?"

"Not me, Ned. I haven't taken a dime on this deal. The forty percent share is held by your father's estate. Our partnership agreement with Jerry allows us to remove him as the managing partner if he's convicted of a felony. We're close to tracking down the guys who did the number on your theater and your actor. Once we do, I think they'll turn on Jerry. If I were a betting man – and I am – I would say he'll do some time."

"Which means the estate would take over the project?"

"Right. And the people I've talked to think this thing could make a mint. Jerry bought the land for a song and wangled all sorts of incentives out of the state and county. He played them like a violin."

"He's got a knack for that."

"Yes, he does. Years of practice, I understand. But I have a few years in the saddle myself."

"So why did you leave us all in the dark?"

"I'm sorry, Ned. It was a judgment call. I didn't want to raise your hopes until I knew we really had something. And until that approval came through, we didn't. Until then, I had to play everything very close to the vest – though I decided to show you those plans after the maid found them in the piano so you could see the vision your father had. I had to be able to control the flow of information in order to make a deal with Jerry. I thought it was better to paint the situation as bleak, then surprise you all if everything came together."

"So you packed me off to Portland to improve your bargaining position?"

"No, no. We had no idea what your father had invested in until one of the accountants stumbled across his e-mail account. You know about the e-mails, right?"

Ned nodded. "I burgled the disk from Bolden's office. My first and only breaking and entering."

"I don't think Roger will be pressing charges. He and I did far worse back in college. Anyway, we didn't learn about your father's account until after you'd taken the job out here. Even then, it took us a while to piece together what had gone on. It was no thanks to Jerry that we did."

"He probably thought he was sitting pretty."

"Sure. He had a dead partner who'd used no lawyers and had nothing in writing. Nice deal if you can get it. He wasn't too pleased to hear from me, I can tell you."

"So what did you swing with Bolden?"

"At first, Jerry wouldn't give me the time of day. He thought I had nothing on him. He and I went a few rounds trying to cut a deal, but he wasn't giving up anything. It looked like I would need some help from the media to get him to listen to reason. I let Jerry know I was prepared to go to the press about his Rolls Royce scheme. He thought I was bluffing. He figured I would keep things to myself so that the whole project wouldn't blow up. He miscalculated.

I called Roger and told him Jerry was working a scam. I said I would send him e-mails that laid it all out, on one condition. I needed the right to put a hold on the story at any time in the next sixty days. Roger would have told most people to go to hell, but he and I did a few things together at Yale that bond you for life – or at least as long as your memory holds out. So he took my terms.

From there it all ran like clockwork. I sent Roger the disk, Roger let Jerry knew what he had, I told Jerry he had one day to cut a deal or word would hit the street, and he bit. I came out here, took a tour of the ranch, and signed the contract. We ended up with a nice check – which is all sitting in short-term T-bills in the estate's name, Ned – and a fair percentage in the project. And I killed the story."

"And sent Selvaggio into a rage. He'd been honing in on Bergren for months."

"It looks like he got his man in the end, thanks to you."

"I had to make it up to him for stealing his story and putting it on stage."

"It was more your story than it was his, Ned."

"I suppose you're right. But Selvaggio and I got to be friends. The only one I've got out here, frankly. He's not a bad guy, for a thin-crust pizza chewing Yankee fan."

"Roger thinks very highly of him."

"He should. His stories have helped that paper sell a lot of phone sex ads."

Farr snorted.

"Is that how his rag makes money? I never understood."

"It's not selling theater advertising, I can tell you that."

"I suppose not. But you said he was your only friend out here. What about that lady friend you mentioned, the actress?"

"It wasn't meant to last."

"Too bad. Was she pretty?"

"Gorgeous."

"Other admirers?"

"Everywhere she went. But that wasn't it. She had some serious family business to attend to. Someone close to her is about to go through a rough patch – very rough. It's going to be hard on the rest of her family."

"Did it end well?"

"I didn't think it would. But it did. It was touch and go for a while, but somehow we managed to offload all the baggage. Not before the bartender at our favorite place almost stuck a knife through me, though."

"A friend of hers?"

"Oh yes. He missed a chance to protect her a long time ago. He wasn't going to make the same mistake twice."

"I'm sorry, Ned."

"Don't be. We sort of put each other back on stage, and that turned out well for both of us. Anyway, neither of us would have been up for a long-distance relationship."

"Long distance? Is she moving?"

"No. I am."

"You're leaving Portland?"

"It's time to go back to Chicago. Portland served its purpose. Yours, and mine."

"Mine? What was my purpose?"

"Don't patronize me, Tucker. You didn't send me out here to take the waters. You wanted to give me a kick in the ass. Which I admit I badly needed. I think you could have scraped together my allowance if you'd really needed to."

Farr chuckled.

"I imagine I could have shaken a few nickels out of the sofa cushions. All right, fair enough. What was your purpose?"

"To write well again. It wasn't happening in Chicago."

"And you think it will now?"

"It already has. It had nothing to do with where I was, and everything to do with what I committed myself to. Portland was a dive into shallow water, but at least I was going some place head first."

"I'm not sure I understand what you mean."

"You'll need to see the play."

"Will I ever get the chance? I hear you decided to do it for one night only."

"In Portland. We had all sorts of offers of places to put it on – high school gyms, church basements, even an empty condo penthouse. But that one night was so awesome, we decided we couldn't top it. We'd said what he'd had to say to people who'd braved an awful lot to hear it. Plus, we made enough money passing the hat that we didn't really need to do another performance here. But there's interest in doing it in Chicago. I got a call from one of the big companies. They'd have to rearrange things, but it looks like they might want it for their next season. It could lead to a New York run."

"Congratulations."

"Thanks. All the national press coverage didn't hurt. Milson's review – he's the guy I replaced – didn't either. Did you see it?"

"No. I guess I was too busy looking at the phone sex ads."

"I happen to have an extra copy. He called me up to say that I'd almost restored his faith in contemporary theater."

"Almost?"

"Well, he said that one extraordinary evening could not undo a decade's worth of mediocrity."

"Ouch. So what did Roger have to say when you told him you were moving back to Chicago?"

"Actually, he beat me to the punch. He fired me before I could tell him. He took me out to lunch and gave me the final chapter of his series on the ways and means of Portland. Then he said the *Columbian* could no longer afford a full-time theater critic.

'I know we have a first-rate performing arts scene here,' he said. 'But these companies just don't advertise. Things might have been different if you'd only discovered some hot young company that could have gotten a real theater buzz going.'

'I did,' I told him. 'But unfortunately, their space was just destroyed.'

He said I was welcome to work as a stringer and do reviews piecework. He said he wouldn't hold it against me that I had appropriated the paper's journalistic content for my own personal use."

"Roger was always a pompous ass – even in college. I'll have to remind him of that at lunch today."

"Oh, don't yank his chain too hard on my account. He gave me a job when I needed one. And the fact is that in this town, they probably can manage the reviews with a few stringers. At least until his hot young company comes along."

The waiter arrived with their orders. Farr tore into his omelet.

"So do you think they'll want any of your original cast in Chicago?"

"Not a chance. Portland is a bunch of country cousins to them. Anyway, my one-night acting career is over, the actor who played the Bergren character is retired and not going anywhere, and my lead actress is off to LA next week. All this media hoopla got her an agent in Hollywood. She wouldn't go to Chicago even if they offered her the part. Not enough television, not enough movies."

"That's Elena Devlin, right?"

"Right. How did you know?"

"Oh, someone mentioned the name to me. I guess you'll be able to say you knew her when."

"She's good. But more important: she's hungry – starving really. She'll do whatever it takes to get her name in lights. There are plenty of better, and better-looking, actresses than Elena, but they just don't want it as badly."

Farr started to say something, then thought better of it.

"Scott will be glad to have you back."

"Sure, if we ever see each other. He and Linda are settling into that house in Wilmette, although the concussion he got out here slowed down the remodeling a little. I predict a kid by next spring, which means he'll be totally out of circulation. He'll start thinking of the city like the rest of you suburbanites do – a sinister place full of lowlifes like drug dealers and writers."

"The roads run both ways, as I recall. Even the trains."

"I'll make the odd pilgrimage to the North Shore. Celia and Art will need some company when they move into the old house. She tells me they're going to turn the fountain back on this spring. I'll have to come out for the first splash. Maybe write a commemorative ghost story for the occasion."

"You think the house is haunted?"

"Shouldn't it be? I don't think my father's spirit will rest until that theater gets built. Now wait a minute. If we can shove out Bergren and take over the ranch, couldn't we go back to the original plan and build the amphitheatre?"

"The ranch was just approved with a museum, Ned. We'd have to go through the approval process all over again. Jerry told me he went everywhere and couldn't get that theater financed. The bankers wouldn't buy it. They all said theater was dead. Ordinarily Jerry was not on close terms with the truth, but on that one I believed him. I'd love to honor your father's memory, but as his executor I don't want to bankrupt the estate – for a second time."

"Ever the businessman, Tucker. Thank God we have someone practical on our team. You're right. Building theaters is best left to incurable romantics with money to burn."

Farr gave a wry smile.

"Perhaps. Anyway, your father will be at peace when his son has a play produced in Chicago. Then he'll have an artistic legacy in his hometown, which meant more to him than anything."

“With any luck, it’ll be more than one play. I think I’m going to do some more writing for the theater. After I finish the novel, of course. There’s no way I’m paying back that advance.”

“You think you can get the book back on track?”

“After I burn about two-thirds of what I’ve already written, yes. But that’s OK. I know where I want to go now.”

“Will you go back to reviewing for the *Weekly*?”

“I’ll do as much as they’ll give me. I’ve already spoken to my old editor. They’ve got some other stringers backing up Schaeffer now, but he said he’d fit me in when he could.”

“I could check around if you want.”

Ned raised his palms in gentle refusal.

“No, I think you’ve done quite enough in the job placement department already, thank you very much. It’s up to me to earn my own Cubs’ tickets and booze now. As a writer. I’ll see what I can do to cash in on being the man of the moment.”

“Fair enough.”

Farr finished off the last of his omelet.

“So why didn’t you tell me what the play was really about?”

“Because you would have told me this was a job for lawyers and accountants – not playwrights.”

“And I would have been right. You didn’t know the deal.”

“Because you didn’t tell me.”

“What would you have done if you’d known? You’d still have written the play, wouldn’t you?”

“Sure. I still had something to say. But plays are meant to be played.”

"And yours will. In Chicago, where no one knows Jerry Bergren from a hole in the wall."

Over Farr's shoulder Ned saw a woman approaching their table. Farr saw his glance and turned around. They both rose in unison.

"I think you know Robin Story," said Farr.

"Good morning, Dirk," she said, serenely.

She wore a white open-neck sweater and a powder blue blouse. Her flaxen hair was beaded with a fine dew, as if she had just emerged from a shower.

"Dirk?" asked Farr with a puzzled look.

"They know me by my pen name out here."

"Oh, right."

"Your pen has been busy, Dirk."

Ned reddened.

"That's not a criticism. We need brave writers. Writers who are not intimidated by their subject. Writers who grasp that the essence of art is making public what is most private."

"I'm sorry if I over-did the private," said Ned.

"You needn't apologize. My life is my art. It's open for any audience to see. As you showed so well."

"You saw the play?"

"Of course. I had no candle, but I found my way there. Milson's review captured my thoughts perfectly."

"Ned tells me a major company in Chicago is interested in putting it on," said Farr. "He's decided to move back there."

"All of my friends are leaving us for the big city. Elena's just told me that she's off to LA next week. We'll miss her – and you, Dirk. You've made a real impact in our lives in a very short time."

She said this without a trace of sarcasm.

"I do have one favor to ask. Perhaps you might consider paying a small royalty to Vox Unum if you're able to produce the play in other cities. We'd welcome the support."

"Of course," said Ned. "It's the least I can do. Will you join us for breakfast?"

"I'm afraid I can't," she said. "Our first meeting is at nine thirty."

"Robin and I are interviewing contractors today," said Farr. "I'm helping to rebuild the theater. You remember when you sent me to see *Doll's House* the last time I was here? You were right. One of the best performances I'd ever seen. I decided to go backstage after the show to meet Robin. We've stayed in touch ever since. When she told me what happened to the SoHo, I knew I had to be a part of bringing it back. We'll need to have crews working night and day, but it'll be ready for Robin's opening. Well, we'd better get going. I'll call you this afternoon, Ned, and let you know how much I made Bolden squirm at lunch. Don't worry about the bill. I'll put it on my room."

Farr turned toward Robin.

"It was a pleasure to see you again, Dirk. Congratulations on your tremendous work. I hope you'll call me before you leave Portland."

The two of them made their way up the narrow aisle that led to the hostess stand. Ned might have been mistaken, but he thought he saw their fingertips brush together. Farr said something quickly to the hostess. Then they turned and took the stairs down to the hotel exit.

Ned caught a last glimpse of Nora's white-blonde hair as she glided through the revolving door.

About the Author

Gary D. Cole was raised in the Chicago area and graduated from Williams College and Stanford Law School, where he acted in numerous theater productions. Cole practiced law at the Central Intelligence Agency before writing a play based loosely on his Agency experience. While a partner at a Portland, Oregon law firm, Cole in 1995 founded a professional theater company, CoHo Productions, that still performs in the black box theater he developed for the company.

In 2003, Cole was appointed by the Bush administration to head the $60 million annual grants program at the National Endowment for the Arts. The administration later withdrew his appointment, reportedly because of two provocative plays filmed by a theater video company founded by Cole called StageDirect. Cole has written a memoir about his odyssey through the arts and politics entitled *Artless*.

Cole now resides in North Carolina, where he founded a Southern theater festival called Theater of the American South. He is married and has two children. *Black Box* is Cole's first novel.